After being scattered by jobs and missions, ̶ ̶ ̶ ̶ come
together to witness their grandmother's wedding to a longtime family
friend.

Silver Bells by Debby Mayne
Carol Scheirer's children and grandchildren left her during her loneli-
est time. Fortunately, an old family friend, Alex Knight, has always
provided her with emotional support. But now Alex confesses he's
fallen in love with Carol and wants to marry her. How will her family
react when she sends them letters inviting them to her Noel nuptials?

I'll Be Home for Christmas by Elizabeth Ludwig
Writer Christmas Scheirer has been too ashamed to admit that her
greed may have led to her grandfather's death. Wanting to make
amends, Christmas returns to Boulder for her grandmother's wedding and comes across a slew of letters written by her grandfather.
She's determined to see these missives published—even if it means
battling with Marcus Taggert, the handsome guardian of her grandfather's estate. How far will Christmas go to put things right?

O Christmas Tree by Elizabeth Goddard
Missionary Holly Rivers was heartbroken when Nick Brohns had
stayed behind in Boulder, leaving her to head to South Africa on her
own. But now that she's returning home on furlough for Grandma
Carol's wedding, she and Nick meet up again—an uncomfortable
encounter for both. Will Holly find that Nick's priorities have changed,
or will she realize that God has a new mission for both their lives?

The First Noelle by Paige Winship Dooly
Left at the altar years ago, party planner Noelle Evans reluctantly
returns home to help with her grandmother's wedding. But she arrives
in Boulder, only to have an accident and find herself in the hands of
Rocky Carmichael, MD—her former fiancé. Can Noelle learn to trust
the man who once jilted her? Or will she run back to her high-pressure
life in the city?

CHRISTMAS HOMECOMING

DEBBY MAYNE

PAIGE WINSHIP DOOLY / ELIZABETH GODDARD / ELIZABETH LUDWIG

BARBOUR
PUBLISHING

©2009 *Silver Bells* by Debby Mayne
©2009 *I'll Be Home for Christmas* by Elizabeth Ludwig
©2009 *O Christmas Tree* by Elizabeth Goddard
©2009 *The First Noelle* by Paige Winship Dooly

ISBN 978-1-60260-564-0

Scripture taken from the HOLY BIBLE, NEW INTERNATIONAL VERSION®. NIV®. Copyright © 1973, 1978, 1984 by International Bible Society. Used by permission of Zondervan. All rights reserved.

Scripture taken from the New King James Version®. Copyright © 1982 by Thomas Nelson, Inc. Used by permission. All rights reserved.

Scripture taken from the New American Standard Bible, © 1960, 1962, 1963, 1968, 1971, 1972, 1973, 1975, 1977, 1995 by The Lockman Foundation. Used by permission.

Scripture taken from the King James Version of the Bible.

Interior Illustrations: Mari Small, www.thesmallagencynj.com

Published by Barbour Publishing, Inc., P.O. Box 719, Uhrichsville, OH 44683, www.barbourbooks.com

Our mission is to publish and distribute inspirational products offering exceptional value and biblical encouragement to the masses.

 ecpa Member of the
Evangelical Christian
Publishers Association

Printed in the United States of America.

SILVER BELLS

by Debby Mayne

To three fabulous women—
Paige Winship Dooley, Elizabeth Goddard, and Elizabeth
Ludwig—who made brainstorming and writing this book
such an enjoyable experience. What a fun team!

For no one can lay any foundation
other than the one already laid,
which is Jesus Christ.

1 CORINTHIANS 3:11 NIV

Chapter 1

"Delightful party, Carol," Gail said as she leaned over for a hug. "Merry Christmas."

Carol smiled. "Merry Christmas to you, too, and thank you for coming."

Terri hugged Carol and whispered, "I'm proud of you. Paul would have enjoyed this."

Finally, Alex Knight, her deceased husband's best friend since the army, took one of her hands in both of his and looked into her eyes. "Very nice, Carol. I'll stop by tomorrow if that's okay with you."

Carol Scheirer nodded and blinked back the tears that threatened to fall. Tomorrow was Christmas, the most difficult time of year for Carol, since Paul's death a little more than five years ago. All but one of her children had scattered, and she often found herself alone to reflect on what she once had—a loving husband, healthy children, and a happy home.

After she said her last good-bye, Carol gently closed the door, locked it, and turned around to face the tree she'd put up for the party. Until this year, she hadn't bothered with

Christmas decorations, other than the small tabletop tree in the front room.

She and Paul had gone to the same church since shortly after they got married—right before he enlisted in the army and headed off to Vietnam. Their friends from church had held her hand and consoled her when she got word Paul had been hit by sniper fire and was coming home an injured soldier.

Carol had to wait several weeks while arrangements were made to transport Paul to the States then move him to the closest VA hospital. When she finally got to see him, half his body was wrapped in bandages, but that didn't matter. Paul was home, and his prognosis was excellent.

Now that the party was over and she had the house to herself, Carol walked toward the tree and touched a couple of ornaments that held the most memories. Each ball—each figurine on that tree meant something to her. She smiled as she gently traced her fingers over the first ornament they'd bought together during a craft fair forty-eight years ago, when she was barely out of childhood at eighteen.

The clock in the hallway continued ticking away the minutes, until finally an hour had passed since the last guest left. It was time to do something she'd been avoiding for five years. Paul had always put the star on top of the tree on Christmas Eve, but since she hadn't put up a tree since he passed away, it wasn't an issue.

Carol went into her bedroom, opened the armoire, and pulled out the carefully wrapped tree topper. As she held the star by the braided golden string on top, it caught the light as it twirled, casting a sparkling shimmer on the wall in front of her.

With a heavy heart and the shiny star in her hands, Carol slowly walked into the living room and stared at the tree. Yes, it was time to move on.

She put the star on the table and went into the kitchen to get her step stool. Before she put the finishing touch on the tree, she bowed her head and asked the Lord for the strength to move forward in life. Then she opened her eyes and allowed the memories to flood, until her knees grew weak, and she had to sit down for a few minutes.

Before Paul's cancer diagnosis seven years ago, they'd assumed they would grow old together and enjoy their golden years traveling. Even after the doctor called with the news of prostate cancer, there was hope. But that hope had faded with the cancer's aggressive spread throughout his body. Carol had no regrets because she'd never left his side. His best friend, Alex Knight, the man who'd saved Paul's life in Vietnam, helped her care for him then cried with her as he passed.

Finally, after nearly a half hour, Carol stood slowly then moved toward the tree. It was time to put up the star and get on with life.

Alex had never seen such strength in a woman, which was what had made him fall in love with Carol Scheirer. She'd given him credit for saving Paul, but in reality it was Paul who'd saved him.

Paul's faith in God, even as he lay in the ditch, bleeding from every limb, was a mystery to Alex, until he visited the Scheirer home after his Vietnam tour ended. The second he walked through the front door, he knew this family had something special—and he wanted to find out more. Since he didn't have a place to call home, Alex settled in Boulder to be near his army buddy. Paul invited him to church then informal Bible studies. It didn't take Alex long to realize what he'd been missing all his life. He committed his life to Christ and never looked back.

On Christmas morning, Alex took his time eating breakfast and reading the newspaper. He didn't want to rush over to Carol's and overwhelm her during this emotional time. He had a box of gifts people had sent, and he wanted to wait to open them with Carol.

Late in the morning, he gathered everything and put it in his car. Then he called to make sure she was ready to see him.

"Sure, come on over." Her voice was soft but a little shaky. He could tell she'd been crying, and it broke his heart.

After he pulled into Carol's driveway, he sat in the car and prayed that the day would be peaceful. He'd long since given up expecting excitement on Christmas. As a child, he'd never failed to be disappointed, and as a Christian adult, he realized expectations were mostly tied in to the commercialism of the day.

He opened his eyes and saw Carol standing in the doorway, waiting. His heart thudded in his chest. One of these days, he'd let her know how he felt about her. Back when Paul was alive, Alex set out to find a woman like Carol—someone who loved the Lord, appreciated the gift of marriage, and wanted children. But he'd never found anyone who came close to matching Carol. It never dawned on him that after Paul was gone, he'd fall in love with his best friend's wife. At first, it bothered him, but after praying about it, he knew it was okay. However, he couldn't find the nerve to tell Carol, so he kept the little secret close to his heart.

He waved, and she smiled as he got out of the car. By the time he popped the trunk, she was there, by his side.

"It's nice having you here," she said. "Paul would appreciate how well you've taken care of me."

"I'm happy to do it." He didn't let on that his actions had long since ceased being about Paul and more about his own feelings. "The way I see it, we take care of each other."

The sound of her soft laughter filled his heart with gladness. His instinct was to reach out and pull her close to his chest. However, he resisted the urge. "I'll get the heavy box. Do you mind carrying the food?"

She lifted it and led the way to the front door. "You didn't have to bring food. I have plenty of leftovers from last night."

"It's not much, but I wanted to do something."

They'd spent the last several Christmases together, but something was different this year. For the first time since Paul died, she had the traditional party on Christmas Eve, with old friends from church. When the Scheirer children were small, they started early so they could get the little ones home and in bed. As the families matured, the parties were more focused on the adults. In spite of the fact that Alex had never married and had a family of his own, he was always invited and never made to feel like the odd man out. There was no doubt in his mind he had Carol to thank for that.

"I'll put these things under the tree then join you in the kitchen."

When Carol turned and smiled, warmth flooded him. He loved everything about this woman—from her quiet confidence to the way she made everyone feel like part of her family. Hopefully, he'd be able to discuss his feelings with her soon.

As he laid each wrapped gift beneath the tree, he thought about all the times he and Paul had wrapped and hidden gifts for the Scheirer kids. He also remembered the time when their oldest daughter, Marie, sneaked out her bedroom window to be with the boyfriend Paul didn't approve of, and he and Paul went looking for her after the other children had gone to bed. The Scheirer family had been through quite a bit, and he'd been there with them for most of it.

After he emptied the box, he stood and admired the tree. Carol must have spent hours decorating it. There wasn't an empty branch in sight. But it looked different—something that hadn't been there last night. The star. She must have put it on the tree after everyone had left.

~ ❦ ~

After Carol put Alex's multilayered salad into the fridge and the tin of cookies on the counter, she finished washing the dishes in the sink and brewed more coffee. Alex still hadn't joined her, so she grabbed a towel, wiped her hands, and went out to see what was keeping him.

There he stood, all six feet of him, staring at the tree. He'd even turned on the lights, something she'd forgotten to do that morning.

Alex turned and motioned for her to join him. "I see you put the star up."

She nodded and sighed. "That was always Paul's job."

"Must've been hard. You could have waited for me, ya know."

Carol swallowed and bit her lip until the threat of tears

retreated. "I know, but I felt like it was something I needed to do." She paused before adding, "Alone."

When she turned to face Alex, she saw him visibly tense. His jaw pulsed, and he looked down.

She realized she'd hurt him. "I'm sorry."

He lifted his hands and offered a slight smile. "No need to be sorry. I understand."

She had no doubt he fully understood what she was going through. Alex had been by her side from the time Paul became bedridden, through the prayer vigils, and all the way to the end—when Paul took his last breath. She would have had a much tougher time getting through the funeral without him.

To her relief, he rubbed his belly and widened his grin. "I'm starving. Let's eat."

Carol put out the salad he'd brought and a platter of cold cuts and vegetables left over from the night before. She wasn't hungry, but she fixed herself a plate anyway. As he ate, she nibbled and tried to make conversation, hoping he wouldn't notice her lack of appetite. But it didn't work.

"Not hungry, huh?"

She slowly shook her head. "This is a rough day for me."

He put down the last piece of his sandwich and folded his hands on the table in front of him. "Let's say a prayer then go and open some gifts."

Alex started the prayer, and Carol finished it. They'd started doing that since Paul had passed away, and it felt right. After they both said, "Amen," Alex stood and reached for Carol's hand.

Once they were in the living room, he directed her to take a seat, while he brought each gift to her, one by one. She chuckled. "You're spoiling me."

He glanced over his shoulder, gave her a thumbs-up, and winked. "It's high time someone did. You deserve it."

They took turns opening gifts from family members and each other. Alex loved the windbreaker from Carol, and he stopped to put it on. As he pranced around the room, modeling it for her, she laughed until her sides felt like they'd split.

Then suddenly, he stopped acting silly and looked her squarely in the eye. "I left the best for last, Carol."

Chapter 2

Her heart hammered as she accepted the wrapped rectangular box from Alex. The way he watched her open it, his gaze focused, a slight grin on his lips, she knew it was something special.

As soon as the paper was off, she flipped the hinged lid of the black velvet box. Lying on a bed of satin was a sparkling, multicolored gemstone necklace.

"This is absolutely gorgeous!" Carol lifted the necklace from the box and turned it over in her hand. "It looks like an antique."

Alex nodded, and his smile widened. "It is. It was my grandmother's and then my mother wore it."

Carol gasped. "I can't accept this. You need to keep it in your family."

"I want you to have it." He stood up and took it from her then opened the clasp. "Turn around. I'll put it on you."

It was so beautiful, she couldn't resist. "This must have a tremendous amount of sentimental value."

"It does." He fastened the clasp then gently turned her

around to face him. "It looks beautiful on you, like it was meant for you."

She couldn't resist taking a peek in the hall mirror to see for herself. It truly was a gorgeous piece of jewelry.

When she turned around, Alex was right there beside her. "I–I'm stunned. I don't know what to say." She ran her fingertips over the stones then turned back around to see it. "Thank you, Alex, but you really shouldn't—"

"It was a gift from Dad's father to my grandmother on their first Christmas together. Then after my parents had been married for years, and my grandmother moved into a nursing home, she gave it to my dad to give my mother."

"Why did you give it to me?" Carol asked.

"Because I wanted to."

They stood and faced each other for several seconds. Carol felt the bond thicken between them as something turned over in her heart. "I'm honored that you want me to have this necklace, Alex, but if you ever find a woman who deserves it more than me, I'll understand."

He offered one of his comical grins. "I have a great idea, Carol. Why don't we spend the day making plans for the coming year—just like you and Paul used to do?"

She nodded. "Most of the time, we never followed through on those plans, but it was fun. Sure, let's do it."

They went back into the kitchen and sat down at the table. Carol still wore the necklace, and she noticed Alex glancing at it when he looked at her. It seemed to make him happy for her to wear it, and it made her happy to see him so pleased.

"We need some paper," he said. "If we have any hope at all to follow through with our plans, they need to be documented."

Carol found a spiral notebook and handed it to Alex. "You can write down anything that sounds good to you."

He tilted his head back and belted out the laughter she'd grown so fond of since she'd known him. She liked Alex when she first met him, and he'd gotten even better over the years. He'd lost all semblance of inhibitions, and his laughter was sincere. His deep, baritone voice had resonance—not only in sound but in meaning. When Alex spoke, people listened.

"What are some things you'd like to do this year?" he asked.

She thought for a moment. "Bowling. I used to like to bowl, but I haven't done it in years."

"Okay, so would you like to join a league, or just go bowling once or twice?"

She laughed. "Let's not get too carried away with this. A night of bowling would be fun."

He jotted down *bowling* then looked up at her. "There's something I've always wanted to do but haven't yet." He lifted the pencil to his chin and pondered for a moment. "I've always wanted to play tourist and see all the sights around Boulder."

"Sounds like fun!" Carol gestured toward the paper. "Go ahead and write it down." She tapped the table. "Add horseback riding to your list. I haven't done that in a very long time, and I love horses."

"How about seeing the sights on horseback?"

She sighed. "Sounds dreamy."

They spent the rest of the afternoon jotting down ideas for things to do—some of them realistic and others that were totally outrageous. By nightfall, Carol realized her sadness had lifted.

After they finished listing their ideas, Alex stood up and handed her the notebook. "Why don't we start out by going to one of those places on New Year's?"

"Sounds perfect," she said.

They gathered all his gifts and stuffed them into the box he'd brought. "I had a wonderful Christmas," he said as they stood by the door.

"Me, too." She looked up and met his gaze. "Thank you for spending the day with me."

Alex smiled down at her. "My pleasure." He walked out onto the porch, took a couple of steps, then turned around to face her. "I'd like for you to wear that necklace when we go out on New Year's."

"Yes, of course."

She stood and watched him back out of the driveway before she opened the door to go inside. He waved from the road then took off.

As she walked through the house and turned off lights on her way back to her bedroom, she thought about how the day had gone from being one of the saddest of the year to a day of pure joy. Alex Knight was truly a remarkable man with an amazing ability to make her smile. She wondered why he was still single.

It wasn't late, but Carol was tired after an emotionally exhausting day. She laid out her nightgown before turning to look in the dresser mirror. The necklace was truly a gorgeous piece of jewelry—much too nice to be taken for granted. It meant more than just a gift. It represented trust and friendship—no, it was something stronger than friendship. It was more like the faith in family, knowing the person will always be there.

She carefully turned the necklace around so she could see the clasp. As she pulled the tiny lever and gently removed it, she knew that this single item stood for that special relationship she and Alex had after more than thirty years of being around each other.

After Carol put the necklace in the drawer where she kept her valuable jewelry, she got ready for bed. The phone rang, and she was tempted to let it go. But she couldn't do that; it might be important.

"Carol, I wanted to thank you again for the wonderful day," Alex said softly. "You're a fine woman. Paul was a fortunate man."

"Thank you for being here for me, Alex," she said. "Good night. I'll see you soon."

He chuckled. "Yeah, we better get started very soon, or we'll never get through half the things on that list."

She hung up the phone with a smile on her lips and giddiness in her heart. For the first time since before Paul's cancer was diagnosed, she felt complete and utter joy.

Thank You, Lord, for seeing me through the difficult times and giving me hope for more good times to come. She swallowed hard, squeezed her eyes shut tighter, and finished her prayer.

They had a quiet New Year's Eve, starting with a short church service then ending with a ginger ale toast at Carol's house. He took advantage of the moment and leaned down for a quick kiss on the cheek. She looked at him, stunned, then smiled back at him. "I had a wonderful evening, Alex."

It was time for him to leave. "Me, too. I'll call you." He tweaked her nose and she crinkled it as she smiled. "Now go get some sleep."

The sound of the alarm clock jolted Alex from the best dream he'd had in years. He opened one eye and flung the covers off before forcing himself to sit up.

Memories of Christmas and New Year's Eve instantly made him smile. Christmas started out somewhat shaky, but she gradually gave in, relaxed, and enjoyed herself. That was what he'd hoped for, but he didn't expect it. He was glad to see that she wore the necklace he'd given her on New Year's Eve.

His family heirloom looked amazing on her. The colorful array of ruby, emerald, lapis, and topaz stones intensified the milky tone of her skin and depth of her blue-green eyes. He'd had the urge to kiss her on the lips a few times, but he wouldn't dare—not yet, anyway. He'd have to settle for an occasional hug.

Alex decided it was time to pursue the only woman who could ever make him happy. It wasn't something he would have even thought about if Paul hadn't died. Paul was the salt of the earth—the best friend a guy could have and a wonderful husband who set examples for other men from church.

A few days before Paul fell into a coma, he'd awakened from a nap and asked Alex to look after Carol. "She's still young and vibrant," Paul had whispered. "I don't want her to be alone for the rest of her life."

Alex nodded as he fought back tears that threatened. Man-sized tears. He didn't want Paul to see him blubbering, so he looked down. "I'll make sure she's okay," he promised.

Paul somehow managed a smile. "Thank you for saving my

life back in Nam. If it weren't for you, I wouldn't have seen my kids grow up."

"That's what any soldier would have done." Alex had a tough time accepting praise, but he couldn't very well brush off the words of a dying man.

Laughter burst out of Paul's pale, parched lips. "That's what you always say, but I know better. You risked your own life so I could see my family again."

Alex patted Paul on the shoulder. "Carol will be back any minute. She had to pick up one of the kids from the airport. I offered to do it, but she needed to get out for a while."

Paul's lips quivered. Alex knew Paul was aware he was about to die, and people were coming in from all over to see him one last time.

He shuddered away the memory as he flipped the switch on the coffeemaker. The last thing Alex needed to do right now was wallow in depressing thoughts. Today was the start of a new chapter in his life—a time of pursuing what he'd been praying for over the past year. He was pretty sure Carol was ready to move on, and he wanted to be part of her future.

After his first cup of coffee, Alex picked up the phone and punched in the number he'd found on the back of a brochure. He asked a few questions then promised to call back within the hour.

Then he called Carol. With each ring, he felt a slight bit of trepidation, but the second he heard her voice, his heart lightened.

"I have a surprise for you."

Carol sucked in a breath, making his heart do its little

flippy thing that only Carol could make it do. "Another surprise? My, aren't you something else!"

"Yeah, but I'm not sure what else I am. Can you be ready in an hour?"

"An hour?" She hesitated. "What's the surprise?"

"Can't tell you. Just be ready in an hour, okay?"

"Well. . .what should I wear?"

He didn't want to give anything away, so he just told her to wear nice slacks and a jacket, like she'd wear to their casual church services. After the surprise, he'd take her out to a nice dinner somewhere with a breathtaking view of the Flatirons. He planned to give her the world—one small piece at a time—in hopes of winning her heart.

Carol stood waiting on her front porch, wondering what Alex's surprise could possibly be. She sensed a change between them, and the anticipation felt like a delicious adventure.

He pulled up the driveway and got out before she had a chance to reach his car. Holding the door, he gestured for her to get in, then he shut it behind her.

"Are you going to tell me where we're going?" she asked as she suppressed a giggle.

"Nope."

"Can you give me a hint?"

Alex turned to her and grinned. "You're gonna like it." He laughed. "A lot."

Chapter 3

Alex drove to the edge of town then turned off on a narrow road. Carol couldn't imagine where they were going, but she certainly enjoyed the scenery.

When they came to a stop in the middle of nowhere, she was even more puzzled than before. She turned to him, tilted her head, and smiled, waiting for him to say something.

"I called a friend who's supposed to meet us here." Alex checked his watch. "We're a few minutes early. It won't be long."

Carol knew better than to keep asking what was about to happen, so she settled back and took in the setting. "This is gorgeous."

He studied her for a few seconds before nodding. "It certainly is."

The implication of his comment felt wonderful, but she tried to push back the feelings that had risen inside her chest. She had no business being attracted to Alex. They were close friends, that's all.

After another five minutes passed, she heard the clopping

sound of horse hooves. She looked in the direction of the noise and smiled at the vision before her.

"Surprised?" he asked.

She nodded. "I've never ridden in a horse-drawn carriage before."

"Neither have I," he admitted, "and I think that's a crying shame. This should be fun."

He helped her out of the car and into the carriage before going to his trunk and pulling out a blanket. The driver kept his attention focused straight ahead as he seemed to know where he was going.

Once they were on their way, Alex slipped an arm around her shoulder. "One of the new guys in my men's Bible study class owns a horse stable, so I called him. I promised to help set up his computer in exchange for an hour-long ride."

Carol sighed. "This is absolutely the biggest surprise. A horse-drawn carriage ride never even crossed my mind."

"Good." He touched her cheek then quickly withdrew his hand. "I'm glad I could surprise you."

As they rode in the carriage, Carol inhaled the sweet, fresh air. They were about fifteen minutes from the origination point when a light flurry of snow started to fall. Alex unfolded the blanket and arranged it around the two of them, creating a cozy cocoon that made Carol feel all was right with the world.

Occasionally, they hit a bump, and Alex tightened his grip on her. There was no doubt in her mind he was a great protector. For most of the trip, they rode in silence, but occasionally, he pointed to something of interest, whether it was a bird or a different angle of the mountains. It was all spectacular.

At the end of the ride, Alex helped her down from the carriage and to the car, then he went over and chatted with the carriage driver, who laughed before he went on his way. Alex joined her in the car.

"How does a warm mug of hot cocoa sound?" he asked.

"Mmm. Yummy."

"I know just the place." Alex started the car and took off toward town.

They spent the rest of the day walking and shopping. Carol admired a scarf, and when her back was turned, Alex bought it for her. He presented it to her with a flourish.

"You shouldn't have."

He unwrapped it from the tissue and gently placed it around her shoulders. "I wanted to."

The cashmere scarf felt soft and warm, and she loved the magenta color. But not nearly as much as she appreciated all the things Alex was doing for her. If it had been anyone but dear, sweet Alex, she would have thought she was being wooed.

At the end of the day, he drove to her favorite restaurant. "I can't believe all this. You're full of surprises, Alex Knight."

"I love surprising you," he whispered. "I have more, but this is it for today."

She smiled up at him and noticed the twinkle in his eyes. "You're a good man, Alex."

~ ❦ ~

The biggest advantage of courting a woman at this age, Alex thought, was having the financial means to do it right. He never would have been able to afford a place this nice when he was in his twenties. However, the last thing he wanted to do was show off or make Carol feel indebted to him for the money he spent. If anything, he felt that he owed her for bringing so much peace and contentment into his life.

At the end of the long day, he drove her home and walked her to her door. "I had a wonderful time, Carol."

She looked up at him. "Today couldn't have been nicer. Thank you for everything."

Alex licked his lips but resisted the urge to kiss her. He wasn't sure she was ready, and he didn't want to spoil what might happen if he took his time.

"Would you like to come in?" she asked.

Another temptation to spend more time with her. He reached out and touched her cheek before pulling his hand back and putting it in his pocket. "I'd love to, but I think it's time for me to go on home. I don't want to risk having you get tired of me."

She laughed. "That will never happen, Alex. I've known you for a long time, and I've never gotten tired of having you around."

His heart leaped, but he still held back. "I'll call you in the morning. Good night."

Carol tilted her head, tempting him even more to kiss her. But he didn't. He backed off the porch then turned and ran the rest of the way to his car. She had the ability to make him feel like a teenager again.

True to his word, Alex called Carol the next morning. She sounded wide awake.

"I was afraid you'd be exhausted after yesterday, and you might still be in bed."

"No way," she said with a lilt in her voice. "I can run circles around women half my age."

"Yes, I know that." He wanted to ask her to spend the day with him, but he didn't want to rush her.

"Now it's my turn to surprise you," she said, snapping him from his thoughts. "Why don't you stop by around six this evening?"

"You don't have to do anything," he said. "Yesterday was as much for me as it was you."

"Don't argue with me, Alex." She paused for a laugh. "You know you don't stand a chance when I have my mind set on something."

"True. Want me to bring anything?"

"No, just come hungry."

At least he knew he'd get a wonderful meal. Cooking was one of the many things Carol did better than anyone else he knew.

Carol needed to run to the grocery store and pick up a few things before fixing Alex his favorite meal, meatloaf with tomato gravy and mashed potatoes with buttered peas. She used to tease him about how he was a heart attack waiting to happen, so he'd challenged her to figure out a way to make the meal a healthy one. She made a few substitutions, and although it wasn't completely cholesterol free, it had a few healthier components than the original version.

She'd gathered her purse and keys when the phone rang.

After seeing her youngest son Michael's name on caller ID, she was tempted not to answer it. He never called unless he wanted something.

After a slight hesitation, she picked up the phone. Her voice sounded tight, even to her, as she answered it.

"Are you okay, Mom?" he asked.

"Sure. I'm fine. What's up?"

"I hate to ask you this, but I'm really in a bind." He paused, giving her an extra few seconds to dread what was coming next. "My business isn't doing so well. I can't compete with some of the bigger companies."

She let out a sigh. This was standard for Michael, but she couldn't bring herself to say no. "What do you need?"

"Well, I know I need to upgrade my software, and since my computer is so old and everything—"

"I just bought you a new computer three years ago, and if I remember correctly, you said it should last you a good six or seven years."

He cleared his throat. "Things are changing so fast these days."

"How much do you need?"

When he told her the amount, she nearly choked. "I don't know, Michael. You should be making money by now instead of spending so much."

"I am making money. . .but not enough to expand. This will be the last time I come to you for anything. I promise."

How many times had he promised this exact same thing? She couldn't count them on both hands. Paul had started turning him down, but after he died and left Carol with enough for retirement and a little extra cushion, Michael's money radar zoomed in on her nest egg.

"Let me think about it. When do you need it?"

Michael coughed, something he did when he was nervous. "Um, it would be nice to have it in the next week or so."

"Sorry, Michael, I can't get to my money that fast."

"I guess I can wait a little longer. When can you get it?"

Carol thought for a moment. "Let me call you back tomorrow. I'm on my way out the door."

"I was hoping. . ." His voice trailed off before he added, "Okay, I'll talk to you tomorrow."

Distracted, Carol forgot her shopping list, so she had to turn around and go back home. All the way to the store, she thought about Michael and how, at the age of thirty-nine, he was still asking for money. She didn't mind helping him out when he was fresh out of college, but when he hit thirty and still hadn't found himself, she became concerned.

Paul had talked to him about responsibility more than once. Carol thought Paul was a little hard on him, but she supported her husband. The last time Michael asked for something when Paul was still alive, the three of them sat down and had a long talk about being a good steward. Then after Paul passed away, Michael didn't give grass time to grow over his dad's grave before he approached Carol. She was embarrassed that Alex had overheard the conversation, and she found herself making excuses for her son.

"He's our youngest, and everyone always babied him," she'd explained.

Alex shook his head. "That doesn't make it okay. Paul

talked to me about it, and I agree with what he said."

Carol didn't want to argue, so she changed the subject. After the insurance check arrived a couple of months later, she gave Michael the money he wanted, and he promised never to ask for anything else.

By the time she arrived at the grocery store, she'd lost the mood to cook. Fortunately, the store wasn't crowded, so she zipped in and out without having to wait too long.

A couple of times throughout the day, she stopped and stared at the phone. She remembered when she and Paul talked about, how one of these days, they'd be able to enjoy retirement without having to worry about the kids. They'd be free to pamper the grandchildren then go off on their merry way. That never happened.

She used her pent-up energy to whip through the house in a cleaning frenzy. Then she soaked in the tub filled with bubbles. Finally, she felt relaxed enough to enjoy having Alex over.

He arrived with flowers and a wide grin. As she smiled back and took them, she noticed his grin had faded.

One look at Carol, and Alex knew something was wrong. Behind her smile was a troubling thought. Anything that bothered her bothered him, as well.

"Smells good," he said as he followed her into the kitchen. He watched as she put water in the vase then arranged the flowers according to color and height.

She glanced over her shoulder and forced another smile. "I cooked your favorite."

"That's good," he said as he took a step closer to her, never taking his gaze off her face. "Now would you like to tell me what's wrong?"

Chapter 4

Carol shrugged and tried not to look directly at him. But he wasn't going to let her off the hook. She needed to stop trying to shoulder her burdens alone.

"Nothing's wrong," she said, her voice a higher pitch than usual. "At least nothing either of us can do anything about."

"I'm a good listener."

She glanced down then looked back up at him, her fake smile replaced by a solemn expression. "It's Michael. He called."

Alex should have known. Of Carol and Paul's four children, two were self-sufficient, one had died a few years ago, and the youngest still hadn't learned to stand on his own two feet. "Let me guess. He wants money."

Carol swallowed hard, pursed her lips, and offered a brief nod. "And not a small amount."

"Of course not." Alex couldn't hold back the sarcasm. "You told him no, I hope."

She quickly looked away. "Not exactly."

"Carol," he said as he closed the distance between them.

"You don't need to support Michael. He's a grown man. He must be getting close to forty."

"He just turned thirty-nine."

"Do you realize that by the time Paul was thirty-nine he was supporting a family with four children?"

Carol nodded. "But Michael is different. He never—"

Alex held up his hands. "You don't have to explain anything. Would you like for me to talk to him?"

"No." Her reply came so quickly, even Carol seemed stunned.

"You do realize last time Paul turned him down Michael came to me, right?"

Carol gasped and looked at him, her eyes wide. "I had no idea. What did you tell him?"

He shrugged. "Same thing Paul told him. Get a job."

"He said his business has fallen on hard times, and he needs the money to compete."

Alex instinctively reached out and touched her shoulder. She tensed, so he dropped his hand. "His business needs better management so it won't keep falling on hard times. Some people aren't cut out to have their own businesses. He has a degree. He can find a job."

"I don't know," Carol said as she turned away from him and picked up an oven mitt. She stood with her back to him before she opened the oven door then closed it again. When she turned back around to face him, she looked like a woman who'd been beaten down—unlike the Carol from the day before. "Michael has always been the sensitive type."

"He needs to get over it." Alex forcefully but gently guided her to one of the kitchen chairs. After she sat, he lowered himself into the adjacent chair. "Paul made sure you had enough money to keep up the lifestyle you've worked so hard to have. If you continue giving money to Michael, you won't have what you need."

Carol looked conflicted, but she didn't respond. She looked him in the eye then stood up again.

"Okay, I understand. You don't want to discuss it. Just know that if you need to talk, I'm here for you."

"Thanks, Alex."

The rest of the evening was peaceful as they avoided the subject of Michael. However, the long silences that frequently hovered were reminders of what they didn't want to discuss. Finally, after dinner, Alex helped her with the dishes then said he needed to go.

"I'm sorry I'm not much fun tonight," she said. "I just can't enjoy myself when I know one of my children needs me."

"Don't forget, Carol, that other people might need you, but you have needs, too. No one is so strong that they can hold the weight of the world alone."

~ ❧ ~

After he left, Carol contemplated calling Michael back and telling him exactly what Alex had said. But she couldn't. Instead, she wrote a note to herself to contact her financial advisor, Weyland, an old friend from church. She planned to help Michael one more time.

The next day, she called Weyland and told him she needed a check drawn from her account. When she told him it was for Michael, he said the same thing Alex had said. "Paul specifically said this money was for you and not the children."

"I know," she replied, "but helping Michael makes me feel better."

He sighed. "I can't tell you what to do with your money, but I can advise you on how to handle this."

"Okay. I'm all ears."

After Weyland told her she needed to consider this a loan rather than a gift, she said she'd consider it and to wait until she got back with him before doing anything. Then she called Michael. He didn't waste a single minute answering his phone.

"Thanks, Mom. I appreciate it."

"This time, it's different," she said, doing her best to keep her voice steady. "I want you to sign a promissory note."

"A what?" His voice cracked, and he let out a nervous chuckle.

"A promissory note. Michael, this isn't a gift. It's a loan."

"I don't know if I can do that. Business is tough, and. . ."

"If you don't think you can pay this back, I'm afraid I'll have to turn you down."

"But, Mom, this will be my inheritance eventually. I don't see why—"

Carol almost couldn't believe her ears. Anger boiled inside as she realized what her son was doing. "Michael! Don't you ever come to me expecting your inheritance early."

"I was just saying—"

"Good-bye, Michael. Don't come back begging for money, ever again." She slammed the phone down with such force, the wall shook.

She lifted a trembling hand to her mouth as the impact of what she'd done sank in. Both Paul and Alex had been right. If it hadn't been for Weyland's advice to demand a promissory note, Michael would have kept coming to her for money until he had what he thought was his share of the inheritance. Knowing that was difficult enough, but now she needed to call Weyland back and tell him not to sell the fund.

Weyland didn't seem the least bit surprised, and he didn't harp on the issue. Instead, he thanked her for getting back to him so quickly and reminded her that he was there if she needed him. The rest of the day was difficult, and her routine chores saved her.

A few days later, Alex called and asked her to go look at some property with him. "I'm thinking about moving farther out, if I can sell my house."

That sounded like fun. "Sure, when do you want to go?"

"How about a half hour?"

"I can be ready." All she had to do was freshen her makeup, brush her hair, and slip into a jacket.

He pulled into her driveway exactly a half hour later. "One of the things I love about you, Carol, is that you never make people wait."

"It seems rude to do that."

She loved the sound of Alex's laughter. As they rode away from town, he told her what he knew about the property. "It already has a house on it, so I won't have to do much. The Realtor said it belongs to an elderly woman, and her kids are motivated to sell it quickly. They want to buy her a condo closer to town."

Carol nodded. "As someone else who's knocking on the elderly door, I can certainly understand their concerns."

Alex belted out a snort. "You are nowhere near old enough to be talking like that."

"I'll have you know I'll be sixty-six on my next birthday."

"Good for you," he said. "I'm sixty-eight, and I feel better than I did when I was forty-eight." He made a muscle. "It's all that working out I do."

She giggled. "I do think people take much better care of themselves these days."

"Besides, the woman who lives in the farmhouse is old enough to be our mother. Her kids are in their sixties." Then he told her the price. "I'm sure it must need some work for that price. Property in this area is generally quite a bit more."

"You're probably right."

"But that's okay. I'm pretty good at fixing things, and I don't mind getting my hands dirty."

"Ooh." Carol inhaled deeply and took in the view before her—the blend of naked winter trees and evergreens against the backdrop of snowcapped mountains. "This is pretty."

"I like it, too." He glanced at his directions then made the turn. "It should be coming up on the right in a few minutes. Be on the lookout for a split rail fence with a yellow reflector on the corner."

About two minutes later, she spotted it. "There," she said as she pointed. "Turn there."

Alex followed the directions, and within seconds, the farmhouse came into full view. "Oh, wow. I didn't expect this."

The two-story house was nothing like he'd expected. He'd pictured a dilapidated old house in dire need of a paint job. What he saw before him was a two-story stone house with green shutters that looked like they'd been freshly painted. The tin roof could use some attention, but that was nothing he couldn't take care of in a weekend.

"This place is amazing," Carol said. He turned to her and saw her wide-eyed disbelief. "There has to be something wrong with it. Either that, or we have the wrong farm."

He checked his watch. "Let's go meet the real estate lady."

Chapter 5

The Realtor opened her arms in a wide gesture. "This is the best deal I've seen in years. If you don't jump on it, someone else will." She looked at her watch then cast a glance toward Carol before leveling her gaze on Alex. "In fact, I have an appointment with an eager buyer in a couple of hours, so I have a feeling this place will be sold by the end of the day."

Carol knew a pressure tactic when she heard one, and this was definitely in that category. But she also saw how this place would be desirable. After all, the price of property anywhere near Boulder had skyrocketed.

"I'm interested," Alex said. "But I'm not making a decision right this minute. I'd like for you to show us the place then let us check it out on our own."

"I don't know," the Realtor said. "I mean, I can show you around, but I'm sure someone else from my office will be here soon with prospects."

Alex gave her a long look. "I never make decisions like this unless I know what I'm getting. If I can't look at what you're charging a small fortune for, then something must be wrong with it."

The ping-pong conversation lasted a couple more minutes until finally the Realtor gave up. "Okay, take all the time you need. Just don't blame me if someone comes along and snatches it out from under your nose."

After the Realtor gave a grand tour, pointing out all the best features, she stepped to the side and watched as Alex and Carol wandered around the house. Then they walked outside and checked the foundation.

Finally, Alex turned to Carol. "With the exception of a few cosmetic issues, I don't see a thing wrong with this house." He made a wide, sweeping gesture. "And the land has enormous potential."

"Are you going to make an offer?" She liked everything about the house, but she didn't want to influence his decision, so she kept her opinions to herself.

He looked around again then nodded. "I think so. Of course it will be contingent on passing a very thorough inspection."

"Of course." Carol remembered when she and Paul had purchased their house and how he'd insisted on hiring an inspector.

By the end of the day, Alex had his copy of the signed contract in his hand. "Now let's go celebrate. Are you hungry?"

As if on cue, Carol's stomach growled. They laughed.

Over dinner, they discussed all the things he could do with the place. "What do you think about the wallpaper?" he asked.

"I like most of it," she admitted, "but the kitchen is a little dark."

He traced the edge of his glass with his fingertips then looked her squarely in the eye. "What color would you like to see on the kitchen walls?" His expression was much more serious than his question implied.

Carol shifted nervously in her seat. "Um. . .anything light and bright. But it's your kitchen, not mine, so what do you think?"

Alex shrugged. "What do I know about kitchens or colors? All I know is that I like the structure and layout."

She chewed on her bottom lip for a moment, then blurted, "A very creamy yellow would be nice."

The grin that split his face turned her inside out. "After the closing, you can help me pick the creamiest yellow they have at the paint store."

They discussed not only colors and the floor plan, Alex asked what she thought about farming and raising animals. She told him that had once been one of her dreams as a child, but since she and Paul had started their family so soon after they were married, they never had a chance to pursue it.

"Yes, I remember you talking about that once—about ten or fifteen years ago," he said. "I thought it sounded like a wonderful dream. In fact, that's one of the reasons I was interested in this property."

Carol wasn't sure what he meant by that, but from the way he looked at her now, she knew he was leaving something unsaid. "Don't get me wrong," she interjected. "I love my house and my family, and I wouldn't trade any of it for all the farms in Colorado."

He chuckled. "You do have a nice family. By the way, how

are the kids and grandkids?" He cleared his throat. "Besides Michael, that is."

"I haven't heard from most of them in a while, so I assume they're doing fine, even though they were busy and couldn't come for Christmas. They all promised they would next year. I just hope Garland and Elaine can eventually make amends with their daughter, Christmas."

"Yeah, me, too."

She thought about the others for a moment. "Holly just left to do mission work. I know Sandy and Clark miss her while she's gone, but they certainly understand her desire to do the Lord's work." She inhaled and slowly exhaled. "And there's Noelle. After Marie died, I tried to talk her into moving back to Boulder, but she said it had too many bad memories. From what I know, she's doing just fine, though. She's a good girl."

Alex nodded. "They're all good kids." He paused for a moment and gave her a look letting her know he was about to broach a subject she didn't want to discuss. "Have you decided what to do about Michael?"

Carol shut her eyes and exhaled before looking at him. "I asked for a promissory note."

He lifted his eyebrows in interest. "Oh yeah? What did he say to that?"

"Unfortunately, he didn't like the idea."

"I can imagine." Alex pushed back from the table and folded his arms. "You do understand, Carol, that sometimes kids need tough love."

Suddenly, her defenses rose, and anger replaced the warm,

cozy feelings she had for Alex. "How would you know what kids need?"

Alex opened his mouth, clamped it shut, then shook his head. Finally, he leaned forward and looked her in the eye. "I might not have children of my own, but I've been with you and Paul since yours were quite young. Paul and I talked quite a bit, and he actually took some of my advice. Sometimes it's easier to see what's going on if you're not right in the middle of it." His tone was serious. And he was right.

"I–I'm sorry. I shouldn't have snapped. It's just that we messed up by spoiling Michael, so it's our fault. Who would have ever imagined he'd be so irresponsible with money?"

"If it's any consolation," Alex said as his expression softened, "I think deep down Michael is a very good person. He's also brilliant when it comes to anything computer related."

"Then why is he struggling so?"

Alex rubbed his chin and looked away for a moment before turning back to face her. "I don't think he understands some basic business principles. All the computer knowledge in the world won't pay the bills if he can't handle the business angles."

"What should he do then?"

"In my opinion, his best bet is to work for someone else."

Carol shook her head. "He tried that, but he didn't like how they wouldn't listen to his ideas."

She watched him ponder that for a moment, then he nodded. "Yes, I remember Michael was always a very creative person, which might make it tough for him in a corporate environment."

"Maybe you can talk to him and give him some ideas?"

Alex looked skeptical. "I don't know if he'll listen to me, Carol. Last time I tried, he was pretty angry."

Carol remembered. "Let me try to talk to him first and explain that you want to help him." She paused and studied his face. "You do want to help, don't you?"

"Yes, of course I do. I'll help anyone in your family."

Relief flooded her. "Thank you so much, Alex."

After Alex took her home, she closed the door behind him and leaned against it. Lately, every time she was with him, her feelings got strange. Whenever he touched her, she felt nervous and giddy. The way he looked at her made her feel like a teenager.

Alex didn't head straight home. Instead, he turned toward the Hillside Chapel, where he'd started attending with the Scheirer family many years ago. As he pulled into the church parking lot, George VanCleef, the pastor, was locking the side door. When George turned, he spotted Alex and waved.

"Hey, George," Alex said. "Got a minute?"

The pastor nodded. "Sure, what's on your mind?"

"I have a dilemma, and I wanted to run it by you."

"Want to stay here or go somewhere else?"

Alex offered an apologetic smile. "Are you in a hurry?"

"No, in fact, my wife is at a baby shower tonight, so I'm going home to a dark, empty house."

Alex pointed to the church. "Why don't we just talk here? It won't take long."

"Okay, I'll go back in and turn on the lights while you park your car."

Less than five minutes later, Alex sat across from the pastor in the tiny office with overflowing bookshelves lining one wall and an assortment of pictures and knickknacks on the opposite wall.

"So, what's on your mind?" George asked as he leaned back in his office chair.

"I've been talking to Carol Scheirer lately. . ."

George smiled as if he knew what was coming. "She's a very sweet woman."

"Yes, very sweet. Anyway, Paul's been gone a long time. Five years."

"That's more than enough time for her to mourn and work through her grief."

Alex nodded. "I'm sure she still misses him, but I think she's ready to move on with her life. In fact, I'm sure she's ready. She put the star on the tree."

"The star?" George looked confused. "Perhaps you better start at the beginning and fill me in on some of the essential information."

Alex explained how the star tree topper had always been Paul's finishing touch on the tree each year, but after he passed away, Carol didn't bother with it.

George nodded as he began to understand. "I think I see where you're going with this."

"Ever since I met Carol, I've looked for a woman like her. Someone who loved the Lord and had her genuine sweet nature. An intelligent woman who wasn't too proud to say when she didn't know all the answers."

The pastor smiled. "In other words, you wanted Carol."

Chapter 6

The pastor's blunt response took him aback. "I would never—"

George belted out a hearty laugh and held out his hands. "I understand what you are saying. You wouldn't have even considered loving Carol as anything other than a dear friend as long as Paul was alive. But now that he's gone. . ." His voice trailed off.

Alex hesitated then nodded. "I care about her more than I ever imagined I could."

"And you're feeling guilty about it, right?"

"Well, yes and no. I don't want anyone to get the idea that this is something I harbored while Paul was still alive. But I know that after all this time, she's free to love again, and, well. . . you know."

George leaned forward with his elbows on his desk. "Yes, absolutely. But that doesn't mean there won't be issues the two of you have to work through."

"That's already obvious," Alex said. "I always got along with a couple of her children, but the other two. . .well, not so much. Sadly, I won't have to worry about Marie, since she died a few years ago, but Michael. . .well, he's another story."

"Michael can be difficult, but not impossible." George leaned back and clasped his hands behind his head. "Have you spoken to Michael?"

Alex shook his head. "Not lately. But he has gone to Carol asking for money."

George lifted an eyebrow. "I guess some things never change." He paused and thought for a moment, then he looked Alex in the eye. "Perhaps rather than seeing Michael as a problem, you can see this as an opportunity."

"For what?" He must have missed something.

"You've always been a good businessman. From what I gather, Michael could use a mentor, since he never seems to have enough money to keep his business afloat."

"So you're saying I should be a mentor to him?"

George removed his hands and nodded. "You could give it a try."

"Carol asked me to talk to him, too, but he's never been open to anything I had to say before."

"He's older now," George reminded him. "Michael is a smart man. Why don't you give it another try?" He paused before adding, "What can it hurt?"

Alex thought for a moment. "True. It's not like I'll lose a relationship, since there isn't one to begin with."

"Let me know how this turns out. If you'd like for me to talk to either Carol or Michael, I will."

"No, that's okay," Alex said as he stood to leave. "I'll handle it. I just wanted your perspective."

After he got home, he called Carol and told her what he'd decided. She sounded guardedly happy and told him she'd talk to Michael and set up a meeting.

The next morning, Carol called him back. "I asked Michael if he could meet you for coffee soon."

"And?"

She sighed. "At first he said no way. Then I reminded him that he was the one who needed help, and if he wanted it, he needed to drop his attitude."

Alex knew how hard that must have been for her, and he was proud of her for standing up to her son. "Did he change his mind?"

"Not at first. He tried one more time to talk me into letting him have his inheritance, but when I kept saying no, he finally gave in."

That angered Alex, but he knew this wasn't the time to let her know. Instead, he forced himself to calm down. "When does he want to get together?"

"This afternoon."

That was quick. "Want him to come here?"

"No, I think you'd be better off talking to him at my house. I'll leave the room so you two can have some privacy."

"I'll be there."

They arranged a time then got off the phone. Alex didn't have long to prepare, but he understood business principles well enough to talk off-the-cuff. Still, he wanted some backup, so he grabbed some books off his shelf and bookmarked a few places in each.

When Alex arrived at Carol's house, she greeted him at the

door and led him inside, where he was accosted by the aroma of cinnamon and vanilla. His nostrils twitched, and his mouth watered.

"I made cookies."

He laughed. "You're such a good mom."

"I'm glad you think so." She cast a glance over her shoulder and offered a wry grin. "I don't know if Michael would agree with you at the moment."

"Is he here yet?"

"Not yet. He said he'd be a few minutes late. You can have a seat in the kitchen. I'll pour you some coffee."

Michael arrived ten minutes after the designated time. If Alex had been a betting man, he would have made a substantial wager on Michael's tardiness being a ploy.

Carol leaned over for a hug from her son then pointed to the chair across from Alex. "You really need to pay attention to what he has to say."

Michael narrowed his eyes and glared at Alex as he folded his arms, then turned to his mother with a softer expression. "Okay, fine."

Carol poured Michael some coffee and set a platter of still-warm cookies between them. Then she left the kitchen. "I'll be in my room if you need me."

"We'll be fine," Alex said.

As soon as she left the room, Michael looked at Alex with disdain. "I don't care what you say, I'm not buying into it."

"Fine." Alex firmly placed the pen on the table and leaned back in his chair. "So you have this whole thing figured out without me?"

Michael shrugged. "I've always had it figured out."

"Then what seems to be the problem?"

"Not enough money." The younger man shook his head. "If Mom would just let me have what's going to be mine eventually, I'd be able to rock and roll with my business."

"That's where the problem lies, Michael." Alex tilted his head forward and looked at Carol's son long enough to make him squirm. "The money is not yours. Your father had enough foresight to plan for the future, which meant making sure your mother would be well taken care of financially for the rest of her life."

Michael flipped his hand. "She has plenty of money. All I want is my share."

Alex grunted. "You're not listening. You don't have a share." There was no way he'd even try to talk to Michael until he got that one point.

They volleyed back and forth for almost an hour before Alex stood. "I can see this isn't going to work. If you ever change your mind and show some willingness to listen to me about a workable business plan, give me a call." Alex tossed his business card on the table then turned to leave. He'd made it to the door when Michael cleared his throat.

"Okay, you win. I can't guarantee I'll do everything you say, but I'll listen."

Alex pivoted to face Michael. "You've got one more shot at my advice, young man. If you so much as mention what you consider your inheritance again, I'm outta here."

Michael's eyes widened. "I understand."

"Good." Alex pulled out the chair and sat back down.

"Here's what we need to do."

They spent the remainder of the afternoon discussing Michael's goals and current business plan, which Alex quickly realized wasn't bad. It was just underfunded. He also learned that Michael had a tremendous amount of creativity, and he didn't appear lazy—just frustrated.

It was almost six o'clock when Carol came back in. Her lips quivered into a smile as she glanced back and forth between Alex and Michael then settled her gaze on the table filled with papers and open books. "Looks like the two of you have been hard at work."

Michael nodded. "Mom, Alex really knows his stuff."

Her smile widened. "I know he does, sweetie. That's why I wanted him to talk to you."

Alex listened to them rehash what he'd talked about, then suddenly an idea struck. But he didn't want to talk about it yet—not until he had time to think about it some more. He stood up to leave.

"Why don't you take these books home with you and review the things we discussed?" he said to Michael. "Work up the financials, and I'll help you figure out how to get what you need." He turned to Carol. "Your son is intelligent, and I think he has a very good chance of making a go of this."

Michael stood and reached out to shake Alex's hand. "I appreciate everything."

~⚜~

Carol almost couldn't believe her ears. She'd arranged the meeting between Alex and her son with the distant hope that wisdom would win out over Michael's crazy dreams of getting rich. She never actually thought she'd see this.

After Alex left, Carol pointed to the books and papers on the table. "Need a box for all that?"

"Sure," Michael said, "that would be nice." His mood was definitely more upbeat than when he'd first arrived.

She went out to the garage and brought in a couple of boxes for him to choose from. After he picked the one he wanted, she removed the others. When she got back to the kitchen, he was putting the last of the papers on top. He patted the stack. "There's some great stuff in here."

"I'm glad Alex was able to help you."

Michael pursed his lips then slowly smiled. "You don't know the half of it. What's really cool is that he thinks some of my ideas are stellar."

Carol had to grin at his choice of words—definitely not his own. "I'm sure they are. You've always been very smart."

He bobbed his head then shrugged. "Smart but lacking the business sense I needed to stay afloat. But I'll be fine now, with Alex's help."

Michael left a few minutes later, so Carol decided to have a sandwich before her favorite TV show came on. She didn't have much time to watch television when her children lived at home, but she found that she actually enjoyed some of the talent shows.

The next morning, right after breakfast, Alex called. "Do you mind if Michael and I get together at your place later in the week?"

"Of course I don't mind."

"I told him I'd come up with a solution to his biggest

problem, and I'll have it by then."

"Want to give me a hint?" she asked.

Alex snorted. "I will when I have everything ironed out. In fact, I'd like to run everything past you before I talk to Michael, if that's okay."

"It's definitely okay."

"Then how about the day after tomorrow? Would you like to go out somewhere, and we can talk about it then?"

"Yes," she said softly. "I'd like that."

The next couple of days seemed to drag, but the time for her to get ready to see Alex finally arrived. She took extra care with her makeup and picked out a turquoise sweater, which flattered her skin tones. Then she pulled out the heirloom necklace from Alex, draped it over her collarbone, and carefully fastened the clasp behind her neck. Then she stood back to see the overall effect. After years of not really caring how she looked, it felt good to be back to her old self.

Alex's appreciative look when she opened the front door made her glad she'd taken the extra time to get ready. It also brought back a shyness she'd gotten over since the early years of her marriage.

"Wow." He cleared his throat and reached for her hand. "You look absolutely stunning."

Heat rose to her face. "Thank you. You look nice, too. Let me grab my coat, and we can go."

They made small talk all the way to the restaurant. Once they were seated with their orders placed, Alex opened up about his plan for Michael.

Chapter 7

Carol stared at Alex in complete disbelief. "You can't be serious."

He jutted his chin and nodded. "I'm as serious as I've ever been. I've been in business practically my whole adult life, and I don't think I've ever seen a better opportunity."

She leaned back and stared at the table. All she'd expected Alex to do was talk some sense into her son, and now he was about to join forces with him. "I don't understand. You advised me not to give him money, but you want to finance the whole thing?"

"It's different, Carol, and you know it. You'd be throwing money at someone who doesn't understand basic business principles."

"So what are you doing that's different?"

Alex leaned forward and looked directly at her, a gleam in his eye and a smile on his lips. "Michael and I will be business partners. He'll be the creative guy, and I'll be the money man with the advice from experience. It's actually an ideal business formula."

She fidgeted with the edge of the napkin as she thought about it. "I still don't understand how it'll help my son grow up."

"I'll keep a tight rein on the money and help keep Michael focused. He's not a lazy man, Carol. He doesn't mind working as long as he knows what he's supposed to do."

"So you're saying he lacks focus?"

He nodded. "That's exactly what I'm saying. I'll help keep him moving forward, and everyone will benefit." He smiled and gave her a chance to process what he was saying. "I'm glad he decided not to take money from you, and I'm pleased to have this opportunity."

"I thought you enjoyed retirement."

Alex snickered. "Not so much. In fact, I've been feeling restless lately, and this is just what I need to get the old excitement back."

"Well. . ." Carol sighed and offered a smile. "If you think this will help Michael and make you happy at the same time, you have my blessing."

He reached across the table for her hand. "Thank you. It means a lot to me."

Carol felt a flood of emotions, from disbelief to relief, as he gently caressed the back of her hand. "I'll help, too, if you want."

"Absolutely! If you really want to help, I'm sure we can find something you'll enjoy. Being on the ground floor of a business is exciting, and I'd love to share that with you."

Carol hadn't even considered going back to work until now, but it actually appealed to her. She'd enjoyed cleaning house and socializing, but now she wanted more.

After Alex told her some of the things he and Michael had discussed, his face suddenly grew somber. "How do you think the others will feel? You don't think Garland and Sandy will be upset about this, do you?"

She thought about it then slowly shook her head. "I doubt it. They're pretty well set in their own lives, so I'm pretty sure they'll be fine."

"Let me know if I need to talk to them."

Carol quickly felt indignant. "I can talk to my own kids, Alex. You don't have to rescue me from them. With Michael, I just—"

He held up his hand to shush her. "I'm sorry. I didn't mean it that way. I was just saying. . .well. . ." He rubbed the back of his neck and made a funny face. "I don't know what I was saying. Open mouth, insert foot."

She laughed. "No harm done."

They spent the rest of their time together talking about the business, Carol's children, and Alex's farm. "I think we'll have a quick closing. The estate needs to be settled soon, and there are no complications on my end."

Carol had more to look forward to than she had in a very long time. Being with Alex gave her an overall sense of well-being, something she hadn't had since before Paul's cancer started.

After dinner, they went downtown for a little walk and window-shopping. Occasionally, they stopped, and Carol had no doubt that something besides the business had changed between them.

Alex took her home and walked her to her door. He lingered on her doorstep, looking down at her—but he didn't make a move. The urge to kiss him nearly overwhelmed her, but she managed to restrain herself from pulling him closer.

Finally, he leaned over for a too-brief hug then quickly bounded down the steps to the sidewalk below. "I had a great time, Carol, but I always do when I'm with you."

"Thank you for everything, Alex."

"I'll call." He rested his gaze on her for a couple more seconds before turning to leave.

After she went inside, Carol replayed their conversations throughout the evening. She allowed her thoughts to linger on the few moments when silence fell between her and Alex. Her insides had crackled with electricity humming throughout her chest and mind each time he looked at her with warmth and an emotion that neither of them verbalized. Romantic thoughts swirled through her head, but fortunately, she hadn't been put to the test tonight. She wasn't quite ready to act on her emotions.

She got ready for bed and prayed for guidance in her relationship with Alex. He'd already overcome the shaky relationship he'd once had with Michael. As she thought about it, she realized most of her son's problems started with the way she and Paul—and even the other children—had babied him most of his life. Nothing was ever expected from him; therefore, he didn't show much responsibility. The other kids had turned out okay, with the exception of a few glitches, like when Marie rebelled as a teenager and got pregnant. But even that had turned out okay after an extensive counseling session with the pastor.

Carol crawled beneath the covers and lay in bed staring at the ceiling as a peaceful sense of contentment flowed through her. Now that all her children and some of her grandchildren were grown, her responsibilities had shifted. Rather than having to deal with their daily needs, she could focus on her own walk with the Lord. In fact, that was what she needed more than anything. She thought about how she'd worried about Michael, then Alex came along, and suddenly after their business meeting, her youngest son showed an amazing amount of maturity. All her worry had been for nothing.

After Marie had died, Garland, Sandy, and Michael had pulled together and let Carol know that they'd always be there for her. Carol knew that Garland and his wife, Elaine, had issues with their own child, so she rarely talked to them about anything that hinted of trouble. Sandy and her husband, Clark, had their hands full as well, but they had a nice family life without strife.

Carol smiled and thought about how all her children had grown up in the same home, yet they turned out so different. The oldest, Marie, and the youngest, Michael, were sensitive and creative in different ways. Marie chose the drama route, while Michael, being the quieter one, started out drawing then turned his passion toward electronic media. Garland was always a good student, and he fit in well with society. Sandy chose a traditional lifestyle, similar to Carol's.

Alex had been through all of the Scheirer family's good times and bad, ever since the children were small. In fact, Michael was a baby when they met. Even though he'd never had children of his own, he held baby Michael as though the child were his own.

Carol drifted off to sleep with all these thoughts and memories swirling through her mind. When she awoke, she felt rested and had the urge to do something different. She called and asked her old friend Gail if she was up for a shopping trip.

"Sounds like a great idea!" Gail said. "And let me treat you to lunch."

Carol laughed. "I'm the one who invited you, remember? If anyone treats, it should be me."

"You had that wonderful Christmas party at your place. Oh well, it doesn't matter. It'll just be fun getting together."

"Like old times," Carol added.

"Yes, like old times." Gail's voice softened.

Carol suspected that a memory of Paul had crept into her friend's mind. But that was okay. Carol was finally able to accept that the only part of Paul she had left besides the children were the memories.

Gail stopped off and picked Carol up, then they headed downtown. The sky was blue with a few puffy, white clouds, and the spring air was cool and crisp—perfect for a light jacket. Carol had a good feeling that all was right in her world.

"I'm glad to see you so chipper," Gail said as she maneuvered her car into a parking spot. "You look fabulous, too."

"Thanks." Carol smiled at her friend. "I feel better than ever."

Gail narrowed her eyes and studied Carol. "You're actually acting like your old self—only better."

Carol laughed. "What is that supposed to mean?"

"I don't know," Gail admitted. "It's sort of strange. You

remind me a little of how my daughter acted during her engagement. Cheerful and somewhat reflective, I guess."

Carol opened her car door. "Let's stop analyzing and do a little shopping."

They flitted from one store to the next, making a small purchase here and there, but mostly window-shopping. Carol found the perfect scarf to wear with the turquoise sweater Alex liked so much.

"Looks like you're into accessories these days," Gail acknowledged.

Carol thought about what she had in her shopping tote— a silver bracelet, a scarf, and a couple of belts. "I didn't think about it much, but you're right. Sometimes all it takes to update an outfit is one little accessory."

They walked a few more steps before Gail pointed to Lucy's Café. "I've worked up an appetite."

"Me, too. Let's eat."

After they were seated, Gail let out a long sigh. "It seems like as I get older, my life centers more around food than anything else."

"I know what you mean." Carol talked about the last couple of times she ate out, and of course, Alex was with her both times.

Gail leaned forward and propped her elbows on the table. "You and Alex are getting closer these days. Is something going on that you haven't told me yet?"

Once again, heat rose to Carol's cheeks, and that flustered her more than anything. She hadn't blushed this much since she was a teenager. "No, not really."

"If things change, you will tell me, won't you?" Gail lifted an eyebrow.

Carol waved off the comment and turned her attention to the menu. As she perused the offerings, she thought about how things really had changed—for her, anyway. And she wondered how Alex felt.

Chapter 8

Y ou know I will." Carol glanced around the room and tried to think of something else to talk about. "This is a good time of year to be in Boulder."

A puzzled look came over Gail, then she tilted her head and laughed. "Okay, I get it. You're not ready to discuss your feelings for Alex. I completely understand."

Carol was happy when Gail flitted from one subject to the next. She loved that about her friends from church. They didn't mind respecting her personal space.

The next several weeks were busy for Carol—between helping Michael and Alex start their new business and feeding her son who hung around the house more than usual. One evening, he'd even suggested moving back into her house to save money. If Alex hadn't been there, she might have gone along with him. However, Alex didn't think it was such a good idea.

"No way." Alex had looked Michael in the eye. "You're a businessman now—with responsibilities that lie beyond work."

Carol held her breath as she prayed for peace. To her surprise, Michael nodded.

"Yeah, you're right. How would it look to potential clients for me to still be living at home with Mom at my age?"

When Michael wasn't looking, Alex cut his glance over to Carol and winked. She grinned.

Michael lifted one of the papers on the table in front of him and studied it. Alex cleared his throat. Both Carol and her son looked at him.

"We need to start out with a prayer." Alex's tone was firm. He reached for Carol's hand then turned to Michael, who pursed his lips before taking both Alex's and his mother's hand.

Silence fell among them for a few seconds before Alex began his prayer of thanksgiving and for guidance in every decision. After he finished, Carol whispered, "Amen." She opened her eyes and saw that Michael still had his shut. She glanced over at Alex who patiently waited.

When Michael opened his eyes, Alex leaned forward. "Ready to get started?"

Michael nodded. Carol noticed that the mood had become somber, which wasn't a bad thing. It was just strange.

After they finished discussing business, Alex closed in prayer. This time, Michael scooted away from the table and folded his hands in his lap.

Each time the three of them got together, Carol was amazed at how knowledgeable and business savvy Alex was. She knew he'd owned several businesses over the years, and he'd turned all of them into profit makers. She never really thought much about how that happened until now. His keen eye and willingness to let things go that weren't relevant to their goal gave him a distinct edge.

"I'd like to provide a long menu of Internet services to clients," Michael explained. His chin lifted as he placed the list of what he wanted to do in front of Alex.

Carol studied Alex as he looked over the list, leaned back, and rubbed his chin. "Very interesting. I can see you did your homework, Michael. Have you calculated how much time you need to spend on each of these?"

Michael shrugged. "Not really. They all kind of work together, so I figured we needed to give the clients choices."

"I can see that." Alex grabbed a nearby pen. "Let's figure out how time-consuming each of these items will be and factor in the profit."

By the end of the day, Michael had willingly pared down his list of options for future clients. He even thanked Alex, which was out of character for him until now. Carol had no doubt how Alex had been so successful, with not only the business acumen but his tact.

"We have to remember that we need the solid foundation of our faith," Alex reminded him, "or this business will crumble."

Carol held her breath as she turned to her son to see his reaction. He reached out, shook Alex's hand, and pulled him in for a pat on the back. "I know. That has become obvious lately."

"As long as we don't ever forget that number one business principle, I have no doubt we'll accomplish what we need to."

"It's not all about the money, either," Michael agreed. "You've reminded me of quite a bit, Alex." He turned to Carol. "Thanks, Mom. You've been great."

After Michael left, she turned to Alex. "Do you realize what you've done in a matter of weeks?"

His forehead crinkled as he cast a quizzical glance toward her. "What do you mean?" He stood breathtakingly close to her.

Tears stung the backs of Carol's eyes as she reached out and gently glided her hand over his cheek. "Thanks to you, my son—my baby son—is growing up. He's finally coming back to faith, and he's taking some responsibility."

Alex lifted his hand to her wrist and circled his fingers around it, making her feel dainty and protected. "It's time, Carol."

She swallowed hard as she glanced down then back up at him. "None of us realized how much we babied Michael until it was too late to do anything about it."

"It's never too late for him to become a man, but he needs to learn from another man. I'm sure Paul would have done the same thing I'm doing."

Suddenly it occurred to Carol that Alex was acting out of a sense of duty. "Don't feel you have to take over for Paul."

"I'm not taking over for Paul. I'm doing it because I think Michael is a very smart man." He tucked his fingertips beneath her chin and lifted it. "And I have to admit, part of my motive is to get on your good side."

Carol couldn't help but laugh. "You've never been on any other side, Alex. You know that."

He slowly lowered his face to hers and gently placed a

light kiss on her lips. Her senses buzzed with a surprising yet delightful sensation.

"Alex." Her voice barely came out in a whisper.

As quickly as he'd moved in for the kiss, Alex stepped back to the table and started gathering his papers. "There are some things we need to discuss soon, Carol, but now's not the time."

Carol didn't trust her voice enough to speak, so she nodded. She walked him to the door, where he turned to her, took her hand and kissed the back of it, then headed for his car without another word.

As she closed the door, Carol had no doubt that at some point over the past several weeks, she'd fallen in love with Alex. And based on the way he acted, he felt something, too.

She headed back to her bedroom to get ready for bed, but the glistening necklace from Alex caught her attention. He hadn't given it to her lightly—on a whim or without some sort of meaning behind it. It was too precious for that.

As she ran her fingertips along the smooth stones, she wondered why he'd chosen her. Alex was an attractive man, and he could have anyone he wanted. The selection of single women—either widowed or never married—at church was ample.

When Paul had been alive, he'd managed to talk Alex into dating a few times, but his relationships never lasted. The women were always willing to continue, but Alex wasn't interested.

"What do you think his problem is?" Carol had once asked Paul.

Paul snickered. "He can't find anyone as good as you." He

put his arms around her and gazed lovingly into her eyes. "Face it, Carol, I married well, and it's hard to find someone who can even come close to matching your qualities."

Carol had always assumed that Paul was talking out of love. She knew she wouldn't have been the best match for just any man. In fact, one of the things that made her want to be such a good wife was Paul's unwavering love. Had the Lord decided to bless her twice?

She giggled to herself at how her tummy fluttered and her heart pounded whenever Alex looked at her. His touches sent her into orbit, made her blush, and gave her the sensation of being sixteen years old again. That's how old she'd been when she first started dating Paul. There had never been another man in her life—until now. How ironic that Alex had once saved Paul's life, and now after Paul had passed away, he'd stepped into her life—not to save it but to bring so much joy.

Carol sighed and put the necklace into her special drawer reserved for her most prized pieces of jewelry—right beside her engagement ring from Paul and the bracelet her father had given her mother on their first Christmas together. Alex's intentions weren't completely clear to Carol, but she knew he cared for her quite a bit.

Alex had to admit he was surprised at how much thought Michael had put into his business. Not only was he creative and intelligent, he understood his market. The only pieces of the success quotient he'd missed were the understanding of sound business principles and the ability to focus on his ultimate goal.

"And relying on the Lord for guidance," Carol had reminded him.

"That goes without saying."

Alex rehashed some of his conversations with Michael, and he realized some things about the Scheirer family dynamics. Although Carol and Paul had brought their children to church and prayed with them at home, once the kids became adults, they allowed more worldly things to pull them away.

According to Carol, after Marie's death, Michael, Sandy, and Garland were so hurt and confused, they blamed God for their loss. It had been especially hard on Garland, who had always been extremely close to his oldest sibling.

Maybe one of these days they'll come around. Until then, Alex needed to concentrate on helping Michael learn the principles he needed for success. Being a business partner put him in a position of teaching Michael without making him sound like a busybody.

He continued mulling everything over in his mind, until it dawned on him. Making Michael his partner wasn't just about helping Carol's son. It also gave Alex a sense of family. Michael was like the son he never had. That thought alone increased his mission and doubled his energy.

Once they settled into a small office in a building Alex owned and had started accepting clients, Alex showed Michael how to take each client from the introductory phase to being an established customer. He encouraged Michael to slow down when the pace became frantic.

"You don't have to take on everyone who wants your services," Alex explained after he'd turned down someone who wanted them to do something he wasn't comfortable with. "We have a business plan and a mission statement, and our clients need to be a good fit, or we'll suffer."

Michael seemed skeptical at first, but when the next several clients requested a listing of others they'd done business with, he agreed. It wasn't long before they had enough word-of-mouth business, and they didn't need to advertise.

Carol was a trouper, too. She skillfully handled quite a bit of the daily work, including phone calls and bookkeeping. A few times, she'd even offered to help with some of the marketing for clients.

At the end of a long week, after Carol left the office, Michael asked Alex to hang around for a chat. "Sure, I don't have anything else to do," Alex replied. "What's on your mind?"

Michael sat down and motioned for his partner to sit in the chair across from him. Once Alex was situated, he felt a strange tension in the air.

"Is everything okay?"

"I had a question that I didn't want to discuss in front of my mom."

Suddenly, Alex's ears began to ring. "What's wrong?"

Michael shook his head and let out a faint grunt. "Nothing, I hope. I just wondered. . ."

Alex narrowed his eyes. "Out with it, Michael. What is going on?"

The younger man inhaled deeply then slowly exhaled before looking directly at his mentor. "I want to know your intentions with my mother."

Chapter 9

Alex wasn't about to discuss his intentions before first talking about them with Carol. "I understand your concern," he began before taking a deep breath and blowing it out. "But that's something your mother and I need to discuss first."

Michael tightened his jaw for a moment, giving Alex the idea he wasn't happy. Then a smile crept over his face, and he nodded.

"I think I can figure it out for myself. I just wanted to hear it from you."

Alex snickered. "Don't assume anything, Michael. Whenever I've done that, I've been wrong as many times as I've been right."

Michael didn't stop smiling. He stood, picked up his briefcase, and edged toward the door. "Whatever. Just know that you have my blessing. Mom seems happy whenever you're around, and I like seeing her laugh."

"You're a good son, Michael." Alex offered a grin of his own. "And thanks for your blessing. Ya never know if I'll need it."

After Michael left, Alex felt the air leave his lungs as a rush of relief flooded him. He hadn't realized how tense he'd become. Now that his feelings were obvious to Michael, he figured it was time to let Carol in on his desires.

He glanced at his watch and thought about calling her, but he held back. She'd just left the office and barely had time to get home, plus it had been a crazy-busy week. The least he could do was give her some time to relax before he sprang anything new on her.

After work, Carol had gone out to her car and waited a few minutes, hoping Alex would come out shortly afterward. But he didn't—and neither had Michael. She thought about going back inside to see if something had come up, but she decided not to. Even if there was more work on her desk, she was exhausted, and the likelihood of making a mistake when she was in this frame of mind was greater.

It only took her ten minutes to get home. She walked past the kitchen and headed straight for her bedroom, where she shed her work clothes in favor of jeans and a sweatshirt. She put on some comfy flats and went back to the kitchen, where she fixed herself a cup of hot tea before sitting down at the kitchen table. The large picture window overlooked her backyard, where memories had been made over the years.

In spite of being well into spring, snow had begun to fall. Carol felt warm and toasty inside the house that insulated her from the chill in the air. She'd never imagined herself working so hard at this point in her life, but she actually enjoyed it.

Carol sipped her tea and continued to reflect on her day,

until the shrill sound of the phone ringing jolted her. It was Alex.

"Glad to know you made it home okay." He cleared his throat. "At least the snow probably won't stick to the roads."

"I hope not," she said. "What time did you and Michael leave?"

Silence fell over the line for a couple of seconds. "We hung around the office for about half an hour after you left. Why?"

"Did I miss anything?"

"Um. . .not really. At least not anything you won't find out about."

She let out a nervous laugh. "What's that supposed to mean?"

"We'll talk about that later. How would you like to go somewhere special tomorrow? According to the weather forecast, it's supposed to clear up." His voice sounded strained—totally unlike she'd ever heard it.

"What did you have in mind?"

"It's a surprise."

"At least let me know what to wear. I don't want to freeze."

Alex chuckled. "Okay, then wear something warm. I'll pick you up around ten. Plan on being gone most of the day—that is, unless you have something else you'd rather do."

Carol couldn't think of anything she'd rather do than be with Alex. "No, I'm fine. All day, warm clothes. Hmm. We're not going hiking, are we?"

"No, not hiking. I figured you'd be exhausted from the busy week we had."

"Hey, if you want to go hiking, I can do it."

Alex let out a snort. "I have no doubt you can do anything you set your mind to do. But no, I have something more relaxing in mind. Just dress casual."

Carol was puzzled by their conversation. Alex sounded like he was hiding something, and it threw her equilibrium off a little. "Okay, I'll be ready."

After she got off the phone, she got up to heat some leftovers. She was about to pull her plate out of the microwave when she heard the doorbell.

By the time she got to the front door, Michael had already let himself inside. "I didn't want to barge in without warning," he explained.

Carol made a face. "You never have to ring the doorbell, Michael. I was just sitting down to eat leftovers. If you're hungry. . ."

He held his hands up. "No thanks, Mom. I just wanted to make sure you were okay. You've worked hard all week."

"We all worked hard," she agreed.

Michael closed the distance between them and placed his hands on her shoulders. "Mom, you're amazing. Even when I acted like an idiot, you were always there for me."

"That's because I'm your mother, and I love you, no matter what." She pulled back a little and looked him in the eye. "I figured you'd eventually find something that made you happy."

He grinned. "Alex is a cool guy. He's helped me more than you can ever imagine."

"All you needed was a little direction." She chewed on her bottom lip for a moment then decided to find out from his perspective what he and Alex did in the office after she was gone. "I noticed that both of you hung around the office after I left."

Michael quickly averted his gaze. "We just had to wrap up a few loose ends."

"You're not going to tell me anything, are you?"

He smiled. "There's nothing to tell."

Carol closed her eyes and shook her head. "Okay, so you and Alex have a secret. That's fine. It's probably just guy stuff that I won't like anyway."

"I have to run. One of the guys from the singles group at church is fixing me up with his sister."

Carol couldn't help but laugh. "His sister? He must really trust you."

He offered an indignant look. "Of course he does. I'm a trustworthy guy."

"Yes, you are, Michael." She gave him a hug then gently pushed him toward the door. "Now go to your apartment and get ready for your date. Wear that navy and light blue plaid shirt I like."

He snickered as he walked out the door, and she heard him mutter, "Once a mom, always a mom."

After Carol closed the door behind Michael, she thought about their brief conversation. There was no doubt in her mind something was up between Alex and her son. Whatever it was, she planned to find out about it tomorrow.

Dinner had cooled by the time she got back to it, but that was okay. She could barely taste it as her mind raced. After she cleaned the kitchen, she headed for the family room, where she watched a little television before getting ready for bed.

The next morning, she awoke before the alarm clock sounded. By the time Alex arrived at ten, she'd eaten a bowl of cereal, showered, and gotten dressed. Then she still had time to run the vacuum through the house and feather dust the furniture.

Alex looked like an overgrown boy standing at her door, hands in his pockets and a big grin on his face. "Ready?"

She nodded. "Let me grab my purse and jacket."

Once they were safely buckled in the car, he turned to her. "You look stunning."

Her face heated up again. "Thank you, Alex."

He held her gaze for a few more seconds before he took a deep breath and turned to face the front. "I hope you have a good time today."

"I'm sure I will. Even if I don't know where we're going."

Alex reached out and squeezed her hand. "We'll be there in about an hour."

All the way to their destination, Alex brought up things from the past—all good things that she'd almost forgotten. "You have a wonderful memory."

"I've been doing a lot of thinking."

"Obviously." She repositioned herself to see him better. "What brought all this thinking on?"

He shrugged. "Whenever something good happens in my life, Carol, you always seem to be there. Most of the time, I think you're the reason I'm such a happy man."

She was speechless. What a sweet thing for him to say.

"When Michael came to me, I have to admit I was a little nervous that he might want something I couldn't help him with." Alex paused and cast a glance toward Carol before turning his attention back to the road. "However, even that has turned out to be something wonderful. I didn't really want to stay retired, but I couldn't find something challenging enough to pursue it."

"I'm happy for both you and Michael." She thought for a moment before adding, "And me. I've enjoyed working again."

"You're doing a wonderful job. It almost feels like we're..." His voice started to trail off, but after he licked his lips, he finished. "It's like we're a family."

Carol felt a catch in her chest. She'd felt it, too, although she didn't dare say it.

"We're almost there," he said. "I hope you enjoy my surprise."

When they pulled onto a dirt road leading to a ranch, Carol looked at him, puzzled. "Are we visiting someone?"

"No, we're going horseback riding."

"Horseback riding?" she said with a giggle. "I haven't done that in years."

"I know. I wanted to take you on a hot air balloon ride, but it was a little too cold. We'll do that later." He lifted a shoulder in a half shrug then let it fall. "Besides, horseback riding was on the list of things you wanted to do."

She laughed. "Life with you is such an adventure, Alex."

Suddenly, his expression changed. His Adam's apple bobbed as he swallowed hard. "I hope you continue to think that way."

Carol felt that the earth beneath her shifted as she got out of the car. Alex's demeanor had her confused. He seemed happy, but solemn.

A woman came out of the ranch house and led them to a barn. "The horses you wanted to try out are almost ready, Mr. Knight." Then she disappeared inside the barn while they waited.

"Why are you trying out horses?" Carol asked. "That is, besides checking things off our list."

"Since I now have a small ranch, I figured I needed horses." He shielded his eyes from the sun. "And I remembered how much you used to love horses."

Carol hadn't ridden since she, Paul, and Alex had taken the children when Michael was still a little boy. Alex was right. She did love being on a horse, but there hadn't been enough time, and the children had her running all over the place.

"So you'll let me come to your place and ride?" she asked.

He nodded. "You can ride anytime you want to, Carol. My place will always be—" He cut himself off as the sound of a whinny came closer. "There they are," he said, pointing in the direction of the barn. "Aren't they beautiful?"

Carol nodded. "Stunning."

He helped her mount the smaller horse, then he got on the other one. The young woman who'd brought out the horses gave him some instructions before going back to the house.

"Let's head over there," he said, pointing to a nearby hill. "It's been a long time since I've been here, but I remember the gorgeous view."

They rode side by side in silence. Carol couldn't remember the last time she felt this peaceful. As they rounded the bend, she gasped.

The vision before her was mind-boggling. The sun reflected

off the Flatirons, casting an ethereal glow of deep purples, blues, and greens in the foggy mist surrounding them.

"Let's dismount here," Alex said. "We can hitch the horses and take a little walk."

Without another word between them, they found a place to tether the horses, then he took her hand in his and led her to a clump of trees. He leaned against it and wrapped his arms around her. With a slight hesitation, he leaned over and kissed the top of her head.

"This is beautiful, Alex. So peaceful and inviting."

He turned her around to face him. Then he gazed at her until she looked directly into his eyes.

"I wanted to bring you here because it's a special place to tell you something I've wanted to say for a long time."

She held her breath as she waited. Alex looked nervous but resigned. . .and happy.

"Carol, I love you with all my heart." As she tried to catch her breath, he got down on one knee and kissed the back of her hand. "Would you consider doing me the honor of becoming my wife?"

Chapter 10

Carol opened her mouth, but nothing came out. Her mind swirled with all sorts of thoughts, although there was no doubt what her answer was. Finally, she knew she needed to give him an answer since he remained on one knee, waiting. So she nodded.

His eyes glistened as a wide grin erupted on his face. The sight of this tall, broad-shouldered man with the full head of white hair on the verge of tears completely undid her. She burst into tears and leaned over for a kiss.

"Yes," she finally managed to say. "I'll marry you."

"This is the most wonderful day of my life," he said as he stood and pulled her back into his arms. "It's perfect."

Then suddenly, as though she'd been splashed with a bucket of ice water, Carol remembered her children. Her hands flew to her face. "I spoke too fast. I can't give you an answer yet."

"What?" His perplexed expression stabbed her heart.

"I have to make sure it's okay with the kids."

Alex took her hands in his. "Your children are grown,

Carol. You have a whole life ahead of you. Why do you have to ask their permission?"

Now the tears flowed down her cheeks. "This will affect them, too, so I think they need to be behind us on this. Alex, I would love to just say yes and ride off into the sunset with you on those gorgeous horses. . .but at this point in my life, I have to consider other people."

Finally, he nodded. "Yes, I understand. It's one of the things I love about you, even though it hurts me at the moment."

"Have you already spoken to Michael about this?"

Alex grinned. "Not in so many words, but he knows it's coming. And I think he's okay with it."

She thought about her other two children who were still living. "I'm pretty sure Sandy will be fine with it, but I'm not sure about Garland. He's always been a little difficult."

"Why don't you call them now?"

"On the phone?"

Alex nodded and grinned. "That's the easiest way."

She pulled her cell phone from her pocket and tried to place a call, but there was no signal. He offered his phone, and it worked. Her first call went to Michael.

"Great news, Mom, but I'm not surprised. Hand the phone to Alex so I can congratulate him."

Carol gave Alex the phone and watched as he grinned and winked at her. "Thanks, Michael. I thought you'd be okay with it." He listened for a moment then laughed. "Will do." After he got off the phone, he handed it back to Carol. "He told me to behave and treat you right, or I'd have him to answer to."

She giggled and punched another number into the phone.

"I'll talk to Garland next," she whispered as her son's phone rang.

Carol made strained small talk with Garland for a couple of minutes. Ever since he'd married Elaine, Carol had felt a disconnect with her second oldest child.

"Did you call me for a reason, Mom? I need to get back out to the garage. I promised Elaine—"

She interrupted him. "Yes, I did call for a reason. Alex has asked me to marry him, and I'd like your blessing."

Carol held her breath while she waited for him to process the news. Finally, she heard him breathing.

"Alex Knight?"

"That's the one," she said with a nervous giggle.

"Are you sure you really want to do this?"

"Yes, absolutely," she replied.

"Then do it. It's your life."

Carol couldn't help but grin. She said good-bye then flipped the phone shut with one hand while pumping the air with the other. "He's fine with it!"

Alex lifted her off her feet and twirled her around. "That's wonderful news. Now all you have to do is call Sandy, and we can go looking at rings."

Sandy's husband, Clark, answered the phone. "She's out back right now, Carol. Is there something I can do for you?"

"I wish there was, but I really need to talk to my daughter."

"Okay, if it's that urgent, I'll go get her." He covered the mouthpiece, but Carol could still hear him call out to Sandy. "Your mom's on the phone, and it's urgent. You better hurry up."

Carol smiled and winked at Alex. She wanted to dance

around the field, but she forced herself to hold back—at least until she got her daughter's blessing.

Sandy answered the phone with a worried voice. "Are you okay, Mom? You're not sick, are you?"

"No, honey, I'm fine. I just have some wonderful news I'd like to share. Alex Knight has asked me to marry him."

Sandy gasped. "You're not getting married again, are you?"

"Why yes, I'd like to." Carol was puzzled at her daughter's response. Surely, Sandy would want her to be happy.

"You can't marry Alex. He was Dad's best friend."

"I know, Sandy, but your father is gone. I'm sure he'd understand."

Suddenly, Sandy's voice grew cold. "It's just not right."

Carol felt like someone had opened the earth beneath her, and she was falling into a bottomless pit. "Would you like to speak to Alex? He's right here."

"No." A few seconds of silence passed before she spoke. "Mom, I don't know what's gotten into you, but I can't deal with this right now. I'll call you back tomorrow."

After she flipped Alex's phone shut and handed it back to him, numbness took over the pain in Carol's heart. She slowly shook her head as she looked out toward the Flatirons. "Sandy wouldn't give us her blessing."

"What?"

Carol shook her head. "I'm as surprised as you, Alex. I don't know what to say."

His jaw tightened as he glanced down at the ground before looking back up at her. "If you want me to talk to her, I will."

"No, but thanks. I'll deal with it."

They rode their horses back to the ranch. When the woman came out, Alex told her he'd get in touch with her soon, then he and Carol left.

"Wanna go look at rings?" he asked.

She thought about it for a moment and was tempted to say yes, but the joy of the occasion had been dampened. "Not today, Alex. Maybe some other time."

He nodded. The day ended earlier than planned, but Carol needed to be alone. She suspected Alex needed some time to think, as well.

After he dropped her off with a light kiss, she went inside and sat down on the sofa to reflect. She knew what she wanted, even though she wasn't about to disrupt her family. The phone rang, and she considered not answering it, but it might be important. So she hopped up.

"Mom, this is Michael. What is going on?"

"Nothing, son, why?"

"I just got a call from Sandy. She told me what she said to you, and I told her she was being selfish."

Carol thought for a moment before she finally spoke. "I'm not sure she's being selfish. It's just that she's never been one for change."

Michael grunted. "She's not the one who'll be changing. She has her life exactly how she wants it. Mom, if you love Alex and want to marry him, you don't need to let her do this to you."

"I'll have to think about it some more, Michael. She's calling me back tomorrow. Have you spoken to Garland?"

"Yeah, after Sandy called, I called him. He has his own life, too, and he doesn't care what you do."

That bothered Carol almost as much as Sandy's reaction. "Garland never spent much time around the house growing up."

"He never got along with Dad, that's why."

For the first time ever, Carol didn't try to soften anything. Instead, she softly replied, "Yes, I know. I really need to go, Michael. I have a lot of thinking to do."

"Okay, Mom, but just remember that I'm behind you all the way—whatever you choose."

After she hung up, she looked around the kitchen and spotted one of the family photo albums lined up on a shelf with her favorite cookbooks. She pulled it down and opened it. As she flipped through the pages, she noticed how the family had started out smiling but began to appear more somber toward the end. Finally, she closed the book and thought about Sandy's reaction.

Sandy had always gone with the flow—rarely rattling any cages—while Marie had rebelled at every turn. Marie had even gotten pregnant while still in high school, and Paul's reaction was shocking. He'd threatened to cut Marie off, until Alex reminded Paul that Marie needed the same kind of love Jesus had for all sinners. That calmed Paul down in a flash.

Garland was the wanderer. As soon as he got his driver's license, he took off, was rarely seen, and almost never did anything with the family—including attending church on Sundays. Nothing Garland did surprised Carol, so she wasn't worried about him.

Sandy was quiet and unassuming, so no one ever knew what she was thinking. Her engagement to Clark Rivers was a bit of a surprise, but Carol did everything she could to show her support. Again, Alex had to talk Paul down from one of his many rants.

The more she thought about the dynamics of her family, the more Carol realized how vital Alex had been to their happiness. Paul had developed a temper after his stint in the army, and he blamed everything on his family. If it weren't for Alex, Carol wasn't so sure the family would have fared as well as they had.

Alex wasn't a Christian when she first met him because he was raised in an unchurched home. However, once he heard the gospel, he latched on to it and never let go. Carol watched him absorb scripture and apply it daily, which made her happier than anything she'd experienced outside of her nuclear family.

As darkness fell over the house, Carol decided she couldn't allow Sandy to govern her life. What gave her daughter the right to make decisions for others, when she had no idea what she was talking about?

With the strength of her convictions, Carol decided not to wait until the next day for Sandy to call. She picked up the phone and punched in her daughter's number. Clark answered and said Sandy was too upset to talk to her.

"That's too bad," Carol said as her body tensed. "She needs to get over it and act like an adult."

After a couple of seconds, Clark let out a little cough. "I'll try to get her. Just a minute."

Carol heard voices in the background, and it sounded like arguing. She was about to give up and drop the phone back into the cradle when she heard Sandy's voice.

"I still don't want you to do this, Mom."

Carol squared her shoulders and lifted her chin. "That's really too bad, sweetheart, because I'm doing it anyway."

"But I thought you asked—"

"All I asked for was your blessing, not permission. I love Alex, and he loves me. In fact, he loves all of my children, including you, so you should be happy for me."

Sandy burst into tears, so Carol told her to go cry it out. After she hung up, she called Alex and asked him to come over if it wasn't too late.

Alex arrived in fifteen minutes. "Is everything okay?"

Carol closed the door behind him, pulled him to her, and circled her arms around his neck, clasping her hands behind him so he couldn't get away. "Everything is just fine, Alex, because I am going to be your wife."

He offered a guarded smile but reached back and took her hands in his before leaning away so he could look at her. "But what about Sandy?"

Carol shrugged. "It's not her life. It's mine, and this is what I want to do."

"I'll talk to her if you want."

"You always offer to do that, and I appreciate it." Carol smiled up at him. "She'll come around. Trust me on this. Sandy hasn't ever embraced change at first, but she's a smart woman."

Carol enjoyed having Alex's appreciative gaze on her for several minutes. Then he spoke.

"She gets that intelligence from you, Carol. You're the smartest woman I know."

"I'm certainly smart enough not to let you get away."

"I love you, Carol." He lowered his face to hers and kissed her.

They chatted for a couple of hours and ironed out some of the details. Since they wanted to include many of the family members, they decided to plan the wedding for the day after Christmas because everyone would still be in town. Then Alex went home. Carol fell asleep and woke up with a smile on her face.

Later that morning, Sandy called. "Mom, I'm really sorry for my behavior yesterday. I can't believe I was such a brat. I'm glad you're marrying Alex. He's a nice man."

The joy in Carol's heart soared to the moon. She told Sandy some of the details and promised to let the grand-children know. As soon as she got off the phone, she sat down at the kitchen table and wrote her granddaughters a letter.

Dear Family,

Remember Alex Knight, the man who saved your grandfather's life in Vietnam? After more than thirty years of friendship, Alex and I are in love, and we plan to marry the day after Christmas. I realize you're all busy, but it would mean the world to me if you could join us on this very special day.

Love,
Grandma Carol

Author and speaker **DEBBY MAYNE** grew up in a military family, which meant moving every few years throughout her childhood. Debby was born in Alaska, and she has lived in Mississippi, Tennessee, Oregon, Florida, Hawaii, and Japan. Her comfort foods are as diverse as her interests. You might find her eating sushi while reading a cozy mystery novel or fried catfish while watching a Tampa Bay Buccaneers football game.

Her husband of almost 30 years has accepted the fact that outside of her faith and family, books are the most important thing in her life. She and Wally have two grown daughters, Lauren and Alison; a son-in-law, Jason; and a granddaughter.

Debby has published 16 books, more than 400 short stories and articles, 6 novellas that have been printed in 7 anthologies, and a slew of devotions for busy women. She has also worked as managing editor of a national health magazine, product information writer for a TV retailer, a creative writing instructor, and a copy editor and proofreader for several book publishers. Debby currently enjoys writing Christian fiction, which allows her the freedom to tell stories without restraining her convictions.

She lives on Florida's west coast with her husband and two cats. To learn more about Debby, visit her Web site at debbymayne.com.

I'll Be Home for Christmas

by Elizabeth Ludwig

To my dad. . .you always welcomed me home. And to my mom, who believed in me.

"And he arose and came to his father.
But when he was still a great way off, his father saw him
and had compassion, and ran and fell on his neck and kissed him."
LUKE 15:20 NKJV

Chapter 1

There it was again. The look on Marcus Taggert's face that said he was totally disgusted. Chris had seen it once before, in this very same office, on this very same spot—only her grandfather had been alive to see it, too.

"I'm surprised you came, Ms. Scheirer."

Heat invaded Chris's face. Why wouldn't he be? She hadn't been home since she'd asked Grandpa for her share of the inheritance. Her throat convulsed. "Yes, well, it has been a while."

"Seven years."

Marcus's eyes were as cold as their surroundings. Hard, like the massive oak desk he stood behind. Intimidating, like the brass plate with ATTORNEY AT LAW lettered beneath his name.

She gripped her purse strap tighter. "I suppose you've heard that my grandmother intends to remarry."

At the mention of Carol Scheirer, Marcus's gaze softened. He took his seat and gestured to one of the rum-colored club chairs in front of his desk, which she slid into, gratefully. "I had heard that," he said. "I'm happy for her. Alex is a good man, and

Carol's been alone a long time."

No thanks to her. A familiar wave of guilt rippled through Chris's stomach. She ducked her head to hide her face and pulled an envelope with Marcus's address from her purse. "Your note said if I was ever back in town, I should stop by. You have something for me?"

"So, you're here for your grandmother's wedding, is that it? I wasn't aware Carol and Alex had set a date."

"December 26, the day after Christmas."

His eyes narrowed. "That's less than three months away."

Not nearly enough time to make amends. Chris returned the letter to its spot beside her billfold and stood. "I'm sorry, Mr. Taggert. This may not have been the best time. I apologize for dropping in this way, I just thought"—she tucked a strand of hair behind her ear—"well, I'm not sure what I thought. Please, excuse me. I won't take up any more of your time."

The door seemed much farther away than when she'd come in. She crossed the navy carpet, her shoes swishing softly in her haste.

"Christmas?"

Confused for a split second, she paused with her hand on the knob. Marcus was looking at her, calling her by her full name, not referencing the holiday. She shook her head. "It's Chris. No one's called me Christmas in years."

He looked disappointed by the information, but he rose to his feet, one hand extended toward the seat she'd vacated. "Please, come back. I do have something I think you should see." When she hesitated, he added, "It's from your grandfather."

Grandpa Scheirer's face fluttered in her memory—his

cheerful smile, twinkling gaze, snow-white hair. She trudged back to the chair and sat.

Brought on by stress, the corner of her eye twitched. It wasn't all that visible, she knew, but it added one more thing to the already hefty stack of weapons Marcus Taggert wielded over her. As if sensing her discomfort, he dispensed with further conversation and retrieved an envelope, yellowed with age, from the filing cabinet.

"I ask that you read it here." His tone was firm, his face somber, but otherwise barren.

"Another letter?" She willed the shaking from her fingers as she reached for the envelope. She snatched her arm back when their hands grazed.

Marcus laid the letter on the desk, his sharp eyes cutting ribbons through her flesh as he slid it toward her. Gingerly, Chris picked up the note and slipped it from the envelope.

My Dear Christmas,

The pain stirred by his bold, strong handwriting slammed her like an avalanche, even after all these years. She swallowed hard and forced her eyes open.

My Dear Christmas,
    Welcome home, my darling granddaughter. How I've missed you! I had hoped to speak these words to you in person, but since you're reading this letter, I can only assume it was not to be. Still, I want you to know that I forgive you, my dear one.

At this, a deep, wet fountain welled up from Chris's chest and spilled down her cheeks. What a fool she'd been to stay away after she heard of Grandpa's illness. How selfish to be so consumed with her desire for publication that she'd refused to see anything else.

"Are you all right?"

Marcus's voice startled her, as though he had no right to be there, an interloper on her lapse into the past. She rubbed her index finger under her lashes. "I'm fine."

Her strangled tone said otherwise.

Marcus reached behind him for a box of tissues and held it toward her. She took one, blew her nose, then wadded it up and dropped it into the trash can he slid around the desk.

"Thanks."

He nodded then sat back and folded his hands over his midsection. Apparently, he intended to wait while she struggled through Grandpa's letter. She picked it up again.

I hope you have found happiness. Though it was difficult to see you go, I would not have tried to stop you from experiencing the world for yourself. I pray it has been kind.

My darling, though I say once again that I have completely forgiven you, I must ask something of you. I must ask that you make amends with your family, especially your father.

Her stomach tensed. Her father's disappointment had been so much sharper than anyone else's.

He loves you, Christmas, even if he can't bring him-
self to say the words. Your leaving hurt the family deeply,
him most of all. Even so, there is something in you that
has always been apparent to me, something that tells me
the future of our family rests in your hands. I have sought
the Lord's will in this. His peace fills me, which is why I
left a gift with Marcus, to be given to you once you prove
that you have indeed changed from the self-absorbed child
you were. I do not say this to hurt you. I'm merely stating
what hopefully you already know.

I pray God has blessed you, my dear.

You have all my love,
Grandpa

Drawing a deep breath, Chris lifted her eyes to Marcus.
He watched her intently, his brown eyes measuring. "You knew
about this?" she said.

"Yes."

"How?"

He withdrew a slip of paper from a drawer in his desk and
passed it to her. "Read it."

As in her letter, Grandpa expressed his love for Marcus and
his family, but he also asked that he do his best to ensure Chris
was worthy of the "gift."

"Is he kidding?" She jerked her hand and rattled the page.
"He expects you to follow me around like a little lost dog? Just
what is this 'gift' anyway, and why is it so important?"

Marcus reclaimed the note and carefully folded then
replaced it inside the envelope. "Your grandfather was a lot of

things, but he wasn't the kidding kind."

"No, I guess not." Chris doused her irritation with a bucket of cool, rational thought. She couldn't up and leave, not without seeing her grandmother and telling her how sorry she was for hurting everyone. But could she go that extra step? Could she truly make amends?

"Well?"

Again, Marcus's voice snapped her from her thoughts. She bit her lip. "I don't know." To her dismay, she felt her chin tremble. "My father was so angry. I–I'm not sure. . ."

His eyes narrowed. "I see."

Her stomach muscles clenched as he got to his feet, towering over her a second too long before he crossed to the door.

"Well, I can't say I'm surprised, though I had rather hoped that you'd care enough to at least try to find out what your grandfather left you." He paused with his hand on the knob. "Have a safe trip back to New York, Ms. Scheirer. Can I call you a cab?"

Searing anger evaporated the tears in her eyes. Bad enough Grandpa favored this arrogant, egotistic snob, but Marcus deemed himself fit to judge her, too? She'd just see about that. Gripping her purse to her side, she lifted her chin and got up from the chair. "No, thank you, Mr. Taggert. I've changed my mind. I'll be staying in Boulder, after all."

Chapter 2

Boulder was colder than New York, even this early in October. Chris took a deep breath, the crisp, dry air scraping down her nose and throat. Traces of anger curled around her limbs, holding her rooted to the sidewalk outside Marcus's office until she could compose herself.

A slight breeze swirled around her legs as the door behind her swooshed open.

"You forgot this."

Marcus held out a cream-colored silk scarf, one of the extravagances Chris had bought for herself before Grandpa's money ran out. She took it in trembling fingers. "Thanks."

"No problem." He shrugged and slid his hands into the pockets of his trousers. "So, where you headed?"

Chris glanced down the crowded street, past the bricked path on Eleventh Street where she and Marcus stood, to the mountains in the distance. Where would she go? The days had grown shorter, and twilight was already settling on the peaks of the Flatirons. She was hungry, she had yet to check into a hotel, and Grandma—well, she wasn't certain Grandma Carol would even want to see her.

Marcus reached back, inserted a key into his office door, and snugged the lock. "How about we get something to eat? There's a pizza place a couple of blocks down the street. They serve great Chicago-style. You hungry?"

She was staring, yet even as she realized it, she couldn't stop. "You're kidding, right?"

He lifted an eyebrow and smiled with a look that said he wasn't. "You've got to be tired after traveling all day. Does your family even know you're here?"

He had a point. She frowned. "No."

"Well, there you go. Wouldn't it be better to give them a little warning, and then go out to see them after you've had a chance to rest up?"

She glanced down at her rumpled slacks. A kid in the seat next to her had spilled Coke all over her on the airplane. Not exactly the impression she wanted to make after seven years. Before she could answer, her stomach rumbled.

Marcus laughed. "I'll take that as a yes." He motioned to the jacket slung over her arm. "You'd better put that on. It's starting to feel like snow."

The lowering clouds seemed to prove that out. Chris fumbled with her scarf and purse then reached for her jacket, but before she could slip into it, Marcus grabbed the collar and held it for her. Left without a choice, she turned and pushed her arms through the sleeves then moved quickly away.

"Thanks."

"You're welcome. Do you like pizza?" He strolled down the

sidewalk as easily as if they'd been lifelong friends.

Chris's steps were less certain, but she followed nonetheless. "Love it."

He smiled at her. "Me, too. Pop used to make it from scratch when I was a kid. I always said he should have been Italian."

Eager to keep the light conversation going, Chris matched his tone. "How is your father? I haven't seen him in ages."

A strange look flitted across Marcus's face. He glanced sidelong at her. "He died four years ago."

Chris's heart sank to her toes. "Oh. I–I'm sorry."

Marcus shrugged, and his eyes took on a faraway gleam. "I still miss him."

There was an emotion with which Chris could sympathize. She dropped her gaze to study the red pavers they walked over. "Was he ill?"

Marcus's face flushed. "Pancreatic cancer. It took him quickly."

What could she say to that? Nothing. "I'm sorry," she repeated.

He only nodded.

A large boulder huddled on the corner of Eleventh Street and Pearl. Tourists crouched in front of it, snapping pictures. Under different circumstances, the lights twinkling from the trees and brightly colored mums clustered around the lampposts in celebration of fall would have made for a cheery scene. Tonight, it only made Chris feel lonely. She sighed and wrapped her arms around her middle.

At the restaurant entrance, Marcus paused and held open

the door, allowing her to precede him inside. A warm blast of yeast-scented air flooded her senses.

"Hello, folks," a cheery voice called, ending the awkward silence that had fallen upon them.

Marcus lifted his hand in a wave. "Hey, Dario. Table for two, please."

"Coming right up." Dario froze and stared. "Christmas Scheirer?" He took off his apron and flopped it onto the counter. "It is you! How are you, gal?"

Dario Conti had been friends of the Scheirer family for as long as Chris could remember. She smiled and stepped into his beefy embrace, almost smothering herself with the intoxicating scent of tomato sauce and herbs.

"Hi, Dario."

His grin stretched across his round face as he moved back to hold her at arm's length. "It's so good to see you. You home for the holidays?"

Marcus laughed. "The holidays don't start for another month, Dario."

"They do around here," Dario snorted. "Christmas starts two weeks after Labor Day. Skips right over Halloween and Thanksgiving."

So, things weren't so different from New York, after all, or pretty much the rest of the country, for that matter. Chris smiled and shook her head. "No. I'm home on a little business, actually."

Dario took her arm and led her and Marcus to a quiet booth near the window. "Well, I'm glad you stopped by. It's been too long. You tell your grandmother hello for me, and give her my congratulations on her engagement." He shook a finger at her, his bushy eyebrows rising to meet his hairline. "I want a wedding invitation."

"I'll tell her."

Dario bustled back to the counter and snapped his fingers at a slender young girl standing next to the cash register. "Selma, take care of our best customers. Anything they want, on the house." His jovial smile stretched even farther.

"That was sweet," Chris said, sliding into the booth.

Marcus nodded in agreement. "He's a nice guy. Good family. They go to my church."

Well, now, that was something Chris never expected. She lifted an eyebrow, unable to keep the surprise from showing on her face.

"Don't look so shocked," Marcus said with a grin. "I'm sure there'll be one or two lawyers in heaven."

Chris laughed. He had a sense of humor. No wonder Grandpa liked him so much. She grabbed a couple of menus and offered one to Marcus. "Know what you want?"

He declined it with a wave. "The house specialty—Chicago-style."

"It's good, huh?"

"The best."

She dropped both menus on the edge of the table. "That's good enough for me."

When Selma arrived, they gave her their order then sat back to wait for their drinks. A modest crowd clustered around a television set mounted in the corner. The theme from *Monday Night Football* mingled with their chatter.

"You a Broncos fan?" Marcus said, tipping his head toward the TV.

"You can't live in Colorado and be anything else."

"Ain't that the truth." Marcus shifted to allow Selma to set their soft drinks on the table. She placed them quietly and disappeared. "Always wanted to see Elway play in person," he continued, "but he retired before I got around to it."

"You're kidding! A Broncos fan, and you never went to Mile High?"

"Oh, I went to the stadium, just not to see a game."

Chris picked up a straw, plucked the wrapper off, and stuck it in her drink. "Why, then?"

"Class field trip." Marcus laughed. "Every boy I knew wanted to grow up to play in the NFL after that, me included."

"I bet." Chris settled against the back of the booth. Intentional or not, Marcus was succeeding at putting her at ease, something she would hardly have imagined an hour ago. "So what happened? How come you decided to be a lawyer? Game too rough for you?"

Marcus's eyes flashed, and he leaned forward to rest both elbows on the table. Chris's breath caught. The way his shoulders pulled at the seams of his suit left little doubt as to his physical condition.

"Hardly," he said, his lips twitching. "I just got tangled up in a different kind of game."

A game indeed, but with the glint in his eye making her heart trip erratically, Chris wasn't at all sure she wanted to play.

Chapter 3

Marcus eyed the attractive woman sitting across from him, his thoughts in a jumble. His heart had beat faster when she walked into his office, just like it had the first time he saw her, yet Chris was nothing like the selfish, arrogant young girl he remembered. This person was smart, well-spoken, even seemed a bit shy. Maybe she did take after her grandpa Paul, like Carol said.

He shook the thought loose. Paul had been a kind man, generous to a fault, which was why Marcus had been so angry to see Chris taking advantage of him. He forced himself to look past the pretty face and smiling lips and remember the pain in Paul's eyes when he'd entrusted him with the "gift."

Picking up his soft drink, he twisted the straw and took a gulp. "So, what's the plan for this week? Will you be going by your parents' place?"

Chris's smile vanished and her lashes fell to cover her brilliant blue eyes. Just as well. Marcus had caught himself staring twice already.

"I'm not sure. I guess it'll depend on how Grandma receives me."

Her voice was soft, sincere, but hard-fought cases in court had taught Marcus how easily people could lie.

"That's the point, isn't it? To at least make the effort at amends regardless of how the family receives you?" His tone came out sharper than he'd intended, and she flinched.

"I guess so."

Talk about a heel. . . Marcus mentally kicked himself. His thoughts regarding Paul Scheirer's granddaughter weren't what was important. Fulfilling his promise to an old family friend was.

He picked up a napkin and twisted the edges to give his hands something to do. "Look, if it makes you feel any better, I know they've all missed you, Carol especially. I don't think you have anything to worry about. They'll welcome you with open arms."

To his surprise, she shook her head and pierced him with pain-filled blue eyes. "You don't understand. I don't deserve that kind of welcome. I'd be happy if they just let me stay."

The music floating from the jukebox perched at the entrance faded, as did the noise of the football game, until all he saw and heard was the utter sadness echoing from the depths of her soul. He tore his gaze away. Fortunately, Selma arrived with their pizza, and he was spared from having to answer.

He served a slice for Chris and one for himself then grasped her hand and breathed a quiet blessing before she could protest. Small and soft, her palm fit snugly in his. He let go the moment he said amen.

"Tell me about New York," he said, trying to appear unaffected by the lingering warmth her touch caused.

"It's beautiful this time of year, though nothing like Boulder." Almost absently, she sprinkled a thin layer of Parmesan on top of her pizza. "But what are skyscrapers and traffic lights compared to mountains?"

Marcus cut off a piece and stuffed it into his mouth. Cheese, olives, and onion mingled to create culinary genius. He took his time chewing then swallowed. "You stayed, though, right?"

She shrugged and took a bite. "I didn't have much choice," she said after a moment. "At the time, all I cared about was pursuing my writing career, and New York was the best place to do that. By the time I realized my mistake, it was too late." She glanced down at her food. "This is delicious, by the way."

He smiled and gestured for her to continue. "So? No book contract, I take it?"

"A few articles here and there, some ghostwriting, and freelance stuff." She shook her head. "Never could break into full-length novels. It's a competitive business." She speared a pepperoni and popped it into her mouth.

Marcus washed down a bite with a swig from his Coke. "Mind if I ask what you write?"

"Not at all." Her face brightened and the sparkle returned to her eyes. "I write fiction—mostly historicals. I love the feel of the past, you know? Delving into a period that has slipped the pages of time? It's like an addiction with me."

An addiction. The description was apt considering she'd

given up everything, hurt everyone, pursuing it. He dropped his gaze and concentrated on finishing his pizza.

"What about you, Marcus? You never answered my question." She took a bite, her curious gaze demanding an explanation.

Much as he hated to admit it, he knew his face wouldn't light up the way hers had when he talked about taking over the family business. He couldn't conjure up the same excitement in his voice, even if he wanted to. "I—"

"Yes!" A cheer went up from the crowd at the TV set, and several hands shot into the air to be high-fived by others.

"Did you see that catch?" one of the men shouted.

"Twenty-five yards and there was no one around."

"I thought for sure it was going to be intercepted."

The commotion continued, but Marcus ignored the celebration and motioned toward the leftover pizza. "We can ask them to box that up for you. I'm sure there'll be a microwave in your hotel."

She tilted her head and looked at him curiously but said nothing more.

Marcus motioned for Selma. "A to-go box, please?" When she returned with the leftovers, he slipped her two bills and waved away the offer of change. "Ready?" he said with a glance at Chris.

She nodded and slid from the booth. Once again, he took her light jacket and held it while she slipped her arms through. It looked good on her. The color set off her blond hair and blue eyes, but it would do little to ward off the chill now that the sun had set behind the mountains. He shook his head.

"What?"

"Excuse me?"

She quirked an eyebrow as she fastened each button. "You shook your head."

"Did I?" He shrugged into his trench coat then held his hand toward the door.

She smiled as she moved past. "Bye, Dario," she called, which Marcus echoed.

Dario waved. "Come back soon. Say hello to your grandma!"

Outside, a light snow had begun to fall. It was pretty, but it probably wouldn't stick. Too early yet. Marcus lifted his collar and pulled a pair of leather gloves from his pocket. He glanced at her hands, too slender to stay warm for long in the falling temperatures. "You want these? They'll keep your hands warm."

Wrapping her scarf around her neck, she shook her head. "No thanks. I'll be fine."

"Suit yourself," he said, and tugged them on. A large, fluffy flake settled on the tips of her eyelashes. Marcus smiled and brushed it away with his thumb. Realizing the intimacy of such an action, he took a step back and apologized. "Sorry. You just—you had. . ." He motioned toward his eyes.

She laughed, her breath curling upward in a wispy white cloud. "Not a problem."

Marcus glanced down the street. Several couples walked arm in arm, the lights from the trees creating a sparkling tunnel for them to pass through. His mom used to love this time of year. Before his dad died, they spent hours raking up leaves and carving pumpkins. Mom claimed it helped her get in the mood for Christmas. Marcus knew she never needed an excuse to celebrate her favorite holiday. Suddenly, he was lonely, and he sensed deep inside Chris was, too.

He turned to her. "Hey, you wanna get some coffee or something? There's a little café down the street with the best apple pie in town."

She hesitated, her teeth worrying her bottom lip. "I don't know. I still haven't checked into a room, and I left the rental"—she pointed ahead a couple of blocks to a white Toyota parked in front of his office—"on the street."

Her eyes widened as Marcus grabbed her finger. Hard to believe they could look any larger, framed as they were by the longest, thickest lashes he'd ever seen. "They stopped checking meters an hour ago. The car could sit there all night and no one would mind."

For the longest time, she simply stared. Then, to his delight, her head bobbed. "Okay. Yeah. I could use some coffee."

"Good." He released her finger, and they started down the sidewalk the way they'd come. "Any idea how long you'll stay?"

"I can't be sure," she said, tucking her hands into the pockets of her jacket. "I'm hoping it'll be a couple of weeks, maybe longer."

"What about your job?" Marcus said, watching surreptitiously as she navigated the icy patches on the sidewalk in her heels. "Don't you have to be back for something?"

She shook her head a tad too quickly. "It's all taken care of."

What did that mean? He had a sneaking suspicion the answer wouldn't be good. Still, since it was too soon to form an opinion of her motives, he'd give her the benefit of the doubt. Besides, in two weeks, he'd have a much better idea of who Christmas Scheirer was, and whether or not she was the kind of person Paul would want to have the gift.

"Here we are," he said, thrusting his chin toward a small store with a green and white awning stretched over the entrance. "Lucy's. Best baked goods—"

That was as far as he got. Chris's foot hit an unsalted patch of ice and shot out from under her, and her hands were still firmly in her pockets, rendering her helpless. Whirling, Marcus caught her before she could fall and pulled her to his chest. She felt good in his arms. Too good. He didn't want to let go. And her hair smelled wonderful. He dipped his head, breathing deep, to whisper to her. "You all right?"

Her breath came in short, white puffs, and her cheeks were flushed and rosy. "I'm fine."

Her scarf had come loose. Marcus gently rearranged it over her ears. "There you go."

"Th–thanks," she stammered.

Too soon, the moment passed, and he no longer had reason to continue holding her. He reluctantly dropped his arms and stepped away. An elderly couple emerged from the restaurant, releasing a cloud of coffee-scented air that made his taste buds tingle.

"Shall we go inside?" Chris said, her voice low.

Marcus agreed, too embarrassed by his schoolboy display to do more than nod. Okay, he told himself as they entered the muted lighting of the café, so he'd been a tad overeager holding Chris in his arms. On the bright side, she hadn't seemed in too much of a hurry to move away.

And where he was concerned, that did make for a bright side, Marcus realized with a grin. A very, very bright side.

Chapter 4

The alarm on Chris's phone beeped early the next morning. Too early. She wasn't ready to get out of bed. Blinking, she tried to read the numbers on the dial. Her eyelids felt like sandpaper. Rolling over with a groan, she yanked the blankets over her head.

No good. She was awake. Thoughts of last night with Marcus flooded her groggy brain and she smiled. Who'd have thought a starchy lawyer type could have a fun side?

She took a deep whiff of the scented cotton sheets. He'd been right about this place. Much better than the Best Western.

Cracking open one eye, she peeked at the clock on the nightstand. Five thirty. She'd gotten exactly six hours of sleep. Less, the night before.

"Ugh." She poked out her arm and turned the offending clock to the wall, but still the hour called to her. If she wanted to get up and out before Marcus started tailing her around town, she'd need to move.

She slid her legs out from under the warm covers, gave her senses a moment to adjust, then headed for the shower. Exactly forty-five minutes later, she pushed out the front door of The Bella Rose B & B and climbed into her cold rental car. A short drive, and she parked outside the Shady Hill Cemetery.

Now, if she could just find. . .

The snow had ceased with the dawn, but a frosty chill remained, preserving the thin blanket of snow clinging to the tree limbs. She wandered down one pathway after another until she found the marker she sought.

PAUL WARREN SCHEIRER
BELOVED HUSBAND, FATHER, GRANDFATHER

Her breath caught. She dropped to her knees, ignoring the bite of the frozen ground and the damp circles the snow melting against her flesh caused. Fingers trembling, she traced the letters until she reached the last word—*grandfather*.

Suddenly, it was as though he'd only just died. Regret for having missed his final days washed over her, flooding her eyes with tears that burned fiery trails down her cheeks.

"Oh, Grandpa, I'm so sorry!" She pressed her face to the cold marble, letting the grief take over. "I was such an idiot. I hurt you, Grandma, Mom and Dad—everyone. Please, forgive me."

Pressure built in her chest and behind her eyes. Who was she kidding? She didn't deserve his forgiveness. She'd lost all of the money he'd given her, wasted seven years of her life, and for what? A job waiting tables and a run-down motel room in a bad part of town? She clenched her fingers.

Pastor Scott was wrong.

The overworked minister of the homeless shelter Chris landed in just after she lost her uptown apartment had counseled her to return to her family. He said Grandma's letter announcing her upcoming marriage to Alex Knight was a sign from God. The time was ripe for making amends.

She scrunched her eyes shut. Amends were impossible, with the one she'd sinned against most lying in the cold ground. "I'd do anything to have you back. I'd do everything differently, make different choices."

Rocking back on her heels, she stared up at the young elm spreading gracefully over her head. Grandma. She would have wanted Grandpa Paul to have shade in the summer since some of their favorite times were spent lounging on a swing under the tree in their yard.

And Chris had robbed her of that—caused Grandpa to be taken too soon.

A tremor shook her at the thought of facing Grandma Carol. She lumbered to her feet, all the weight of seven years' worth of guilt pressing down on her shoulders. It was too much to hope for the family's forgiveness, but she'd at least try to honor Grandpa's last request. She'd make her apologies, return to The Bella Rose, and book a flight back to New York. Maybe then she could finally put this mess behind her.

Marcus paused with his hand on the cemetery gate, torn between hurrying to Chris and letting her pour out her grief. The snow muffled her quiet sobs, but they were still enough to render him motionless.

Coming to a decision, he dropped the latch and backed away. She needed this time. To rob her of it would be cruel. He drove back to the bed-and-breakfast and sat down in the parlor with a cup of coffee, prepared to wait all day if necessary, for Chris's return.

In fact, it was less than an hour. The door opened, and a burst of cold air ushered her in. He jumped to his feet, caught himself, and approached her slowly. "Good morning."

"Hi."

She refused to look him in the eye. Not a good sign. He pushed his hands into the pockets of his jeans and tried to appear casual. "Been out for a walk?"

"Something like that." She rubbed her hand over her reddened nose. "Listen, I need to get out to Grandma's place. Do you think you could take me? I–I'd rather not drive just now."

What was going on inside that head? Her eyes were still swollen from crying, and she looked ready to burst into a fresh bout of tears at any moment. The last thing she needed in this condition was a confrontation whose end was uncertain.

He tossed a look toward the dining room where the proprietress of the inn had only just begun setting out breakfast. Silently, he thanked God for a sudden flash of inspiration and rubbed his palm over his belly. "Um. . .sure. I can take you. But would you mind if we get something to eat first? I'm starving, and who knows when we'll eat again. Plus, that bacon smells heavenly, don't you think?"

Her blue eyes dull, she followed the direction of his stare and conceded with a halfhearted nod. "All right, as long as we don't wait too long, okay? I'd like to get this over with."

"Fine with me."

He held out his hand for her jacket, which she slid out of before crossing to the dining room. Only a handful of guests occupied The Bella Rose, so apart from the owner, they had the table to themselves. Marcus poured Chris a cup of coffee and set it down next her plate.

"Thanks," she said, sipping from the brew without adding cream or sugar. She lifted an eyebrow and watched him over the rim of her cup. "Aren't you having any?"

Marcus shook his head. "Already had a cup." Actually, it'd been more like two, but he wasn't about to say so.

She nibbled at her toast when it arrived. At first, Marcus feared he'd been foolish to delay, but as her body thawed from being outdoors, so did her mood. She dug into her eggs, and when she finished, she set down her fork and laid her hand over his on the table.

"Thank you, Marcus."

Heat crept upward from his fingers. "For what?"

Her lashes swept down over her eyes. "For giving me a chance to prove that I've changed. It—means a lot." Her gaze lifted to meet his squarely. "And for this." She motioned toward the breakfast dishes. "I had a rough morning. This gave me time to calm down and think about what I want to say to Grandma Carol."

"You're welcome."

A blush stole over her cheeks, and she pulled her hand away. Marcus couldn't stop looking at her. Her face was made even more beautiful by the sunbeams streaming through the bay window. Devoid of makeup, and without dim lights to cast shadows over her thoughts like the night before, she was as transparent as glass.

He had to admit, he liked what he saw.

Chapter 5

Chris peered out the car window, her hand frozen on the door handle. Grandma's house looked the same. She'd expected it to be different, somehow—smaller, as if diminished by Grandpa's absence.

"We can take a minute before we go in."

She turned to look at Marcus. For the first time, she noticed the kind slant to his lips and the warmth radiating from his gaze. No doubt clients flocked to him, since he wasn't the typical person one expected to meet in a lawyer's office. She squeezed his fingers. "You're a good man, Marcus Taggert."

His eyebrows winged upward. She wasn't surprised. She'd shocked herself with the words. But if there was one thing she'd learned in New York, it was to appreciate genuine kindness, given with no strings attached.

Pulling on the handle, she climbed out of the car and set her feet on the path leading to Grandma's door. When she hesitated, Marcus joined her, his hand warm on her back as he walked her to the door.

"I'll be praying for you," he ducked his head and said for

her ears alone, as he rang the bell.

A quick thanks was all she had time to mumble. The door flew open, and Grandma Carol stared out.

"Christmas!"

Shock registered in Grandma's blue-green eyes. Her hand flew to her neck, her fingers settling on a multicolored gemstone necklace Chris had never seen before. In her other hand, a bit of lace fluttered.

"Grandma. . ." Chris's voice faded to a whisper.

"Who is it?" a voice from inside called.

Chris swallowed hard, forcing the words past the lump in her throat. "Hello, Grandma. It's good to see you." Unable to look her in the eye any longer, she dropped her gaze and fumbled around inside her purse. "I—I got your letter." She held up the crumpled envelope, stained beige by her tears as she'd read and reread the message inside.

Grandma Carol's eyes welled with tears of her own, no doubt born from the sorrow Chris had caused. Her hand lowered.

"I want you to know," she said, barely loud enough to be heard, "that I'm so sorry for. . .everything. I don't expect you to forgive me. I just hope someday—"

She got no further into her practiced speech. Grandma Carol made a little sound before wrapping Chris in a bone-crushing hug.

"Oh, sweetheart. You've come home! You've no idea—"

"Mom? Who is it?"

The door opened a little wider and Chris was suddenly face-to-face with her father. What was he doing here? She backed from her grandmother's grasp straight into Marcus's solid form. His hands on her shoulders steadied her.

"You can do it," he said, his breath warm against her neck.

But her gaze was riveted to her father. "Hi, Dad."

Pain, heartrending and tangible, vibrated in his brown eyes. "Christmas."

More than anything, she wanted to launch herself into her father's arms, to lay her head against his chest and sob out all the pain of past failures. Instead, she remained frozen on the stoop, waiting.

Grandma broke the silence. "Well, don't just stand there, come inside. Come." She grabbed Chris's hand and pulled her into the foyer. "Elaine? We have a guest. You'd better have a look."

The savory scent of a roasting chicken floated through the house. Mom appeared in the hallway, wiping her hands on an apron.

"Who is it?" she began then halted when she spotted Chris. "Darling!" Instantly, joy shone from her face and she rushed forward to envelop her in a hug. "What are you doing here, I mean, I'm glad to see you, but I never expected—" She broke off, laughing, and then, as though a thought struck her, fell into silence, her eyes wide. Her gaze flitted from Chris to her husband. "Is everything okay?"

"Fine, Mom," Chris said, ashamed that her lack of communication had caused her mother to worry. "This is just"— she cast a surreptitious glance at her father, who stood in the entrance to the den with his arms folded—"a visit."

"Whatever the reason, we're so glad to see you. Marcus,"

she said and turned to him, "how are you?"

"Just fine, Elaine."

"Well, come in and sit down, both of you." Grandma Carol reclaimed Chris's hand and led her into the den. "Where have you been? What have you been doing? Sit here"—she patted a leather sofa next to the fireplace—"and tell us all about it."

Chris sank onto the seat, mostly because her wobbly knees refused to hold her, with Grandma on one side and Mom on the other. Her dad took up residence at the fireplace. Marcus sat in the chair across from her, and thankful for at least one friendly face, she focused on him. "There's not much to tell," she began.

A grunt rumbled from her father. "In seven years? Surely there's something."

"Garland!" her mother said sharply.

Her father shrugged and directed a pointed look at Chris. "Well?"

Never in her life had Chris been able to stand up to her father, but today, she found the strength. She lifted her chin and looked him in the eye. "I've written a book. I'm working on getting it published."

"But you haven't sold it yet."

Her stomach fluttered. "No, but I'm hopeful. My agent says—"

"You have an agent?" Grandma Carol interrupted.

Chris tore her gaze from her father. "Yes. Her name is Adrianne Clark. She owns a large literary firm in New York."

"What kind of book is it?" her mother said.

By her nervous smile, Chris figured she asked despite her father's displeasure.

"A historical. Civil War."

"You always did like delving into the past," Grandma Carol said with a laugh.

Her father snorted. "Never could get your head out of a book. Maybe if you'd spent a little time concentrating on the present, you'd take more of an interest in what's been happening with your family."

Grandma Carol shook her head. "Garland."

"It's true, Mom. Christmas hasn't phoned or visited in seven years." He looked at Chris. "Do you have any idea how hard that was for your mother?"

From the corner of her eye, Chris saw her mother lift a tissue to her nose. "It's fine, Garland."

Her dad straightened. "No, it's not. We've been worried sick. Mom, you, too. Are we all going to sit around and pretend like she never left? Like she didn't break Dad's heart by—"

Marcus rose, his tall presence drawing all eyes to him. "Carol, Elaine, it's been good to see you both." He tipped his head to each in turn then looked at her father. "Mr. Scheirer, I'm sure there's a lot you need to work out with your daughter, but for now, this has been quite a shock. Why don't we postpone this discussion until you've all had a chance to recover?"

Too numb to speak, Chris nodded and rose. Avoiding her father, she looked at Grandma Carol and then at her mom. "Will tomorrow be all right?"

"Of course, dear," Grandma Carol said. "I'll call you. Where are you staying?"

"At The Bella Rose." Chris gave her a quick hug, followed by another for her mother. Finally, she looked at her father.

"It's good to see you, Dad."

"You, too," he said, almost apologetically, though he remained where he stood.

Heart throbbing, Chris headed for the front door. She was barely aware of Marcus as he opened the car door for her and helped her inside then circled around to the driver's side. The streets passed in a blur, matching the unfocused whirling of her thoughts.

"You okay?" Marcus said at last.

"Fine."

She wasn't. Facing her father had been so much worse than she'd feared. His anger, she expected, but his disappointment? It was too much to bear. Tucking her hands in her lap, she took a quivering breath and focused hard on stemming her tears.

Chapter 6

For almost thirty minutes, Marcus drove in silence, letting Chris cry out her anguish and praying. Finally, he pulled into a roadside park and drew her into a hug.

"It's all right, Chris. You did it. The worst is behind you."

She shook her head and pulled away. "No, you don't understand. I'm not sorry that I went to see them. I just wish I hadn't caused everyone so much pain. I was such an idiot, and an even bigger fool for daring to come back. How can I ever expect any of them to forgive me? It's not reasonable. It's not—"

Her voice rose in pitch. Desperate to stop her from beating herself up, Marcus did the one thing he could think of—he kissed her.

Chris's lips were made salty by her tears. Still, he lingered, gently caressing the side of her face with his thumb. "Don't," he urged. "Don't think about the past. It's over, Chris. You've apologized. Now, forgive yourself."

Her breath caught, but gradually, he felt the tension drain from her body and she sighed, long and deep. She straightened with a weak laugh and rubbed her finger under her watery eyes. "Thanks."

He smiled back. "You're welcome." Tugging a Starbucks napkin from a pocket in the door, he unfolded it and handed it to her. "Sorry. It's all I've got."

She laughed again, a little stronger. "It's fine."

Dropping the transmission into gear, he pulled onto the street while Chris took out a compact and began making repairs to her face. Moments later, she flipped the visor mirror closed.

"Where are we going?"

"Mom's."

She lifted her head to look at him. "What?"

"If it's okay with you." He cast her a quick glance. "I just don't think it's a good idea for you to be alone."

He saw the hesitation on her face, held his breath while he waited for her answer.

Finally, she nodded. "Yes, all right. If you're sure she won't mind."

"I know she won't." He squeezed her fingers then turned his attention to the road.

Marcus's mother lived on the outskirts of Boulder in a two-story house Chris's grandpa Paul had helped his dad build. His mother met them at the door.

"Hello, sweetheart," she said, pressing her cheek to his as they hugged.

He turned to Chris. "Mom, you remember Christmas Scheirer?"

"I do, though if I remember correctly, you prefer Chris, right?" She smiled and held out her hand.

Chris took it. "It's a pleasure to see you again, Mrs. Taggert."

"Melody, please." She waved them inside. "You're just in time for lunch. Have either of you eaten?"

Marcus shot a look at Chris. Mom's outgoing demeanor was easing her tension just as he'd hoped. She smiled and shook her head.

"Good. I'll get some extra plates."

Lunch was simple fare—smoked turkey sandwiches and homemade potato salad—but Chris seemed to enjoy the light conversation that passed between him and his mother, and even joined in when the stories turned to her grandpa Paul and Marcus's father, Walter.

"So, how long *did* they know each other?" she asked, taking a bite from her sandwich.

Mom counted the years on her fingers. "Let's see, they were in the war together, Vietnam," she clarified, "but they knew each long before that, right Marcus?"

He nodded. "Wasn't Dad in college that they met?"

"Yes, I think so. That means they knew each other forty-some years." Both hands fluttered through the air.

Chris brushed the crumbs from her lips with a napkin. "Wow. That's a long time to continue a friendship."

"Not so long when you have so much in common." Mom shrugged. "Paul and Walter were more like brothers than friends. Their bond reminded me of King David and his love for Jonathan. There was nothing they wouldn't do for each other." She gripped Chris's hand and spoke softly. "I wish you could have known them when they were young. It was fun seeing them together."

Chris gave a wobbly smile. "I bet."

"In many ways," Mom continued, settling back in her chair, "your grandfather was a lot like you."

Her eyes widened, and Chris leaned closer. "Really?"

"Oh, yes." She picked up a chip and ate it. "Marcus remembers, don't you, dear?" She waited for his nod. "Paul wanted to take the world by the horns. Never shied away from a challenge. Your going to New York to pursue your writing career sounds just like something he would have done in his younger days."

Startled, Marcus watched his mother nonchalantly pick up her sandwich and take a bite. Why hadn't that thought ever occurred to him? She was right. Paul wouldn't have hesitated to do just what Chris had done had he wanted to be a writer, yet Marcus had always derided Chris for her choice. He looked at her for the impact of his mother's words.

Tears welled in Chris's eyes, but she quickly dropped her gaze to hide them. "I'd like to think that's true, though, knowing him, I doubt he would have gone about it the same way."

"Maybe not," Mom said, wiping her hands on a napkin, "but you only knew him when he was older and wiser." She gave a wry grin. "I knew him in his wild and crazy days. Don't discount the benefit of years, Chris, and don't be too hard on yourself. Like most of us, Paul was made wiser having lived through his mistakes."

A cloud lifted from her troubled expression. Chris covered his mom's hand and smiled. It took her a moment, but she finally managed a strangled, "Thank you."

His mom patted her arm in response. "You're welcome, dear. Now, who wants coffee?"

Chapter 7

Chris put the finishing touches on her makeup then went downstairs. Already, Marcus waited for her in the parlor, his broad back turned as he conversed lightly with Mrs. Hanaby, the proprietress of The Bella Rose.

Pausing on the bottom step, Chris let her gaze wander over his solid form. He looked so different dressed in jeans and a casual black sweater. More approachable. Maybe that wasn't a good thing. She pressed her fingers to her lips where the memory of his kiss lingered then shook away the thought. He'd only been trying to help. It wouldn't do to make more of it than that.

She moved off the last stair as Mrs. Hanaby left, headed toward the kitchen. "Good morning."

Marcus turned his head and greeted her with a smile that dispelled her notion of his simply being kind. This look said he was truly glad to see her. What had changed?

"Good morning. Ready for a day of Christmas shopping?"

Chris nodded. Late last evening, Grandma Carol had called as promised and invited the two of them to spend the day with her in Boulder. Chris fell asleep looking forward to a little time alone with her grandmother. She still had so much she wanted to say.

"I'm ready. The question is, are you? Shopping with two women wouldn't be high on the list of many men."

Marcus laughed as he helped her into her coat. "That's because the two women wouldn't be you and Carol Scheirer."

Chris snorted. "Okay, Mr. Smooth-talker. I'll remind you of that when we're loaded down with presents."

Grandma Carol was dressed and waiting for them when they reached her house. Pulling Chris into a hug, she told her how glad she was that Chris had accepted her offer and that she looked forward to the day. "Oh, and Alex said to tell you hello," she finished.

Chris smiled, grateful all over again for her grandmother's generous spirit. "Thanks, Grandma. I'm looking forward to today, too."

Pleasure shone from her grandmother's face as she turned to Marcus. She opened her arms wide, and he stepped into them. "About time you came around. I thought for sure we'd see you at lunch last Sunday."

"I meant to come by," he said, "but I got caught up helping Pastor Dave deliver meals to the shut-ins."

She patted the side of his face warmly. "You're a good boy, Marcus. How's your mother?"

"Doing fine. Said to tell you hello next time I came around."

Chris watched in silence as they chatted for the next several minutes. An unusual feeling, one bordering on jealousy, stirred in her stomach as she listened. Marcus was obviously close to her family, closer than she'd been the past seven years, and it filled her with regret. She was relieved when Grandma Carol suggested they get going.

Before long, Marcus had them parked and walking the sidewalks of downtown Boulder. "Any place special you want to go?" he asked.

Chris glanced at Grandma Carol, who shrugged. "Let's just play it by ear," she said.

At the first store, a clothing shop, Chris found a creamy cashmere cardigan.

Marcus joined her at the checkout counter. "That's nice."

Chris shook her head. "It's not for me. It's for my mom. I borrowed one similar to this from her and never returned it. It was her favorite," she finished softly, her fingers smoothing the fuzzy material. She swallowed down a knot in her throat. It wasn't much, but maybe Mom would understand the meaning behind the gift.

After leaving the clothing store, Grandma Carol asked to be taken to an electronics store where she could purchase an external hard drive for Alex. "He and Michael are so wrapped up in this new business they're doing together. I'd hate for them to lose any of their hard work."

Marcus agreed, and while Grandma Carol browsed the computer section, Chris perused the navigation systems. Her fingers lingered over one brand, and then another. Finally, she gave up and gestured to Marcus.

"What do you know about GPS?" she said when he approached.

Marcus frowned. "For you, or someone else?"

She shook her head and grinned. "My dad. He's notorious for getting lost on the road then refusing to ask directions. This will be as much a present for my mother as it is for him."

He answered with a soft laugh and picked up a mid-priced model Chris had been considering. "This is a good one, and you can program addresses into it that you use often, like home or family."

Her gaze fell to the brightly colored box. "It helps you find your way home," she whispered, almost to herself. Would her father understand how hard she'd been seeking that road these past seven years?

Marcus tipped his head toward her. "What?"

She blinked and cleared her throat. "Nothing. It's perfect. Thanks, Marcus." She took the GPS from him and joined Grandma Carol at the checkout.

"Find everything you need?" Grandma asked as she pulled her billfold from her purse.

"I think so. How about you?"

Grandma Carol patted a plastic bag next to the cashier. "Right here. Alex is going to be so pleased." She withdrew her hand. As she did, she caught a charm from the bracelet hanging on her wrist on the cuff of her jacket. "Oh, dear. Can you help me with this, Christmas?"

Careful not to damage the piece, Chris untangled the charm. It was one she remembered well. Every Christmas, Grandpa Paul gave Grandma a new charm for her bracelet, and the grandkids always loved to see what he'd chosen that year. This one, a delicate heart engraved with the date, was one of Chris's favorites.

"There you go," she said, straightening.

Grandma Carol breathed a sigh of relief. "Thank you. I'd never forgive myself if I lost it." Her fingers absently caressed the tiny gold heart. "Have you finished here?"

Chris nodded, though her eyes remained fixed to Grandma Carol's wrist. Suddenly, she knew just what she wanted to give her, but it wouldn't wait for Christmas. "I have one last stop I'd like to make. Do you mind?"

"Of course not, dear. Where would you like to go?"

Smiling, Chris squeezed her grandmother's hand. "It's a surprise."

After whispering the next destination to Marcus, Chris settled on the backseat and enjoyed the easy banter that passed between him and her grandmother. He was such a familiar figure, as though he'd always been a part of her life. Having heard his mother speak of her grandfather's friendship with Marcus's father, it was no longer such a surprise that the Scheirer family lawyer also attended their family picnics.

The car rolled to a stop in front of Drummond's Jewelry. A soft sigh escaped Grandma Carol. "This is where your grandfather. . ." She trailed off.

Chris leaned forward to squeeze her shoulder. "I know, Grandma."

Marcus slid from the car and opened their doors. Taking Grandma's arm, he walked her to the entrance and helped her inside.

"Carol Scheirer! How have you been?" Philip Drummond's

voice boomed across the store. Hurrying around a glass display case, he wrapped her in a bear hug.

"Hello, Philip." Slightly out of breath from his boisterous greeting, Grandma fanned her face and laughed. "It's good to see you, too."

"You here looking for engagement rings? I hear there's a wedding in the works." He gave a broad wink that set Grandma to giggling.

"I'm sure Alex and I will be in to do that soon, but today it's my granddaughter who could use your help." She took Chris's arm and pulled her forward. "Philip, do you remember Christmas?"

He studied her over the rim of his round glasses. "My, but haven't you grown into a pretty young thing." His eyes widened and his gaze shot from her to Marcus. "Wait, are you two—? Don't tell me there's two weddings on the horizon!" His large palm slapped the counter and he gave a bark of laughter that made Chris blush.

Refusing to even look at Marcus, she quickly shook her head. "No, sir, it's not that. I just wanted to pick out something for my grandmother."

"What?" Grandma Carol said. Surprise registered on her face.

Chris nodded. "I hate that I never thought of it before." She took a deep breath and gestured toward the bracelet. "I'd like to get you a charm since Grandpa Paul. . ." Her voice lowered, "well, since he can't."

Tears sprang to Grandma's eyes, and she gripped Chris hands tightly. "Oh, sweetheart, there's no need—"

"Please, Grandma. I want to, and one for every year that I've been gone, every year Grandpa would have bought one had he lived."

The jewelry store went silent. Chris froze, counting her own pounding heartbeats while she waited. Finally, Grandma Carol pressed her palm to Chris's cheek.

"One charm, that's all, for the year that you came back. The missing ones will serve as a reminder that we should never, ever allow anything to come between us as a family."

Chris nodded and selected a slender gold cross in honor of Pastor Scott, whose message of Christ's love and forgiveness had prompted her to come home. They waited while Mr. Drummond ordered the date engraved on the back. When it was finished, he attached it to the bracelet, right next to Grandpa's heart.

Back in the driveway in front of her home, Grandma Carol gently stroked the new addition to her charm collection. "I can't thank you enough for your thoughtfulness, dear. This means the world to me, and it would have to your grandfather."

Chris wrapped her in a hug and pressed a kiss to her warm cheek. For a second, she lingered in the embrace, breathing deep of the comforting scent of peppermint and cinnamon that always seemed to cling to Grandma. "I love you."

It was all Chris could manage.

Grandma Carol withdrew far enough to cup Chris's face in her hands. Her blue-green eyes steady, she somehow managed to convey without a word how far she had already removed herself from the past. "I love you, too, Christmas Scheirer. I always have."

Marcus had already unloaded their purchases into the hallway, so Chris simply joined him in the car and waved to Grandma through the window as he pulled away. All day long, he'd been a silent shadow, observing, but not intruding. At no time had Chris been uncomfortable in his presence. In fact, she'd appreciated his willingness to chauffeur them around. Once she'd regained control of her emotions, she turned to offer her thanks.

"For what?" Marcus said, his strong hands gripping the steering wheel firmly.

"For not letting Grandma know your presence was anything more than just social." He glanced at her and Chris dropped her gaze. "I realize this probably isn't how you would have chosen to spend your day off."

"I'm not so sure about that," he said.

Pondering his cryptic response, Chris said nothing until they arrived at The Bella Rose. She reached for the door handle. "Well, thanks again—"

"What are your plans for supper?"

Chris stared at him in surprise.

"You have to eat, right?" he said, swiveling toward her on the seat. "I do, too. No sense us eating alone. How does a steak sound?"

Her mind swam in fuzzy circles. "Good, I guess."

"Great. I'll give you an hour to get changed and freshen up then pick you up around. . . ," he said, pausing to glance at his watch, "seven?"

Chris nodded.

A wide grin spread across his face. "Good." He jumped

from the car, opened the door, and helped her out. "See you at seven."

After he left, Chris winged her way past the foyer, up the stairs, to her room.

Another evening spent in Marcus's company.

Her heart fluttered at the thought, but she had no time to wonder why it should react so. Marcus would be back to pick her up, and she had exactly forty-seven minutes to get ready.

Chapter 8

The restaurant Marcus selected was cozy and elegant, but not too formal. Perfect for the light gray slacks and pink blouse Chris had donned. Still, she'd managed to slip on the icy sidewalk outside and, if not for his hand on her elbow, would surely have fallen.

"Thanks again for catching me," she said, once they were seated at a snug table in a corner of the restaurant.

Marcus smiled at her over the top of his menu. "My pleasure."

Her mouth went dry. She reached for her water glass and took a sip. My, but the man could make a girl's heart flutter.

"Do you know what you're having?"

She told him, and when the waitress arrived, he ordered for them both.

"I have something for you," Marcus said after their drinks were delivered. "I bought it after I dropped you off."

Chris watched curiously as he pulled a large gift bag from under the table. She'd seen it on his arm when they came in, but had been too embarrassed to ask.

"For me?"

He nodded and handed it to her.

Her fingers shook as Chris removed a layer of tissue paper. To think he'd even bothered getting something sent a rush of excitement through her.

She went still as she peered into the bag. "What—?"

Marcus smiled at her, his brown eyes twinkling with mirth. "Boots. You'll kill yourself eventually if you keep wandering around town in those things." He pointed at her slender-heeled shoes. "I hope you're a size eight."

"Seven and a half."

"That's without socks."

Chris pulled the boots from the bag. Aside from being clunky and brown, they had a ring of fur around the top that looked like it had been scalped from a hapless bunny.

"Like 'em?" Marcus asked.

What could she say? They were hideous. Chris swallowed hard and fought to meet his gaze. "They're—um. . ."

Suddenly, Marcus's lips twitched and Chris knew he was struggling to control his laughter. She plopped the boots into her lap and forced a serene smile. "They're perfect. Thanks."

Marcus burst into laughter. Before long, Chris had joined him.

"You don't have to keep them," Marcus said, when he'd calmed enough to speak. "I just couldn't resist. I'll return them tomorrow."

"Absolutely not," Chris said, hugging the boots close. "I intend to wear them everywhere we go."

She paused, aware as she spoke the words of how they

sounded. He seemed not to notice and shortly after that, their salads arrived, so the awkward moment passed without comment.

"Tell me about yourself, Marcus," Chris said, tucking into her salad with gusto. She hadn't realized until she got a whiff of sizzling beef how hungry she was.

He shrugged and spread a thin layer of butter over his dinner roll. "Not much to tell. I took over the family practice straight out of law school, and I've been working at the firm ever since."

The words appeared straightforward, yet something about the way he said them made her think there was more he wasn't telling.

"What about you? You always wanted to be a writer?" he asked before she could question him further.

She swallowed and nodded. "It actually started when I was younger and loved to read. Writing just seemed like the natural progression."

He paused with his fork in midair. "What kind of stuff are you interested in?"

"The classics, mostly, and historicals, which is what I write. Mysteries are fun, too."

His fork lowered and interest sparked in his eyes. "Have you read *Silas Marner*?"

She nodded. "George Eliot. It's one of my favorites."

"Mine, too, but I've never been able to find a first edition to add to my collection."

They spent the next hour discussing what they'd read, what they liked, and enjoying a meal cooked to perfection.

When they'd finished, Chris felt she knew Marcus better than ever before, yet something still confused her.

"I don't understand." She placed her spoon in her empty dessert dish and pushed the plate away. "You obviously love the written word, but you went into law. Why? Why not work in a library, or teach, or"—she waved her hand—"I don't know. Something having to do more with books?"

His coffee cup rattled as he replaced it on its saucer. For a moment, he did nothing but run his finger along the rim. Finally, he crossed his arms, leaned back in his chair, and studied her. "What do you remember about my father?"

She hesitated, thinking. "Not much, I suppose. He was Grandpa's lawyer."

Marcus nodded. "He poured his whole career into building up that practice. I always knew he wanted me to take it over. I loved him so much, I couldn't refuse. I went to law school."

He dropped his gaze and drank from his cup. Chris knew by the note of finality in his voice that he would say no more, but there was no need. She understood. Marcus had given up his own dream in order to honor his father's request. And to think she'd been envious earlier, when she'd seen the way he and Grandma Carol got along.

She placed a light touch on the back of his hand. "Your father would be proud." *Not like mine,* she added silently.

His dark eyes met hers. "Thanks."

"You're welcome."

Their waitress appeared with their bill, which Marcus paid before escorting Chris to the car. The air outside had turned cold with the setting of the sun. Marcus switched the heater to full blast then leaned across Chris to turn on the heated seat.

"Better?" he said, his face inches from hers.

Intoxicated by his nearness and the scent of his cologne, Chris could barely manage a nod.

He rubbed her arm. "Good. Give it just a minute. The car will thaw out soon."

He returned to his seat, taking the warmth of his body with him, but Chris remained all too aware of him the entire way home. Her skin tingled where he'd touched her even when they pulled into the driveway of The Bella Rose several minutes later.

Marcus walked her to the door. "Sweet dreams, Chris," he said so softly it felt like a caress.

She tipped her head to look up at him. "Thank you, Marcus, for a wonderful day and"—she held up the gift bag—"for my boots."

He smiled and leaned closer. For a moment, Chris thought he would kiss her good night. Instead, he reached behind her and turned the knob. Stumbling over the threshold into the cozy foyer, she clutched the bag to her and watched as he shot her a wink before darting down the steps to his car.

Chris's heart continued to pound as she closed the door. The other guests had already turned in, so she slipped out of her shoes and made her way upstairs to her room.

Taking a pair of cotton pajamas from her suitcase, she readied for bed. After such a tiring day, she had no doubt she'd pass out the moment she hit the pillow. In fact, lulled by the hum of the furnace, it wasn't long before sleep tugged at her eyelids.

Visions of Marcus's face danced in and out of her subconscious. A slow grin settled over Chris's lips as she fell asleep. Her dreams would never be the same.

Chapter 9

A light snow drifted past Chris's window the next morning. She let the curtain fall back into place and scurried across the cold floor to the bathroom. Maybe by the time Marcus arrived to take her over to her parents' house, she'd have warmed up.

Smiling, she shoved her feet into the boots he'd bought. They weren't half bad. Her feet fit snugly inside them, and navigating the icy streets would certainly be less treacherous. She stood to admire her reflection in the long, oval mirror. With her jeans tucked into the tops of the boots, she looked taller than her five-seven frame. The mirror did wonders for her figure, too. She'd have to take it home with her.

The thought cut short her chipper mood. She didn't have a home, which was how Pastor Scott had talked her into coming back to Boulder in the first place. Yet, was this really where God wanted her to be? Pastor Scott seemed to think so.

She shook her head and went downstairs. Establishing her newfound faith was a lot tougher than she'd anticipated, and it required a lot more work. *"Being a Christian won't be easy,"* Pastor Scott had said. Boy, was he right. Today she'd be meeting with her parents. Alone. No Grandma Carol to help smooth things over.

She said a quick prayer. When she lifted her head, Marcus was pulling into the drive. She grabbed her coat and ran out to meet him.

He was even more handsome than the image in her dreams, if that was possible. She blushed at the memory and climbed into the car without looking at him while he held the door.

He was lighthearted and kept up an easy flow of conversation, though it proved difficult for Chris to focus on what he said. The nervousness creeping into her belly increased the closer they came to her parents' house.

Bit by bit, the roads they traveled grew in familiarity. Chris could drive them with her eyes closed. Three miles, turn on Baker, through the stoplight, right on Willoughby until you get to. . .

One car sat in the driveway.

Her stomach fluttered. Dad's older model Chevy pickup was conspicuously absent. When she called to let her parents know she was coming, she figured he'd take the day off.

"Did they know you were coming?" Marcus said as he unfastened his seat belt.

"Yeah, they knew." She unclasped her own seat belt and waited while Marcus circled the front of the car to open her door.

She was glad for his company as she climbed the stone steps leading from the curb to the bricked path winding across her parents' front yard. Dad took great pride in his lawn. By the look of the perfectly trimmed hedges and immaculate flower boxes, not much had changed.

Mom opened the door on the first knock. One of her hands was covered in flour, and she wore a spattered apron over her fuzzy pink sweater. "Hello, sweetheart," she said, pressing her cheek to Chris's. "Marcus, good to see you. Come on in. I would take your coats..." Giving a soft laugh, she motioned to her flour-crusted fingers.

"I've got them, Elaine," Marcus said. "The den okay?"

"Perfect," Mom said. "On the couch is fine." She bustled down the hall, past the den and formal dining room. "I'm baking cookies."

Chris gave Marcus her coat then followed Mom along more slowly. At the entrance to the den, she paused, her eyes taking in the family photos arranged over the fireplace. Her senior picture still sat directly to the left of Grandpa Paul and Grandma Carol's wedding photo.

"You know how the church always hosts its holiday fundraiser in October?" Mom's voice drifted from the kitchen.

Chris tore her gaze from Grandpa Paul and went to join her and Marcus. "Yeah?"

"Well, this year, they decided to do a bake sale. We're hoping to raise enough money to buy one toy for every needy kid in Boulder." Her arm swept through the air toward the counter, where, already, stacks of homemade Christmas cookies sat awaiting frosting.

That explained the scent of warm sugar and vanilla. Chris laughed, picked up a cookie, and took a bite. It melted in her mouth. "Mmm...that's what you get for making the best

Christmas cookies in Boulder."

Mom's baked goods were so popular, people lined up at church functions, family get-togethers, and social gatherings to get one. She laughed and tossed Chris an apron, another to Marcus. "And that's what the two of you get for stopping by just when my cookies are ready to frost."

Marcus blinked in surprise. "Are you sure you want me to help, Elaine? I'm not much good around the stove."

"You won't be at the stove, dear," she said, pressing a spatula into his hand. "Sprinkles are over there."

Chris could barely stifle a giggle as Marcus struggled to fit the slender apron around his middle. "Let me help," she said, crossing to stand behind him.

"I'm not sure this is a good idea," he twisted far enough to whisper. "When it comes to cooking, I'm a klutz."

Chris patted a fancy bow into place. He'd kill her when he realized what she'd done, but that more than likely wouldn't be for hours, and the giggles she got would make up for the pain. "Oh, I don't know," she whispered back as she took his arm and turned him to face her. "It'll give me and Mom something to talk about."

In fact, baking cookies provided exactly the right mood. Nestled inside the warm kitchen, with the comforting scent of butter and sugar tickling her nose, and Mom's chatter keeping things light, Chris felt herself relax. Together, she, Mom, and Marcus formed an assembly line. Mom put the cookies in the oven and took them out. Chris arranged them neatly on cooling racks. Marcus, perched on a stool, finished the job with a thick coat of icing.

Outside, the snow continued to fall. Her dad usually came home for lunch. Chris wondered if he would, seeing how slush clogged the streets. Maybe he'd use that as an excuse to stay away. She tossed a glance toward the window.

Something cool and moist landed on the back of her hand.

She looked down at the bright green splotch. "What—?"

A second splotch joined the first. Chris glared at Marcus. "What are you doing?"

Marcus very slowly lifted his spatula and took a lick. "Who, me?"

Chris lifted her hand. "Mind explaining this?"

At the oven, Chris heard her mother chuckle.

Marcus leaned over to inspect the damage. "Looks like green frosting." He examined the bottle of food dye Mom had been using to color the icing. "Evergreen, to be exact."

"Oh, really?" Amusement gurgled up from Chris's belly but she refused to let him see. Instead, she reached for the spatula protruding from the bowl of red icing and with slow, measured movements, smeared a thick layer down the length of his nose. "Then what do you call that?"

One side of Marcus's mouth turned up in a grin. "That, madam, is what I call a challenge."

Chris squealed. He leaped off the stool but before he could reach her, she zipped around the counter and hid behind her mother.

"Mom! Stop him!"

"Oh, no," Marcus laughed, wielding a bowl overflowing with frothy yellow confection. "You started this."

"I did not! You did."

Mom joined in the laughter, one hand pressed against Marcus's chest to keep him at bay, the other curved behind her to hold Chris at her back. "Now, Marcus, I have to say, it did appear as though you were the cause of all this."

Marcus froze, and a look of utter shock formed on his face. He pointed to himself. "Me?"

Mom nodded. Over her shoulder, Chris stuck out her tongue.

"Oh, well in that case. . ." His lips turned up into a wicked grin, and he swirled his finger through the thick frosting.

Chris felt her mother stiffen. "Now, Marcus. . ."

"Yes?"

"I wouldn't do that if I were you."

"Do what, Elaine?"

This couldn't be good. Chris backed up a step and took her mother with her. "You heard her, Marcus."

"I heard her, all right." He lifted a glob of icing from the bowl.

"Marcus!" Chris and her mother squealed in unison, but it was too late. He slung the heavy glob through the air. It landed with a splat on Mom's apron. At the look of total surprise on her face, Chris could hold her amusement no longer. She burst into laughter right along with them.

"What in the world is going on?"

Garland Scheirer towered in the doorway, his briefcase dangling from his hand. In the now quiet room, the hum of the dishwasher sounded loud.

Chris was the first to speak. "Hi, Dad."

"We were making cookies," her mom finished.

Collecting herself, Chris unstuck her feet from the floor and walked over to the sink to wash her hands. While she did, her mother took the briefcase and coat from her father and led him to a chair at the table.

"I've made you a sandwich. Do you have time to eat?"

He nodded and shot a glance at Chris. "I took the rest of the afternoon off."

That was a surprise. Dad rarely, if ever, changed his mind about anything. What could have prompted him to come home, when he'd obviously decided she wasn't worth missing the time at work? Beside her, Marcus took the washcloth from her shaking fingers. When his touch upon her hand lingered, she looked up at him.

He knew all along, she realized with a start. Somehow, he'd sensed when she began to worry and did something to stop it.

Thanks, she mouthed.

He smiled at her then turned to the table. "Elaine, do you mind showing me that lease agreement you were telling me about for the lot next to the church?"

She agreed, and they disappeared into the den, leaving Chris alone with her father. She joined him at the table, pulled out a chair, and sat.

"So, how was work?"

"Busy," he grunted. He took one look at the sandwich and pushed the plate away.

As though she'd been transported in time, Chris dropped her gaze and stared at her fingers. It was her way of hiding from the disappointment she knew she'd read on his face.

"Dad—"

"There's something I want to say, Christmas. Something I've been—needing to get off my chest."

Here it comes, she thought. She said a quick prayer and braced herself for the onslaught. "Okay."

Her dad's strong fingers curled around her hand. She jerked her head up to look at him. Instead of the anger she expected, tears stood in his eyes, and his face was drawn and weary.

"I'm sorry, Christmas, for everything."

"W–what?"

He shook his head. "I knew how much you wanted to write, but I never supported you. Maybe if I had, you wouldn't have had to go to your grandfather. You wouldn't have left." His shoulders slumped, and he dropped his head into his hands. "You are my only child, and I let you down. I wasn't there for you. I'm so ashamed."

For a second, Chris couldn't speak, and then, as if her heart splintered into a thousand pieces, she began to cry. She grabbed both of his hands and squeezed.

"Oh, Dad, I made my own choices. None of this was your fault."

He lifted his red-rimmed eyes.

"I never came back because I thought you blamed me for Grandpa's death."

His mouth opened in shock. "What?"

The words were difficult, but Chris knew she'd never be able to move forward unless she spoke them. She brushed away the tears and took a deep breath. "I broke his heart when I asked for my inheritance. I might as well have told him I couldn't wait for him to die. I was horrible, and stupid, and selfish, and it's my fault that he was too weak to fight the cancer that killed him."

"Chris—"

She pulled her hands away and squared her shoulders. "I will make it up to this family, Dad. I can't bring Grandpa back, but whatever it takes, somehow, I'll make it up."

A small groan ripped from her dad's throat. He jumped up from the table, drawing Chris with him, and enveloped her in a fierce hug.

"It's not your fault, sweetheart. I never blamed you. No one did. Can you ever forgive me for my stubborn pride?"

Tears flowed freely from both of them now that the dam had broken. For Chris, it was as though seven years' worth of fear and heartache came pouring out. Placing her hands on his trembling shoulders, she rose on tiptoe and planted a kiss on his cheek. "We both need forgiveness."

Eyes questioning, he said nothing.

Everything she'd learned from Pastor Scott about Jesus' redemptive love came flooding back, and Chris couldn't wait to share it with her father. She smiled at him. "We have a lot of talking to do, Dad."

Chapter 10

Chris's steps were lighter the next day. Her boots tapped cheerfully along the sidewalks of downtown Boulder. The people she passed returned her smiles, and she walked into Reader's Choice Used Books with a song on her lips.

"Good morning," the lady behind the counter called. "What can I do for you?"

Chris loosened her scarf and cast a quick look around the store. "Got any classics?"

The woman's eyes brightened. Wendy, as her name badge said, pointed toward a shelf protected by a thin sheet of glass. "I'll get the key."

Chris stood aside to wait. Marcus wouldn't be joining up with her until after lunch. A call from the law office had pulled him away, and she'd decided to use this time to find something special to give him. Her way of saying thank you.

The store smelled of old paper and dust. Over the windows, wooden shutters filtered the weak October sunlight. There weren't many patrons pacing the worn floorboards, but the ones who did seemed engrossed by whatever treasure they held in their hands.

"Here it is," Wendy said, holding a small silver key aloft. "Were you looking for anything in particular?"

Remembering Marcus's face as they talked over dinner, Chris smiled. "Anything by George Eliot?"

The lady looked perplexed for a moment, and then brightened. "I do have something." Her fingers ran over the spines of the books lining the shelf. "Now, what did I do—here it is." She pulled out a tattered book.

Excitement flared in Chris's chest. Not in the best condition, but it had *Silas Marner* embossed on the cover. A quick glance at the date told her what she needed to know. "I'll take it."

Wendy's eyes gleamed as she carried the book to the cash register. "So, can I gift wrap this for you?"

Chris hid a smile. Wendy was in the right line of work if she read romance in every purchase. Then again, the last thing Chris wanted was for Marcus to think she'd bought the book attempting to bribe him into releasing Grandpa's "gift."

"Actually, you can. Nothing too frilly, though."

The gleam changed to a knowing nod. Oh well. *Let her think what she likes,* Chris reasoned as she left the store with the book tucked under her arm.

The clock mounted to the dashboard of her rental said she still had thirty minutes before Marcus left the office. Plenty of time for another visit to the cemetery. She swung off the main street and veered toward Shady Hill. Not that she couldn't tell Grandpa all about her conversation with her father from her car—she just felt better sitting next to his grave, closer to him somehow.

A lone figure huddled next to the marble grave marker when Chris approached. Even from a distance, she recognized Marcus's broad shoulders and sandy brown hair. She slowed her steps as a playful thought skipped into her head. Maybe she could sneak up on him and—

"It's not that I don't believe she's changed," Marcus was saying, "she has. I'm just worried that I won't be as unbiased as I need to be." He placed his hand on top of the marker, as though he were squeezing an old friend's shoulder. "You really did a number on me with this one."

He was talking about her, Chris realized, and suddenly felt like an intruder. She glanced back at her snowy footprints. Maybe if she backtracked. . .

"I think I'm falling for her, Paul."

Chris froze. Her heart thumped so loud she had to strain to hear Marcus.

He shook his head. "No, that's not exactly right. I know I am. I mean, she's fantastic—fun-loving, considerate—I wish you could see her now, the person she's become. You'd be so proud of her, Paul, which makes me think I should just go ahead and give her the gift. But have I really waited long enough? What if it's all an act?"

With each word, Chris became more uncomfortable. Marcus thought he was alone, and she was eavesdropping.

She withdrew the way she'd come then made her way back to Grandpa's grave, but this time, she whistled softly and hailed Marcus from several feet away.

"What are you doing out here?" she said, clutching the front of her coat together. "I thought you were going to meet me at The Bella Rose after lunch."

His hand lingered on the headstone as he stood. "Just visiting with an old friend."

Chris smiled and joined him at the graveside. Though the sky was clear, the snow that fell the night before cast a quiet blanket over everything, making the setting even more peaceful and intimate.

"Do you come here a lot?" she said after a moment.

Marcus nodded. "Sometimes. Dad's buried over there." He pointed to a rise several yards away. "Can't come see one without the other."

"May I?" Chris said, turning her shoulders in the direction he pointed.

"Sure."

He walked with her up the hill, past the many markers bearing names Chris didn't recognize—and many she did. A bench had been placed facing Walter Taggert's headstone. Marcus brushed off a place for her then one for himself.

"I like this place," Chris said, scanning the evergreens dotting the path.

He quirked an eyebrow. "Well, now, that's something you don't often hear said about a cemetery."

She laughed at his mocking expression and bumped her shoulder against his. "I mean it's peaceful. A person can think here."

He lowered his gaze and appeared to be studying his gloved hands. "What do you think about?"

"I don't know—life, I guess. And death."

He glanced sidelong at her, and Chris felt the need to explain.

"I used to have some pretty messed up ideas about, you know, the afterlife. Everything I believed came from movies, and friends." She shrugged. "Pastor Scott set me straight."

"Who?"

She hesitated. Despite the closeness she felt toward Marcus, she wasn't quite ready to admit how she'd met Pastor Scott. "He's a preacher I met in New York."

"Ah."

She looked away and traced her finger through a fluffy pile of snow on the bench seat. "Do you believe in heaven, Marcus?"

"I do."

She stopped to read his expression as he spoke.

"But I don't believe it's for everyone. Only those who know Christ can know His heaven."

Peace filled Chris's heart as she listened to Marcus explain why he thought the world needed a Savior. It thrilled her to think their faith was so similar, as though God had intended for them to believe as one all along. Sometimes she asked questions, other times, it was him. They talked so long Chris's fingers and nose went numb. When her cell phone rang, she had to fumble with her gloves in order to get it open.

"Hello?"

"Christmas? This is Grandma. You need to get to the hospital right away. Your mother's had an accident."

Marcus cast a worried glance at Chris. She didn't look good.

Her face was pale, and the trembling in her fingers had nothing to do with the cold. He turned up the heater in his car anyway.

"Did Carol say what happened?" he said.

Chris shook her head. "Just that Mom was taking decorations down from the attic to sort out the broken stuff and fell off the ladder."

He turned his attention to the road and pressed on the accelerator. When they arrived at the hospital, he pulled up to the emergency room entrance. "Go in without me. I'll park the car and meet you inside."

She hopped out without argument and ran in. Marcus found a space not too far from the main doors and followed along more slowly.

God, he prayed, shooting a glance at the overcast sky, *this family is just starting to come together. They don't need any more trouble right now. Please.*

Motion sensors whooshed the doors open a few feet before Marcus reached them. Around the lobby, someone had arranged hay bales and pumpkins, a reminder that though the mall might be advertising sales in time for Christmas, it was still only October. He inquired at the desk after Elaine, and when he had the information, he strode down the hall to the room where the nurse said she was being treated.

"Mom, why didn't you just wait until one of us could help you?"

Chris's voice sounded shaky. Sure enough, when Marcus turned the corner, she was bent over her mother's bed with tears tumbling down her cheeks. On the other side of the bed,

Garland and Carol hovered like two agitated hens. Rather than intrude, he eased himself beside the entrance to wait.

"That's what I told her," Garland said, frowning at his wife. "You know I don't like you lugging those boxes down by yourself. What if Chris or I hadn't been here? What if Mom hadn't planned to stop by?"

Elaine made a clucking sound. "It's a sprained ankle, Garland, not a broken neck."

"It could have been," he said, his voice sharp.

"Dad," Chris chided gently.

Garland gathered his wife's other hand to his chest. "I'm sorry, sweetheart. I just wish you weren't so stubborn. There's no need for you to tackle all the decorating by yourself." He turned to peer at his daughter.

Marcus had to look twice. Sure enough, Garland's eyes were awash with tears.

Garland covered Chris's and her mother's clasped hands with his own. "Not with Chris here."

Carol's breath caught in a soft hiccup as she slid her arms around her son's shoulders.

Marcus backed away from the door. He'd seen enough. Elaine's fall was an answer to prayer. Chris really had changed. He sensed it. So did her family. Once this ordeal at the hospital was over, he'd take her by the law office and give her Paul's gift.

Chapter 11

Weariness weighed on Chris's shoulders like a boulder. She sank onto the seat in Marcus's car, the sigh of the soft leather matching the one that escaped her lips. Mom was resting comfortably, at home, and Grandma Carol had convinced Dad to get some sleep. The bed at The Bella Rose was going to feel extra good tonight.

"Thanks for staying," she said as Marcus turned out of the driveway. "You were a big help today."

He shrugged. "Not so much. You took care of all the paperwork and had your mother's painkiller prescription filled. Your parents are grateful to have you home."

A smile spread across her face. It did feel good to be able to take some of the worry off her father, like she was really needed.

The headlights swung onto a street leading away from the bed-and-breakfast. She pushed up in the seat. "Where are we going?"

"My office. Do you mind? There's something I need to pick up."

How could she say no after all he'd done for them today?

She shook her head, but when Marcus pulled to a stop in front of the practice and held out his hand to her, she looked at him in confusion. "You want me to go in with you?"

"If you don't mind. We won't be long, I promise."

She was a little surprised by the request but took his hand and let him help her up the icy steps.

Inside, an old-fashioned radiator rumbled noisily. "I keep meaning to replace that thing," Marcus said. He flipped on a light and wove his way to his office.

Chris waited by the door, her cold hands tucked into the pockets of her coat. Like most places, the law office looked different by night, forbidding and a little spooky. From within, shuffling sounded, followed by a loud thump. "Did you find what you needed?" she called.

Marcus emerged. In his arms, he carried a large chest fastened with a brass lock. "Here it is."

She laughed and went to help him set it on one of the long tables. "What is that?"

Brushing dust off the top, Marcus laughed as she covered her mouth and sneezed. "This" —he fumbled in his pocket until he produced a key—"is your gift."

Chris's laughter faded as she stared at the key he placed in her hand. "Grandpa's gift?"

"It felt like it was time."

She lifted her head to look at him. He was so incredibly handsome in his dark trench coat, the scarf around his neck hanging free—but what attracted her most, the thing she couldn't tear her eyes from, was the look of approval she read in his eyes.

She swallowed down the lump in her throat. "Marcus, are you sure?"

He nodded. "Paul would want you to have it."

Chris laid her hand on the lock and paused. Something didn't feel right. Though she no longer thought of Marcus as a stranger, she wasn't sure she wanted to open the chest with him watching over her shoulder. "Um, would you mind terribly if we took this back to the bed-and-breakfast? I think"—she rubbed her hand over the top of the chest—"I want to open this by myself."

"I understand," he said softly.

Relief filled her as he picked up the chest and carried it to the car without asking for more explanation. Marcus was a true friend, she realized, so different from the people she met in New York. He didn't demand anything of her, or hang around waiting to see what she would do for him. He simply wanted the best for her.

Back at The Bella Rose, he wished her good night before promising her he would pray. The words filled her with comfort as she settled onto the floor of her room, across from the chest. Apprehension made her insides quiver. The contents of the chest were important to Grandpa Paul. He'd thought long and hard before deciding who to entrust them to. What if she couldn't figure out what he wanted her to do?

Her fingers trembled as she inserted the key into the lock. It snapped open. Drawing a deep breath, she lifted the latch and threw back the lid.

Hundreds of letters occupied the space. Stack upon stack, many bound by lengths of brightly colored ribbon. Her weariness forgotten, Chris lifted out the first bundle. They were to Grandma from Grandpa Paul, addressed via an APO box. Military letters he wrote while he fought in Vietnam.

She glanced at the mountain of cards and envelopes. Surely, he couldn't have written them all. She drew out half the collection until she reached a few written in a hand she didn't recognize.

"Albert Scheirer." She breathed the name on a whisper. Her great-grandfather. The letters were addressed to Mirabel Scheirer, her great-grandmother. The postmark said 1943. The letters were from World War II.

Her heart thumped louder. Grandpa Paul had left her over a thousand pages of history. Her hands shaking, she carefully opened the first envelope and began to read.

~❦~

Outside her window, a bird sang merrily, rousing Chris from the place on the floor where she slept. She sat up and rubbed her bleary eyes. What time was it?

The clock on her nightstand read seven thirty. She'd fallen asleep sometime after four. With a groan, she lumbered to her feet, rubbing the sore spot on her lower back where it hurt from sleeping wrong, and climbed into the bed.

"Go away, bird," she grumbled, but it refused to budge. Even when she tossed a pillow at the window, the feathered fiend chirped gaily.

"Fine, I'll go to church," she groaned, dragging herself from the quilted coverlet to the bathroom.

A half hour later, she'd showered and dressed but her eyes still felt grainy. She thought about Pastor Scott, back in New York. He would forgive her for skipping one Sunday, right?

Maybe he would, but God might not be so understanding, and she had a lot she needed to talk to Him about.

At the church, wave after wave of well-wishers stopped to inquire about her mother. Chris filled them in as best she could before settling into a pew near the front.

"Lord," she breathed quietly, "please show me through Your message what I'm supposed to do with Grandpa's letters."

The pastor, a stocky, balding man with rosy cheeks and a ready smile, stepped to the pulpit following the music. Chris had always liked him. He was friendly and peppered his sermons with plenty of humor, but today, he surprised her by asking the congregation to turn to a passage in Habakkuk.

"You all know where Habakkuk is," he said, his eyes twinkling. "It's the part of your Bible where all the pages stick together because you never study there."

Soft laughter rippled across the overflowing auditorium.

As Chris flipped through her Bible to find the scripture, she had to admit he was right. Who read from Habakkuk, anyway? But as she skimmed the words, her heart began to pound.

"Then the LORD answered me and said: 'Write the vision and make it plain on tablets, that he may run who reads it. For the vision is yet for an appointed time; but at the end it will speak, and it will not lie. Though it tarries, wait for it; because it will surely come, it will not tarry.'"

Though the pastor spoke on, Chris barely heard. She squirmed in the seat, anxious to get to a telephone so she could tell Marcus the good news. Suddenly, the last seven years, living in New York—all of it made sense. She knew what God wanted her to do. God wanted her to publish her grandfather's letters.

Chapter 12

Fury pounded through every one of Marcus's nerve endings. "You want to what?"

Chris blinked. She even had the gall to look surprised that he was angry. "Th—the letters are remarkable, Marcus, a piece of living history. I've already spoken to my agent, and she thinks—"

He held up his hand. "Wait, you spoke to your agent *before* you mentioned this harebrained idea to me, or your grandmother, or anyone?"

"Well, I wanted to see if Adrianne thought it would sell. She does, Marcus. She's excited about the idea and asked me to put together a proposal."

Marcus laid both palms on the old-fashioned writing desk and shoved to his feet. Fighting a fresh rush of anger, he paced the patterned carpet of The Bella Rose's parlor. Less than an hour ago—had it really only been that long?—Chris had called, begging him to come over, saying she had a wonderful idea for her grandfather's gift. Some idea. She hadn't changed after all.

"Chris, you realize those letters were very personal, written during a time when your grandfather, and your great-grandfather, believed they might never return home. How do you think they would feel having their private thoughts and fears displayed for all the world to see? Or are you too consumed by your own desire for publication to even think about that?"

Tears sprang to her eyes. Marcus refused to be fooled. He'd been sucked in by her wiles before. He folded his arms and reminded himself what an actress she'd proven to be.

She came to stand in front of him. "I'm doing the right thing, Marcus. It's what Grandpa would have wanted. It's what the Lord wants. This morning's sermon confirmed it."

He was angry with her, angrier with himself for being so gullible. He jerked his hand up to stop her. "Don't. Please don't bring the Lord into this."

Turning to the window, he examined the swirling mounds of snow collecting along the edges of the frozen driveway. Frozen. Exactly the way his heart felt the moment Chris opened her mouth and started spouting her plans for Paul's precious letters. How could he have been so wrong about her? By allowing himself to fall in love, he'd let himself—and Paul—down.

Chris felt as though a stone had been rolled over on top of her heart. "Marcus, if you'll just hear me out—"

He shook his head, already sliding his arms into the sleeves of his coat. "Save it, Chris. You'll never convince me. I only hope your family, and Paul, can forgive you." He spun and left, his words echoing hollowly inside her head.

She sank onto a chair, stung by his lack of faith in her. Could he be right? Had she misunderstood what the Lord had been trying to tell her?

Rising, she snatched her coat off the hall tree and strode to her rental car. There was only one way to find out.

Despite the chill in the air driven by sharp gusts of wind, several cars hunkered in the cemetery. Chris parked and walked the remainder of the way to Grandpa Paul's grave. Tears blurred her vision as she peered at the stone carved with his name.

"Why?" The word felt sharp in her throat. "Why did you leave the letters to me?"

Rubbing her gloved hands over her face, Chris thought over every bad decision she'd made since leaving home. Finally, she knelt next to the grave and laid her hand over the marker.

"I lost the money, Grandpa, every bit of the inheritance you gave me. I spent it on an apartment and trying to get published. I even threw a couple of big parties trying to impress agents and magazine editors."

Hot tears were rolling down her face, but Chris let them fall unchecked. She was through trying to justify her decisions. She needed to make amends, and confessing to Grandpa was the start.

"I believe publishing those letters is what you intended all along, but what if Marcus is right? What if it's selfishness on my part that's keeping me from seeing the truth?"

Overhead, barren limbs stirred by a brisk wind clacked noisily. Chris peered at them, wishing she could interpret their woody chatter. Sighing, she traced the carving on the headstone with her finger.

BELOVED HUSBAND, FATHER, GRANDFATHER

Beloved Husband. Grandma! She needed to talk to Grandma.

"Thank you, Grandpa," Chris said, kissing her fingertips then pressing them to Grandpa Paul's name.

Chris called before departing for Grandma Carol's. Alex was visiting, but once Chris told her what she wanted to speak to her about, she quickly invited her over. After Chris arrived at the house, she settled onto the floral couch, Grandma and Alex seated across from her.

"I must say, I'm not surprised he left the letters to you," Grandma Carol said, passing Chris a steaming cup of tea. She poured a second cup, stirred in two lumps of sugar, and gave it to Alex. "After all, no one else in the family loves history the way you do."

Chris took a sip from her cup to give herself time to think. "That's true, Grandma, but Marcus says—"

Grandma Carol shook her head, cutting off what Chris had been about to say. Reaching out, she clasped Alex's hand. "Alex and I have been talking and we agree on this. Paul gave the letters to you, to do with as *you* saw best."

Her unwavering support lifted Chris's spirits and renewed a confidence she hadn't realized she'd been lacking until this very moment. "You're sure, Grandma? No matter what I decide?"

Grandma looked at Alex.

"You've prayed about this, Chris?" he asked. "You've sought the Lord's will, and you feel certain this is the path He's laid before you?"

Chris nodded. "I have, Alex, and for the first time in my

life, I want to do everything the Lord asks of me." *Even if it costs me a future with Marcus.*

A smile spread over Grandma's face, and peace filled her gentle blue-green eyes. "Well, then, that's all we need to know."

"Not quite," Chris said, drawing a breath. Before she accepted her grandmother's blessing, she wanted her to know the truth about—everything.

Chapter 13

A *Heritage of Faith: The Life and Legacy of Paul Warren Scheirer.*

Chris put the finishing touches on her proposal then hit SEND. Adrianne was expecting her message. Hopefully, Chris would have an answer before the day was out. Closing the lid on her laptop cast the room into unexpected gloom.

She glanced at the clock. Five thirty. It was later than she thought. Okay, so it would be tomorrow before she heard from Adrianne. Fumbling for the lamp switch, she clicked it on and retrieved her phone from the corner of the desk where she had it charging. No messages. No missed calls.

She sighed. It had been four days since she and Marcus argued. She'd left several voice mails, but he had yet to answer a one.

Next to her phone lay a fat manila envelope. A rough draft of her idea for the manuscript lay inside, with photocopies of the letters Chris had chosen to use inserted throughout the pages. Also in the envelope was the edition of *Silas Marner* Chris had bought for Marcus two weeks ago. She rested her hand on the package, sadness crowding her heart. She'd hoped to give the draft to him in person, but with her plane leaving for New York in just over two hours, there was little chance of that.

Her suitcase sat ready at the door. Chris gathered the last of her belongings and made her way downstairs. She'd chosen the late flight on purpose, to give her plenty of time to say her good-byes.

Mrs. Hanaby followed her out to the rental car. "You're sure about this, dear? I know your parents would be glad to see you settle here in Boulder."

Chris popped the trunk and stowed her luggage inside. "I'm sure. I need to go back. I promised Pastor Scott I would help him at the shelter." There were no secrets now that she'd shared everything with her family.

Mrs. Hanaby nodded, her silver curls bobbing. She laid her weathered hand on Chris's arm. "I understand. Take care of yourself. Come and see me again, soon."

Chris gave her a hug. "Thanks, Mrs. Hanaby. I really appreciate everything you've done."

The older woman smiled, her cheerful wave in the waning daylight the last thing Chris saw in her rearview mirror as she pulled away from The Bella Rose.

~ ❧ ~

"Happy Halloween, Miss Scheirer."

Old George's toothy smile did much to lift the weariness from Chris's shoulders. "Happy Halloween, George."

Bright lights winked from a jack-o'-lantern in the corner, a subtle reminder that the holidays, and Grandma Carol's wedding, were just around the corner. She shifted the laundry basket filled with blankets to her hip and gave George a cheery wave.

"I'll take that." Pastor Scott joined her in the hallway of the Helping Hands Homeless Shelter and took the heavy basket from her grasp. "I thought you were headed home an hour ago. You've got to be tired after fetching candy for trick-or-treaters all night."

"I was—am—I'll go home after I finish collecting the laundry."

Pastor Scott quirked an eyebrow. He was single, handsome, and in his mid-forties. Chris could easily see herself giving him her heart, if it hadn't already belonged to Marcus.

He smiled, crinkling the skin around his deep blue eyes. "I can do that. You've been working too hard."

Chris followed him through the large kitchen, replete with stainless steel appliances, to the utility room. Already, the shelves lining one wall were loaded with the fresh sheets and blankets Chris had spent most of the day washing. "I don't mind. It helps keep my mind off other things."

"Marcus?"

She nodded. She had no secrets from Pastor Scott.

"Think you'll see him when you go back for your grand-mother's wedding?"

"Possibly." She shrugged. "Probably. His family and ours have always been close."

Pushing the blankets into the washer, Pastor Scott added a capful of detergent and switched the machine on. "All the more reason for you to seek an answer from the Lord." He held up his hand when she opened her mouth to protest. "I appreciate everything you've done around here, but staying busy is no substitute for spending time on your knees." Eyes narrowed, he leaned against the washing machine and crossed his arms then his ankles. "Want to talk?"

She should have figured he'd sense her unease. She sank onto a ladder-back chair situated next to the door. "I'm worried."

"Is it your grandmother?"

"No." She shook her head. "For the first time, I feel like things are well on their way to being healed between me and my family. It's Grandpa's book."

He straightened. "You heard from your agent?"

She nodded. "Adrianne pitched the idea to a few editors. Several houses expressed interest in seeing a proposal. Adrianne thinks we'll have a publisher before too long."

"Chris, that's great!" Pastor Scott took her hands, lifted her to her feet, and wrapped her in a hug. "So, why aren't you more excited?"

She grimaced.

"Marcus, again?"

She sighed. "What if he's right? What if it is only my selfishness that makes me think I'm doing the right thing?"

Rubbing his hand over his chin, Pastor Scott frowned. "Well, I guess there's only one way to be certain."

Chris's heart rate sped. "You mean. . ."

He nodded. "That's right, Chris. You're going to have to face him."

Chapter 14

The lonely whine of a revving jet engine whirred outside the car rental office. Chris took her keys and headed for the sporty compact the agent behind the counter pointed toward.

"Miss? You dropped something."

Chris looked over her shoulder. Sure enough, a white envelope fluttered from her pocket to the floor. She bent to pick it up. "Thanks," she said, grateful the agent had taken the time to call her attention to the letter. Of all the notes Grandpa Paul had written, this one was her favorite, and she would have hated losing it.

Racing through the cold wind and swirling snow, Chris hopped into the car, started the engine, and flipped the heater to high. While the car warmed, she took off her gloves and blew into her hands. Grandma expected her around three. That left her two hours.

She removed the letter from its envelope and scanned the familiar contents.

My Dearest Carol,

How I long for sight of your sweet face! I hope all is well with you, my darling girl. I pray for you daily.

Weariness has become our constant companion here in this forsaken land known as Vietnam. The rainy season has begun. With the clouds, a deep depression has come to overshadow me and my comrades. I long for home as never before.

Chris paused to wipe a tear from her eye. Loneliness resonated in Grandpa's words. The weight of his longing was like a tangible thing, and it reverberated deep within her being. She resumed reading.

Yet I battle onward, clinging to the hope my Lord and Savior instills in me day by day.

A figure waits on the road before me. Should I die before I see your face again, dear one, I know that figure beckoning to me will be my precious Jesus. If, however, God should see fit to restore me to my home, I look forward to running back to your welcoming arms. Pray for me, beloved, for though I long to see my Savior's face, I would not wish that you bear such grief.

Though she'd read the words before, she suddenly felt as though the message were meant just for her. She lifted her head in surprise and peered out the windshield. Could it be? Had Grandpa's letters been beckoning her home all along?

Winding through the airport exit, Chris pointed her car

toward the highway and Shady Hill Cemetery.

A familiar silver Toyota sat near the entrance by the wrought iron gate. Heart pounding, Chris climbed from her rental. Marcus?

The snow that had been steadily falling piled in fluffy drifts along the path leading to Grandpa Paul's grave. Thankful she'd thought to wear the boots Marcus gave her, Chris hurried forward then skittered to a stop when she caught sight of him.

Tall, lean, Marcus cast a long shadow over the wreath someone had placed on Grandpa Paul's headstone.

Drawing a breath to steady herself, Chris stepped forward and cleared her throat.

Marcus spun around. For just a moment, Chris thought he looked hopeful. "Chris?"

"Hello, Marcus."

"What are you. . . ?" He paused and fidgeted with a thick packet of papers in his hands. The tattered edges revealed the extent of use they'd been given.

Breathless, her heart pounding, she pointed. "Is that—"

Marcus glanced down. "This?" When he lifted his eyes, a deep remorse shone from his gaze. "Your draft for the manuscript. I read it—finally."

A lump too thick for her to speak around rose in her throat. She nodded.

"I'm so sorry, Chris. Instead of hearing you out, I assumed the worst. I had no right. . ." He broke off and looked down at the rumpled pages again. "This is beautiful," he said softly. "I should have listened to you." His head lifted and he met her gaze. "Paul would have wanted this published."

It was too much. Her tears spilled over. "You didn't return my calls."

He extended his hand, but Chris couldn't move, as though her feet were frozen to the ground. Still, he reached for her. "I'm sorry, Chris. I was angry, and bullheaded, and. . .wrong. Especially about you."

More than anything, Chris wanted to place her hand in his, to fill his empty palm, but she had to know. "What—what made you change your mind?"

The pleading in his gaze softened. "Your grandmother. Somehow, she must have sensed there was something wrong between us. She called and practically ordered me to read what you'd written. Called me all kinds of a fool for ever letting you go back to New York." He stepped closer. "She was right. I realize that now. I only hope I'm not too late to tell you. . ."

The tears fell faster. Chris managed a strangled, "Yes?"

A trace of uncertainty flickered in his warm gaze, but then the line of his jaw hardened and he squared his shoulders. "Being around your grandmother these last few weeks has made me realize how much I want a wife and family of my own, but not just any family, Chris. You. I want you. I fell for you the moment you walked into my office. It took your grandmother reaming me out to make me realize it." He glanced at his outstretched hand. "I love you, Chris. I know I hurt you by failing to believe in you, but if you can find it in your heart to forgive me. . ."

Forgiveness.

Hadn't Chris been shown more forgiveness than any person had a right to expect? Before he could finish, she gently laid her hand in his and squeezed. "There's nothing to forgive, Marcus. I more than earned your doubts. Now, I hope I can earn your faith, too."

Relief flooded his face. "You have it, Chris. I'll never doubt you again as long as we live. That is. . ." A rosy flush crept over his face. Tucking the manuscript under his arm, he took both of her gloved hands.

Their breath mingled on the crisp air, forming a puffy white cloud that spiraled and spun into the clear blue sky. He was so close, Chris felt certain he could hear the pounding of her heart.

"Christmas Scheirer, I haven't had a long time to get to know you, but it's been long enough for me to realize how much I want to. Think you can put up with my pigheaded stubbornness?"

She smiled, loving the endearing way his lips curled with chagrin. Slipping one hand free, she laid her palm against his cheek, warm, even through the soft material of her leather gloves. "You're not pigheaded, Marcus Taggert. Stubborn, maybe, but you're definitely not pigheaded."

His deep laughter sent ripples of pleasure through Chris's midsection. She could spend a lifetime getting used to hearing that. Thanks to Grandma Carol, she just might.

Marcus pulled her into his arms. As his head dipped closer, Chris knew beyond a doubt he intended to kiss her, and not just the cover-her-mouth-so-she'll-stop-babbling-kind he gave her last time, either. She put her hand to his chest to stop him.

"There's just one more thing," she said, heat rising to her cheeks.

His face bunched into a puzzled frown. "Yeah?"

"I need you to know. . ."

He definitely looked concerned now. "What is it, Chris? You can tell me anything."

"Really?"

He nodded, his thumb tracing the line of her jaw. "Really."

"Okay, then, what I want you to know is. . ." Her fingers slid to the buttons on his coat as she fumbled for the words.

Understanding dawned on Marcus's face.

Emboldened by his astounded look, she lifted her chin and looked him in the eye. "I love you, too, Marcus Taggert, and I can't wait to spend the rest of my life with you."

He did kiss her then, and with joy and peace bubbling up from deep inside Chris's soul, she knew she'd never again leave Boulder. This was home, now and forever, right next to Marcus's side.

Elizabeth Ludwig began her career writing historicals and romantic suspense. In 2004, she was named a finalist in ACFW's Noble Theme Contest. Other notable accomplishments include two top ten finishes in ACFW's 2005 Noble Theme Contest, General Historical and Historical Romance categories, respectively.

Her first novel, *Where the Truth Lies*, which she co-authored with Janelle Mowery, was released in spring of 2008 from **Heartsong Presents: Mysteries!**, an imprint of Barbour Publishing. Books two and three of this series were *Died in the Wool* and *A Black Die Affair*.

In 2008, Elizabeth was named the **IWA Writer of the Year** for her work on *Where the Truth Lies*. She is a regular contributor to the popular literary blog, **Novel Journey**, named one of Writer's Digest's 101 Most Valuable Web sites for Writers, 2008.

Elizabeth is an accomplished speaker and dramatist, having performed before audiences of 1500 and more. She works full-time and currently lives with her husband and two children in Texas.

To learn more about Elizabeth and her work, visit her at www.elizabethludwig.com.

O Christmas Tree

by Elizabeth Goddard

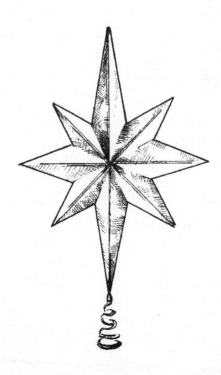

This story is dedicated to my beautiful daughter, Rachel, whose missionary heart has taken her around the world.

Commit your works to the LORD
and your plans will be established.
PROVERBS 16:3 NASB

Chapter 1

Had it been Nick Brohns or the subtle shift in altitude that stirred her from an uncomfortable sleep?

Holly Rivers blinked. Another dream about Nick—great, just great. Though the dream had gone, the image remained, his handsome German heredity obvious in his thick blond hair and piercing blue eyes.

At least she'd slept on her flight from JFK International Airport. Otherwise, she'd be grumpy when she saw her family, who insisted on meeting her at the airport in Denver rather than waiting for her connection to Boulder. Fortunately, the weather promised to cooperate.

Holly yawned and rubbed her eyes, detesting her dry mouth. The puny pillow she'd used was crammed between the seat and the window. She tugged on it, but it refused to comply. Pillow fights were nothing new, she'd even participated in a few, but this was ridiculous.

"Yes!" The pillow's surrender and her outburst came simultaneously, with the unfortunate consequence that she pummeled the seat back in front of her.

"Sorry," she said to the seat, hoping whoever sat in front of her wasn't too miffed, and stashed the offending near-flat, white rectangle under her seat. How could they even call it a pillow?

For the most part, the last leg of her flight from South Africa had been without incident. She hated flying, but there wasn't any other way to travel to the other side of the world and make good time. As long as the flight was free of turbulence, she could forget her anxieties and enjoy watching the landscape or the vast blue ocean during the day, or at night, the stars or lights below. But twenty-two hours of travel, including connections and layovers, most of it spent on a jet, not only zapped Holly's energy, it gave her plenty of time to think about her quandary.

"Did you sleep well?"

Holly stretched and peered at the redhead next to her, swirling a cup of ice. Barb had introduced herself when they'd taken their seats at the beginning of the flight.

Holly's dry mouth turned thirsty. "When did you get that?"

Barb gave Holly an apologetic look. "I'm sorry. You were sleeping, and we thought it best not to disturb you."

Sighing, Holly pressed the button to straighten her seat back. "That's all right, we should be landing soon."

According to her watch, it was eight o'clock in the evening and they were due to land within the hour. She'd reset her watch to reflect every time zone she traveled. The FASTEN SEAT BELT sign lit up, and flight attendants patiently collected the last of cups and snack wrappers as they checked to make sure passengers were secure in their seats. Holly gripped the armrests, feeling the plane's slow descent into Colorado and bracing herself for the turbulence experienced when flying into mountainous regions.

Back pressed into the seat, she closed her eyes, imagining the joy of reunion on her family's faces. She'd not seen them in a year. Anxiety, not just over the flight, jockeyed to displace her elation at coming home.

If she couldn't hide her discomfort, they might notice. Grams would certainly know something was wrong, but that was all right because she needed to talk to her grandmother.

A year ago Grams had given her a scripture to think about. *Commit your works to the Lord and your plans will be established.* Holly had committed herself to serve God and given up one of her greatest desires in order to serve Him in South Africa. She'd given up Nick Brohns. Among the many things she'd learned this past year while there, maybe God had at least one more thing to teach her.

But she never dreamed that a year later she'd still be hung up on Nick. Nor had she imagined that Grams would be getting married before her. A lump grew in her throat, making it hard to swallow.

What *was* God's plan for Holly?

~❧~

The moon his guiding light, Nick Brohns strode through the rows of Colorado blue spruce until he came to the end of the field. Though the Brohns Family Farms grew more Scotch pine, Nick preferred the spruce. Apparently the governor of Colorado agreed because someone from his staff had contacted the farm, wanting one of their Christmas trees for the

Governor's Mansion in Denver. The problem was, the only tree that would fit their bill was the tree Nick had had his eye on for years. So far, he'd managed to keep it off-limits to those looking for a tall tree to grace their home—and it would need to be a lofty home—for Christmas. He feared that was about to change.

As he trudged between the trees, he inhaled the resinous odor filling the air. Finally, he stopped at the end of the field where the blue spruce stood seventeen feet tall.

His blue spruce.

He wasn't sure why he'd decided the tree was special. Maybe because of its symmetrical shape or the most distinctive bluish-silver foliage he'd ever seen on a tree.

This tree outshone all others, regardless.

Maybe his fascination all boiled down to the fact that he just loved trees. The thought led him back to Holly because she'd always called him Tree Man. Nick blew out a breath. Hands gloved, he hung his thumbs on his jean pockets. No matter how hard he tried to forget her, his thoughts returned to her face, an expression, or something humorous she'd said.

Missions had been in her bones from the beginning, sending her to the far reaches of the world. It had always been her dream to go to South Africa, and she'd gone all right, leaving him behind. It was easy to blame the tree farm for that. But he knew his lack of communication skills hadn't helped. Nor the illness that plagued his father.

The tree glowed silvery in the moonlight. Because this tree was unusual, he'd saved it for a special occasion. He thought he knew what it was, but that time had passed a year ago, leaving

Nick feeling empty and the Christmas tree standing.

Christmas season at the Brohns Family Farms officially opened on Thanksgiving weekend—a little over three weeks away. In addition to distributing trees wholesale to retailers and brokers, they provided the public access to certain fields to select and cut trees via hayrides. The farm offered a unique time for families.

He fought the urge to glance at his watch and calculate how much longer it would be before Holly arrived at the Denver International Airport. From there, it was another hour drive home.

The last thing he needed was a distraction—especially not this distraction.

Footfalls crunched behind, coming closer until Tim Caldwell stood next to Nick, eyeing the tree. "Thought I'd find you here, Tree Man."

Nick shrugged, staving off the pang Tim's reference caused, though to Tim's credit, he hadn't called Nick Holly's special name very often.

Tim laughed. "I still don't get what you're looking at. What's so fascinating?"

Nick looked up into the lofty branches and sighed. "I suppose if you understood my fascination, I'd be calling you Tree Man."

Tim elbowed Nick, then began updating him on The Spirit of Christmas Charities, an organization to help needy families over the holidays, starting with Christmas trees provided by Brohns Family Farms. As Tim spoke, Nick nodded absently, feeling guilty that he couldn't stay focused on Tim's words.

"Hello? Earth to Nick. Or maybe, tree to Nick."

Nick looked at Tim and focused. "I'm sorry. What were you saying?"

Tim swiped his hand down his face. "Man, you've got it bad. And I'm not talking trees this time."

"Don't know what you mean."

Tim chuckled. "Whatever you say."

Nick grinned. "I appreciate all you're doing to help with the charity."

Tim grinned. "This is going to be great. You'll see."

"I hope you're right." Nick was pleased that other area growers had agreed to participate in his brainchild, but the extra effort to keep things organized would have done him in without Tim's help. Together, they'd worked hard to get everything ready for the first charitable season. After Holly left, fulfilling her desire to help the needy of the world, this charity idea seemed to be God's answer to Nick's hollowness upon being left behind.

He turned his back on the spruce and made his way through the rows of trees that, as they'd grown the past couple of seasons, had narrowed the path. A cloud moved over the moon, partially shrouding the light, making Nick wish he'd brought a flashlight as he crunched through the light layer of snow that had fallen earlier in the day.

They continued in silence, heading to the office where Tim's truck was parked. Nick had only to walk a few yards to his home on the property. He'd moved into the large converted barn, expecting to one day live there with his wife and family. He'd grown up in his parents' house only twenty yards away.

Tim reached his truck. "Say, how about lunch tomorrow?"

Nick paused before answering. Tomorrow was Saturday. His family had been invited to a small welcome home gathering for Holly at the Rivers' tomorrow. More than anything he wanted to see her again but wasn't sure if that would be a good idea, considering he'd tried to close the door on his hope for a future for them. Since the families had been friends for years, though, he couldn't exactly stay away without good reason.

He looked down, acknowledging that Tim still waited for an answer. "I have plans." More than likely, she'd moved on and chosen someone who could serve in the mission field with her. That was for the best.

"I know what's on your mind, buddy. I'm just surprised you're still hung up on her." Tim climbed into his truck but before closing the door, he said, "Be careful."

Nick nodded, glad the night shadowed his grim expression. Tim knew him too well. After locking up the farm office, Nick strolled toward his house.

Alone.

He usually ate dinner with his parents but had mostly missed it lately due to the busyness of the approaching season. More than once, he wondered if he'd made a mistake in moving out. But he hadn't known of his father's diagnosis of Alzheimer's until a year ago—a diagnosis that had changed everything for his family, for his plans with Holly.

Nick shook off the thoughts as he marched up the front steps of his porch. Though he didn't know exactly what time Holly would arrive—he didn't have her flight number—it would be sometime tonight. Was she already here?

He let himself in and flipped on the lights, then crossed the quaint living room to the bureau where he found the small box nestled in the bottom of the drawer. He ran his fingers over the soft velvet before opening it to reveal the diamond engagement ring—his grandmother's ring—given to him so that he could ask the woman he loved to marry him. When his mother had given it to him, she'd thought he was in love with someone else. She'd been so anxious to see him married that she'd been presumptuous about his feelings for Angie two years before.

Then, just over a year ago, he discovered that he was in love with his closest friend, Holly Rivers. How could he have been so wrong, believing that God meant for him and Holly to be together? He'd had no choice but to sit back and watch things unfold—and they had, sending Holly to Africa without him.

He heard the back door open and the kitchen lights came on. His mother appeared at the counter. "You're sure getting home late. I brought you some leftovers."

Nick strode into the kitchen, quickly shoving the box into his pocket. But he couldn't as quickly put away the thought that plagued him. South Africa had been Holly's dream—a dream she believed was God's call on her life. If he had asked Holly to stay and marry him, he would have stood in the way of that dream, of God's plan for her life—something he could never do.

Then why did he regret it so much?

Chapter 2

Making her way through the revolving doors that opened into the baggage claim area, Holly searched for her family in the throng. She couldn't wait to see them. Travel-worn people congregated near the conveyors to watch for their belongings with friends or relatives. She'd brought her family gifts from South Africa. For her mother, she'd purchased hand-painted place mats. The guy had carved a potato into a shape right there in front of her, then dipped it into paint and pressed it onto the mat, creating a richly colored design. If her mother didn't want to use them for the table, they would be beautiful framed.

Her father would be amused with the African-made drum, and Grams would love the elephant carved out of fake ivory. Holly thought it would make a special addition to her collection. They were supposed to be Christmas gifts, but she didn't think she could wait that long.

Familiar faces caught her attention, their smiles bright as they saw her at the same time. Holly glimpsed her younger sister, Cassie, tagging behind her parents as they wove toward her through the crowd.

Holly dropped her carry-on as she slipped into her mother's arms. "Mom, it's so great to be home."

Looking thin in her smart beige pantsuit, her mother swiped at a few errant tears as she held Holly at arm's length. "Sorry, hon. I promised your father I wouldn't cry."

"And I told you not to make promises you couldn't keep," he said, grinning.

Her mother swatted at him but kept her eyes—and her grip—on Holly. "You look wonderful. I hate to say this, but South Africa's been good to you."

"Well, maybe it's just the work and not the place." Her father held out his arms. "I'd hate to think that the other side of the world could be as good to you as we are."

Once her mother was willing to release her, Holly went to her father. "I've missed you, too, Dad."

Cassie wiggled between them and forced them apart. "Hey, don't forget me."

Laughing, Holly stroked Cassie's polished blond locks. "I'm sorry I missed your birthday. How's it feel to finally be a teenager?"

"Like Mom says, I've always acted like a teenager."

"Well, let's hope you grow out of that soon, then." Holly looked past her parents and Cassie. "Grams couldn't come, huh?"

"I'm sorry, hon. We weren't sure how late you'd be—if there would be delays, or—"

"Mom, it's all right. I would have been surprised if she came." Though she'd clung to the remote hope of seeing Grams tonight, Grams would know something was bothering her and would want to know what, right away. Holly was sure she was too tired to be coherent about her conflicting emotions. Eventually, though, she'd have to explain that her team leader had sent her home on leave to pray about where God wanted her.

The team leader's assessment that she hadn't been focused enough on the job still stunned her, and tears welled. She felt like a complete failure. Not wanting her mother to see, Holly turned her attention to the conveyor and her luggage. She spotted Dad pressing his way to the front of the pack.

Her mother squeezed her arm. "I know you're disappointed."

Grams was probably the only person who could help her work through this. "I understand, really. I just can't wait to see her and—"

"Can you believe she's getting married, Holly? And before you, too." Cassie beamed with excitement.

Holly opened her mouth, but her mother spoke first. "Cassie, you shouldn't say such things."

Shame washed over her that she'd also considered the selfish thought. "Yep, it's hard to believe. And even harder to believe that the wedding will take place while I'm on furlough. I couldn't be more thrilled."

At sixty-six, Grams was getting married again—a second chance at love, though she'd already been blessed with a lifetime of it with Holly's grandfather who'd passed on several years ago. The woman had been everything a grandmother should be, her closest confidant. She deserved the best.

"Well, I'm just glad you're home. The missionary base—I can never remember—"

"Just say Joburg, though it's actually ninety miles northwest of that."

"Okay, let me rephrase it then." Her mother chuckled. "South Africa can live without you for a couple of months."

"I'm surprised you let Cassie stay up this late. Doesn't she have school tomorrow?" Holly slapped her forehead. "I've been traveling too long. Of course, tomorrow is Saturday."

"Yeah and we've got a surprise for you." Cassie's eyes grew wide, and she cast a sheepish grin at her mother.

"Cassie Elaine Rivers!" Her mother's gentle scowl quickly melted into a huge smile.

"A surprise?" Holly ruffled Cassie's hair. "Since you blurted it out, might as well spill the rest."

"Why don't we go to the car since I'm paying for parking by the hour." Holly's father shouldered two of her bags and towed her duffel on wheels. "We've got plenty of time to catch up."

"Dad, I can carry something."

"Nope. I've got them."

He led the way through the airport exit doors and over the crosswalk to the nearby parking.

Holly settled into the front seat next to her father then buckled in.

"Mom, can I tell her now?"

"Well, she doesn't know what it is, so we can still surprise her." From the backseat, her mother's voice sounded heavy with exasperation.

Her father kept his attention focused on the exits from the Denver airport as he spoke. "I've never liked surprises. And in that, I think Holly takes after me."

Her mother sighed. "Looks like I'm outnumbered. Oh, all right, I don't suppose it will hurt for you to be prepared. We're having a welcome home party for you tomorrow. Well, a welcome home lunch to be exact."

Holly forced a smile, wanting to appreciate their efforts, though she could have used at least one day to rest and get her bearings back home.

"And guess who we invited?" Cassie asked. If her father wasn't one for surprises, Cassie wasn't one for secrets.

Nick.

Holly shifted in the seat, her heart suddenly pounding. "Well? Who's coming?"

Cassie seemed to act younger than her age tonight, probably overcome with excitement for her older sister to be home again. "Well, Grandma for one, and the Brohns!"

"That sounds like fun." Their families were close, Nick's father and hers longtime friends. Would Nick come, too? And if she saw him—no, *when* she saw him—how would she react? A year hadn't diminished her feelings for him. And that was the problem—she wasn't sure if Nick shared those feelings. Somehow she needed to find out.

Holly chewed on a nail and stared out the window. Raindrops began to collect on the windshield. With an hour drive from Denver to Boulder she wouldn't be talking to Grams tonight. No one but Grams knew of her true feelings for Nick. No one but Grams had known she'd wished for, even expected, Nick to proclaim his feelings.

Nick pulled to the curb at the Rivers' colonial-style home

where several other vehicles filled the driveway. He checked phone messages while waiting for his parents to step from their SUV. Once they were out, he released a breath. He'd tried to come up with an excuse to miss lunch, but his mother was becoming suspicious. He could tell because she kept watching him.

His father tapped on the window. "You coming?"

He nodded, then disentangled himself from the seat belt. How many times did he have to remind himself that nothing actually *had* happened between them? Because nothing had changed—he'd not told her how he felt, allowing her to fulfill her dreams—he should be able to act the part of good friend. Just like they'd always been. He slid from the vehicle and hesitated before shutting the door. Sure. Right. He was supposed to act normally while being in the same room as the woman he loved and hadn't seen for a year.

Ahead of him, Carl and Amelia Brohns tromped up the steps with eagerness. His mother's good spirits on this particular outing with his dad had a lot to do with the fact that they were in safe territory, Nick was sure. If his father suffered with a memory lapse or any other signs of Alzheimer's, they were among friends.

His breath amassing around him in white puffs, Nick stopped to collect himself, adjusting the collar of his coat. Clouds heavy in the sky, the forecast said snow late that evening.

"This wasn't a good idea," he mumbled under his breath then took the first step onto the porch.

His mother quirked a brow in his direction while his father pressed the doorbell. Not good. He'd worked hard to hide his miserable state of mind since Holly left.

"You seem nervous." His mother readjusted his collar as though he'd made a mess of it. "But I'm sure that's understandable. A close friend is back in town. A beautiful friend, at that. You know, I never understood why the two of—"

Nick coughed into his hand, drowning out the rest of his mother's words. She hadn't known of his intentions toward Holly. The last thing he wanted today was to feel like a figure in a snow globe, his emotions on display for everyone to see. At least his mother's suspicions didn't run deeper than mere nervousness at seeing Holly again.

The door opened, revealing her bright-eyed younger sister, beaming a smile at them. She held the door open as they entered the Rivers' expansive home. "Come in, come in."

After she took their coats, Nick thanked her then fought to remain cool as his eyes scanned the great room with its traditional furniture. He'd expected the house to be filled with people even though his mother had told him the Rivers wanted a small gathering for Holly's first day back. Only a few of their family and friends were scattered about the large open area, which included the kitchen.

A huge welcome home banner that looked like Cassie had created it with all her love, including every color in the spectrum, hung from the vaulted ceiling. It brightened the room, otherwise decorated in muted tones. He spotted his dad talking to Holly's father in the far corner, next to twin leather chairs. Nick made to join the men. He'd noticed more memory lapses in his dad than usual and planned to stay near him for the most part. Still, there wasn't anyone he trusted more with his dad than Mr. Rivers.

Mr. Rivers gripped his hand. "It's great to see you, Nick. I hear you're doing wonderful things for our community over at the farm."

"Well, the Christmas season hasn't exactly started yet, but we're getting ready, yes."

"I'm talking about the new charity you've started, of course."

"Yes, sir." Warmth filled him at the mention, though it embarrassed him to take any credit. "It's surprising, I know, that poverty has become a serious issue and right here at home." Still, Nick had never felt that his idea to provide Christmas trees, food, and toys for the season was enough.

"Mind if I ask what inspired you?"

Your daughter. "Just want to do my part." Would he have guessed that after Holly had gone off to help those in need, Nick felt worthless even though he'd stayed to help his father, help his family?

Mr. Rivers gave him a thoughtful smile, looking right through him, it seemed. "It's a noble cause, son."

Nick hoped the secrets of his heart weren't easy to read.

While his dad became caught up in a conversation with someone else, Mr. Rivers tugged Nick a short distance away to speak privately. "Staying here to help your family because of your father's condition is noble enough."

Was the man trying to say he shouldn't have attempted the charity, or what? Had Mr. Rivers known all along the reasons Nick had stayed behind?

"I'm—not sure what to say."

It was strange to have this conversation here and now. The

families were friends, spent time together, and attended church together. But Nick had thrown himself into work to stave off the pain of his personal loss—both that of his dad's illness and of the woman he loved—and he hadn't exactly given Mr. Rivers a chance to speak with him before.

"I understand why you felt compelled to do more."

"You do?" Nick considered the comment. Where was Mr. Rivers going with this? He glanced around the room, almost thankful that he'd not run into Holly because one brief conversation already had him feeling cornered.

"Sure I do. You'd planned to go to Africa, too, and then your father's diagnosis came." Mr. Rivers' smile faded. "I'm sorry on both counts."

"I appreciate. . ." Nick's next words caught in his throat. So Mr. Rivers had known that much.

He still smarted when he thought how he'd been told about his dad's illness. Apparently, his dad had been adamant about keeping the news from Nick so that he would continue with his plans to travel to South Africa, working with a group of missionaries. Working with Holly. Nick hadn't worried about the farm then, because things had always run smoothly under his dad's exceptional management.

His mother, however, feared being left alone to deal with his dad's deteriorating health. Not that he blamed her for that. But even knowing that his dad would be angry with her for telling Nick, she begged Nick to stay—and then extracted a promise from him not to tell anyone his real reason for changing his plans.

Shocked at the news and overwhelmed by his mother's

desperation, he'd agreed to her plea. It had happened so fast, he'd not had time to consider a solution. All his plans for the future had been sealed away then. Though he'd considered sharing the truth with Holly and asking her to keep things to herself, how could he ask her to promise something that he'd not kept? Plus, asking her to keep the devastating news from her family—with their fathers being close friends—was too much.

All he could think to tell her was that the farm couldn't do without him after all. The words he'd spoken had taken the place of the proposal he'd planned. To make matters worse, she'd ended up staying much longer than a few months. He'd wondered if she'd ever come back.

"Nick?"

Realizing he'd been lost in thought, Nick looked up at Mr. Rivers, but the older man's attention was elsewhere and the expression of love on his face told Nick all he needed to know.

The reason for the gathering, herself, stood in a wide arched doorway. Dark curls framed a face set with large, teardrop eyes, and a smile that outshone all others.

Her eyes eagerly scanned the room and came to rest on Nick.

All the blood rushed to his head as he held her gaze. Suddenly, she was the only other person in the room.

Too late to guard his heart. He wasn't sure how, but he had to focus on something else.

Someone else.

Yeah, right. He'd had a year to do that.

Chapter 3

She stood staring at Nick, feeling unprepared for the encounter. Or was it his return gaze that made her. . . uncomfortable? Her emotions tumbled like a boulder down a mountain, soon to fall into a deep ravine. If she didn't want to break apart in front of everyone, she had to act and quickly.

Holly tugged at the back of her sweater and adjusted her broomstick skirt. "Hello, everyone."

A hush spread around the room as all eyes turned on her. She covered her mouth, embarrassed at the attention, hoping no one had noticed her lingering look at Nick. A laugh escaped and the group erupted.

"How's the missionary?"

"It's great to see you."

"Glad you could join us!"

Even though her parents had only invited a few close friends and relatives, she was overwhelmed. Given the long flight and jet lag, her mother let her sleep in, but then she'd overslept. She was surprised that Cassie hadn't found a way to disturb and wake her. She'd rushed to get ready before everyone arrived, but ended up late to her own party regardless.

The room felt hotter than she'd expected.

"Welcome back, Holly." With a warm smile, her mother's best friend, Margaret Fletcher, grasped her by the elbow and steered her into the small crowd.

"It's good to be back. I'm. . .humbled by all of this." Holly had fully expected Margaret to be there—her mother couldn't manage any sort of gathering without the woman who had a knack for parties. She was flash and elegance all rolled into one.

After a number of hugs, well-wishes, and pats on the back, conversations returned to a life of their own. She breathed a sigh and searched the room again for Nick. Why hadn't he made his way to her yet? Disappointment squeezed her heart. He'd certainly had as much opportunity as the others. But then she saw that he was caught up in a conversation with her father. By their stern expressions it looked serious.

Though he'd never told her what his feelings were, her heart was raw at what seemed like a rejection. Maybe she'd imagined the change in their relationship from friends to something more before she left. Maybe he didn't share the attraction she'd felt between them.

Mouth suddenly dry, she headed to the buffet where hot cocoa, apple cider, tea, and coffee were set up with an array of flavored creamers. Holly would have to make sure her mother knew how much she appreciated everything. After pouring herself some apple cider, Holly perused the guests over the rim of her cup.

Where was Grams? She desperately needed to talk to her. It was hard keeping her emotions in check, especially since she was drained from travel. But if she didn't have an outlet soon, she might explode, which was the last thing she needed at the welcome home party. She certainly didn't want anyone to know of her failure.

When it had come time for her to commit to another year in the field, her team leader suggested she take time off to consider where her real calling lay. After prayer and reflection, she knew he was right, but even now she ached over his words.

The whole thing reminded her of the time she took a scuba diving class, hoping to become certified. The instructor told her he wouldn't certify her. She was able to do the dive with the appropriate skills, but apparently lacked what the instructor believed was an essential ingredient—confidence, to put it in his words. Diving had been something she'd dreamed of doing. But it didn't come close to how she felt about Africa. The million-dollar question, which repeatedly nagged her: Hadn't Africa been her dream for as long as she could remember? Nick had always called her a dreamer because of it.

But once in Africa, it was her unresolved feelings for Nick that left her frazzled. One way or another she needed closure.

One thing she knew already was that their comfortable friendship of the past ten years wasn't the same. What had she expected? Everything to return to the way it was? If he would just come over and talk to her. Say something, anything—she didn't care what—then she could relax. At least for now.

When her mother strolled past, carrying a tray of lasagna to the table, Holly snagged her. "Where's Grams?"

Her mother set the dish down then glanced at her watch. "She had an appointment earlier, but promised she'd be here in time. I think we'll have to start lunch without her."

"Is there anything I can do to help?" The question was out of her mouth before she realized that the other women were putting the finishing touches on the table and buffet. "I'm sorry. I always do ask too late, don't I?"

"It's endearing, hon." Her mother pinched her cheek then hurried into the kitchen again.

Holly frowned, swirling the remnants of apple cider in her cup. About as endearing as a missionary whose heart was somewhere else. Standing alone, waiting for lunch to be served at her own party, she understood the old cliché of feeling alone in a crowd. Conversation was difficult when she had nothing to say, but she'd not seen any of these people in a year. Relationships required regular maintenance. She rubbed her temples.

"Are you all right?" The familiar, smooth voice came from behind, sending a swirl of warmth and panic through her.

A soft smile lifted the corner of her mouth as she spun to face Nick. *I've missed you.* Just how much, startled her. "I'm fine. Just—jet lag."

Nick winked. "You were always a dreamer. Now, you've accomplished your dream, haven't you?" His smile enveloped her while his eyes searched her face as though he'd forgotten what she looked like.

She felt herself flushing under his silent perusal and looked away. "I suppose I did." *Then why do I feel like I've failed, like something's missing?* "So, how've you been?"

"Business is good, but nothing to get excited about. At least not as exciting as going to an exotic country." His blue eyes bored into hers as he nodded and grinned. Though a lone dimple flashed in his cheek, he seemed reserved.

There was so much she wanted to tell him. Going to South Africa hadn't been what she'd expected, especially without Nick. "I'm sure I won't be able to get out of sharing about my adventure with everyone."

A nervous laugh escaped her. It was wrong, all wrong. It should have been easy to talk to him. They'd shared so many easy times together.

Now. . .it was like talking about the weather with a stranger.

Holly's father cleared his throat. "May I have everyone's attention, please? I know you've come to welcome Holly home, but I'm sure you're hungry, too, so I'll get right to the point." His comment drew laughter. "Thank you for taking time out of your busy schedules to join us in welcoming our beautiful daughter back to this side of the world."

"Hear, hear!"

"We're very proud of her for answering God's call, even when it hurt." Silence filled her father's long pause this time. "Let's pray."

Holly stood frozen, listening to her father's prayer. What could he have meant? What did he know of her struggle? She squeezed her eyes tighter, fighting the urge to peek at Nick. Did he know how hard it had been for her to leave him behind? She chided herself for harboring pain from the past, for entertaining even a small hope of a chance with Nick.

She and Nick? They seemed worlds apart, now.

The smell of lasagna made Nick's mouth water and his stomach rumble. Holly's mother had made her favorite dish for the welcome home party. After filling his plate with the aromatic Italian food, he searched for a place to eat. Almost everyone was already sitting at the large dining table or one of two smaller tables set up especially for the occasion, or in chairs, holding a plate and a drink. Nick didn't trust himself to sit anywhere but at a table with a plate of lasagna. A room covered in white carpet was a disaster in the making, and he didn't want to embarrass himself in front of his parents' friends at their party, or—in front of Holly.

As the guest of honor, Holly sat at the end of the formal dining table. There was an empty place next to her, but that spot was for someone special, maybe her grandmother. Besides, why would she want to spend more time talking with him? She'd seemed so stiff only a few minutes before. Too much had transpired. He couldn't fix it in one conversation, if ever. Of course, he'd had a chance, but he'd said the wrong thing at what could have been the right time.

Nick spotted an open place at one of the extra tables. Once he made himself comfortable, sitting across from Cassie and her young cousin, Jamie, he finally took a bite of lasagna.

Someone squeezed his shoulder. He looked up to see Mrs. Rivers.

"What are you doing sitting there? Why, I thought you knew your place was next to Holly."

Nick took a swig of his iced tea as he digested what she'd said. "I didn't know. I'm sorry."

Since he'd already started eating, he assumed a simple apology should suffice. He didn't want Holly to be forced into spending time with him unless she wanted to. Probably her mother just expected him and Holly to act like the good friends they'd always been, because she hadn't known something else had kindled between them.

Nick's inaction prompted further insistence from her mother. "Here, let me help you." Mrs. Rivers took his plate and utensils and strolled to the dining table.

Great, just great. This was drawing the very attention Nick had attempted to avoid. To protest now would be an insult. He tugged at his collar as he made his way over to sit next to Holly, feeling like the room had grown suddenly overcrowded, stifling even.

Already engrossed in conversation with a woman Nick had never met, Holly barely glanced up when he seated himself. What if their discomfort with each other became more apparent? All eyes would be on them, and the snow globe was about to be shaken.

The lasagna had turned to flavorless mush, and instead of the appetizing aroma of an Italian dinner, all he could seem to focus on was Holly, and the light citrus fragrance she had always worn.

Forgetting that he'd been hungry, he watched her animated facial expressions as she talked with the woman.

Finished chatting, Holly pushed some of the lasagna around on her plate then looked at him just as she stuck a forkful into her mouth, smiling as she chewed. He wanted to laugh at the familiar gesture as her smile relaxed him. Maybe he could make it through this party after all.

She swallowed and leaned closer. "Sorry about the assigned seating."

He shook his head and sighed. "No one. . ." He was going to say that no one had made him sit next to her, but he couldn't deny it. He had, in fact, felt uncomfortable about her mother's insistence. "I figured you were saving the place next to you for someone else."

Her mischievous smile faded along with the color in her face, and she went back to looking at her plate and eating. What now? It seemed like he could never say what he felt and when he did, it was the wrong thing to say.

He should never have let her go away without telling her how he really felt. Now a year stood between them, distancing any romantic notions he'd held on to, and it seemed like an eternity.

He set his fork down and considered her. Maybe she felt the same as he did—confused about where things stood, or didn't stand, between them. Or maybe she'd truly found her place in South Africa. Perhaps a partner to share her life with there, as well. But what they both needed was a few minutes alone to talk. Nothing worse than ill-communicated intentions—exactly what had gone wrong a year ago. Except for one thing. He doubted anything he said would have stopped her from going without him.

And that was the crux of it.

He'd already resolved that he wouldn't keep her from doing what she believed was God's call on her life. When she finally looked up at him again, he saw the questions in her eyes and with them he allowed hope to kindle—was it possible she'd stay here now? Had she decided that Africa wasn't for her, after all, or that her time there had been fulfilled?

But now wasn't the time to talk about any of it, and neither had a year ago been. Would it ever be the right time? Some people were considered to be a bad judge of character. Nick Brohns, on the other hand, was a bad judge of timing.

When everyone finally lingered over empty plates, Mrs. Rivers's friend, Margaret, moved to stand next to Holly. "Tell us some stories from South Africa."

Mrs. Rivers took Holly's plate along with several others. "Yes, hon. We can eat our dessert—cobbler or brownies—and drink coffee while you tell us everything."

Holly grinned and clasped her hands, releasing an exaggerated sigh. "Well I suppose I knew this was coming."

She rose from the table and moved into the great room, settling into a plush oversized chair. Some gathered in the room, sitting around her while others hung back, waiting in the dining room, Nick assumed, for the dessert. He leaned against a wall near the kitchen, his hands jammed into his pockets. He wouldn't miss hearing this for the world, no matter how awkward things were between them.

Holly's sister and cousin sat on the floor next to her. "Oh, oh. Can you say something in South African?"

"It's Afrikaans, actually. But be forewarned, I seriously can't do the accent to go with it." Holly smiled, looking thoughtful. "Let me see. Well, as a missionary, I would say, *het jy al regtig tot die kennis van die liefde van Christus gekom?*"

"Oh, that sounds nice. What does it mean?" Margaret

stood next to Nick, drying a dish.

"It means, 'have you already really to the knowledge of the love of Christ come?' But we would say it, 'have you really come to know the love of Christ?'"

"You learned all of that in a year?"

Holly nodded. "I still have a lot to learn. But others where I minister speak Zulu."

"How do you say Merry Christmas in that language?"

"That's an easy one. *Sinifesela uKhisimusi oMuhle noNyaka oMusha oNempumelelo.* Merry Christmas and Happy New Year."

The girls giggled as others murmured words of approval.

Holly's expression once again became animated as she told stories of exciting adventures, including a safari in which the Jeep she'd been riding in was charged by a rhinoceros. Oohs and aahs filled the room along with objections and disbelief.

Holly laughed, throwing her head back in delight. "I promise. I'm dead serious."

Nick laughed along with her, feeling her joy. Holly continued but the tales turned more serious. She described how the people where she ministered lived in shanty towns, but even in their great need they seemed happier than Americans. Yet her heart ached for them. They needed most of the basics: shelter, running water and sewers, clothing, shoes. She ached for the African children with distended stomachs due to malnutrition. Once, she'd held a two-year-old starving boy all day long, shooing flies from his face as she accepted his many kisses to her cheek.

How could she not love that little boy?

Nick felt his own heart ache with longing to be used by God like Holly.

This was Holly at her best—the Holly Nick. . .*loved*.

He coughed into his hand, hoping to hide the word that he was certain had almost been on his tongue. But it had only remained in his heart. For the first time, he hoped it would die because. . .Holly loved South Africa.

He watched her for a long time, as though she were that shining star at the top of the Christmas tree that he could never reach as a child. Only his father could reach the top of the tree to put the star on, though Nick was allowed to remove it from the box and hand it to him.

Even if God hadn't called her to the mission field, how could he compete with South Africa?

Maybe what Nick needed to do was hand over his heart's desire, giving it to his heavenly Father.

Chapter 4

At the memory of Bongani with his large brown eyes and distended tummy, Holly's eyes brimmed with tears and her throat grew tight. Though she'd hoped to convey her strong feelings for the people of South Africa, she'd not meant to be overly emotional. For distraction, she ruffled Cassie's hair as her sister sat beaming on the floor.

She wondered what Nick thought of her stories. Why, she wasn't sure. Maybe she wanted him to know that her leaving when he couldn't go wasn't for nothing. She wanted him to see how much going to the mission field had meant to her. If only he could read in her eyes how much he meant to her, too. Against her better judgment, she risked a glimpse.

He had his back to her. Had he even been listening?

Someone cleared her throat in an attempt to gain attention. Holly's grandmother stood in the living room, her smile wide and arms open for none other than Holly. Her heart leaped for joy. She rushed to Grams' arms, feeling the woman's love engulf her—something she'd missed terribly in Africa.

Grams was the one she'd always confided in, the only

one she talked to about everything. When she lived at home, Holly would call to talk every day, even though she knew it sometimes hurt her mother's feelings that she was closer to her grandmother. Grams squeezed tighter when Holly tried to end the embrace, surprising her with her strength, but finally, she released Holly. "How's my girl?"

Holly wanted to say that she was much better now that Grams was here, but everyone was listening. "I'm fine. I've missed you."

As she realized just how much she'd missed Grams—and everyone else—all her emotions surged to the surface. If only she'd had time to rest more before seeing everyone. Embarrassed, she wiped at the tears.

Grams winked, whispering, "We'll talk later, don't worry."

"I was—so thrilled to hear that you're getting married," Holly said. "Nothing could make me happier."

"Now, dear. We both know that's not quite accurate, but I accept your well-wishes." With a pat, she went to greet other guests.

"Holly." Cassie tugged at her sleeve. "Jamie and I are wondering if we're going to go on a hayride like we always do. We waited this year until you came back."

Holly scanned the room for Nick, who'd always taken the families on a joint hayride at the farm, usually before their busy season opened. "I don't know, sweetie."

"Oh, look, there he is. Hey, Nick. . ." Cassie beckoned to him.

Nick stood near the door, helping his mother with her coat as his father donned his. Once finished, Nick and his parents made their way to Holly.

His mother hugged her. "We're so glad you're home and safe, dear. Come to see us soon."

"It was good to see you, and thank you for coming. I'll come by as soon as I can."

His father nodded at Holly, but something in his expression made her think he was trying to remember her. Surely, she was wrong. Not long after she'd arrived in South Africa, she learned of his illness. A tendril of dread crept through her, reminding her of what Nick must be going through. She masked it with a smile, unsure what to say.

In Holly's estimation, Nick had been obviously uncomfortable today. It was as though they'd broken up, but they'd never been an item to begin with. Holly scratched her head. She wanted to suggest they go without her, but that wasn't an option, given they'd waited for her to get home before going on the hayride.

Before Holly could say anything, Cassie asked, "Nick, can you please take us on our yearly hayride now that Holly's back?"

A slight crease appeared between his brows.

Holly rushed to Nick's aid. "Cassie, wait. Why don't you let—"

"No, she's right. We haven't done the Rivers-and-Brohns hayride this year." His smile was disarming, but his eyes searched hers.

Her heart caught in her throat. Memories tumbled over her from last year's hayride, nearly crushing her. Those last few moments with Nick—what he'd said or left unsaid—had changed everything between them.

And she'd left for South Africa two days later.

A week after Holly's welcome home party, Nick picked up the phone to return a call to a local Christmas tree provider, even though he was several hours late doing so. He was thankful that most of the other suppliers were anxious to be involved with The Spirit of Christmas Charities. He'd spent months in preparation, including establishing the charity's nonprofit status. Success was in the details, most of which could only be taken care of on the last few days leading up to opening day. Having to go on a hayride tonight wasn't helping his stress level. It had been a busy day, nothing going as planned.

He much preferred the outdoors to the office, but his dad had been reluctant to work after his diagnosis. As a result, Nick spent as much time out of doors as he could during the day and put aside working in the office until later. Anything that required his attention there had to wait until the evening.

He'd hired an additional employee to assist Rose who worked as bookkeeper, receptionist, and helped with the sales and market-ing. Angie was going through a divorce, had a son, and needed the job. Surely, she knew his one-time infatuation with her had long since died. More than once, he hoped he hadn't made a mistake in hiring her, but he needed the help, too.

So far, his schedule had worked, though Nick felt his dad's absence every day in the business he'd founded decades before. With their busy season quickly approaching, Nick wasn't sure he could stick to it. How would they manage since his dad couldn't be more involved? His diagnosis was difficult for all of them.

The door to the office building swooshed open. Probably

Tim, who'd offered to help him tonight after running a few personal errands.

"Nicholas Anderson Brohns." His mother used the same tone as when he was a boy.

Still holding the phone to his ear, he turned to face her as she stood in the office, a frown on her face. After several rings, not even voice mail responded, so he hung up.

"Why aren't you preparing for the hayride tonight? Holly and her family are probably on their way right now."

"Everything is already set up. Tim is going to—"

"What's Tim got to do with this?"

"Mom, I've got so much to do to get ready for our big season, now with the additional responsibility of this charity." The words were true enough.

"Did I hear someone say my name?" Tim closed the door behind him, dressed to spend an evening outside in the cold, driving the wagon.

Hurt filled his mother's eyes. "No offense, Tim, but this is family time. When two families, friends since the dark ages, get together to celebrate the holidays like we do every year, then I want my son—"

"What are you talking about?" Tim scratched his jaw and looked back and forth between Nick and his mother. "I'm here to help Nick catch up with some phone calls and paperwork." He shrugged out of his coat.

Nick narrowed his eyes.

Tim smiled and winked. "Go. Get ready for some fun. You look like someone who needs it."

Nick's mother smiled. "There. See? Tim has just offered

to free you up so you can spend some much needed recreation time. I've got to get back to the house in case they show up. I'll see you there."

Once his mother left, Nick explained to Tim what he'd been working on and needed to accomplish.

"I've got it. No need to hover or use me as an excuse to avoid Holly."

"Thanks. I owe you." Nick eyed Tim as he shoved his arm into the sleeve of his coat.

"Well, if I'm ever avoiding a relationship, I'll remember that."

Back at his house he took a quick shower and shaved, knowing that his parents would keep the Riverses well entertained if he ran late. Why had he thought he'd be able to get out of the hayride?

He ran a comb through his hair and realized he was grooming himself as if for a date, not a hayride. A heavy sigh escaped. Wanting something he couldn't have was difficult. That's why he thought it best to keep his distance tonight, but his family wouldn't understand.

He stared at the mirror, unseeing, as images of last year's hayride with the Riverses played before him. Holly standing next to the blue spruce, looking beautiful. Holiday earrings accenting her rosy cheeks. A shiny lip-glossed smile gracing her lips. She even acted unusually shy. Their relationship had changed in the two months before they were set to accompany a team to South Africa. He'd fallen in love with her. And he was almost certain she shared his feelings.

His gut stirred at the memory. But that night, as she

had looked into his eyes with so much expectancy, he could have—*should* have—declared his love for her. Maybe they could even have gotten married before going away. But a tragic diagnosis for his father and a promise to his mother had tied his hands with regret, leaving him without the words he needed. She'd dreamed of going to South Africa. He wouldn't take that from her.

Nick jerked away from the mirror. He couldn't stand the memory of the hurt in her eyes when he told her, without explanation, that he wasn't going. And now? They were like two strangers, two magnets pushing apart.

As he pulled a cream-colored sweater over his shirt, he consoled himself with the fact that at least tonight they wouldn't be alone—they'd be surrounded by family, which might make Holly less uncomfortable. But on the other hand, would it be better if he told her everything, got it all out in the open? He wasn't certain if it would serve any purpose.

Lord, help me know the right time. Give me the right words.

Did she even still care about him?

He yanked on his coat and made his way to his parents' house, where the Riverses would meet them first. He entered the kitchen door in the back, extra voices telling him they'd already arrived.

But when he stepped in to the living room, only Holly, Cassie, and Jamie were there. Holly stood by the fireplace, holding a cup of hot cocoa that his mother always made for such occasions. The firelight danced across her delicate features as she chewed her bottom lip, deep in thought.

She appeared despondent. He hoped he wasn't the reason,

but he didn't dare presume to be at the forefront of her thoughts. After all, she'd chosen to stay longer on foreign soil than any of them had thought.

Still, he knew exactly how to change her somber mood.

Chapter 5

"Where is everyone?"

Holly jumped at the sound of Nick's voice, hot cocoa sloshing out of her cup. Thankfully, it only spilled on the stone hearth and not the white carpet. What was it with everyone and their white carpets here? She decided she almost preferred the dirt floors she'd seen to having to worry about staining expensive floor coverings.

She laughed, teasingly shoving him. "Why do you always do that?"

The corners of his mouth twitched as he lifted his hands in mock innocence. "What did I do?"

"*You* know what. You startled me."

He laughed, removing his coat and tossing it over the sofa back. "Like I've always said, you need to be more aware of your surroundings."

"To answer your question, your mother went to help your dad with something. She asked me to wait here and said you'd be here soon. I hope that's all right."

"Of course it is." He flashed his lone dimple.

She always loved that. Maybe Nick had returned to the way he was before she'd left. Relaxed. It felt good. Maybe they could have their friendship back, if nothing more.

Cassie and Jamie got up from the sofa and strolled coolly, like only teenagers can do, to stand next to Nick. "Nick, you remember my cousin Jamie, right? She was at Holly's welcome home party."

"Yep. You girls are dressed up tonight. Are you sure you're supposed to go on a hayride with the likes of me?"

Cassie giggled and Jamie blushed, grinning. Holly hadn't noticed it at the party, but now that she had a moment to observe, she realized Jamie had a crush on Nick. She put her hand to her mouth to hide her smile.

"Why thanks, Nick. I assure you, we wouldn't want to be anywhere else." Cassie laid it on pretty thick, batting her eyelashes and smiling up at Nick.

Oh, brother. Holly wanted to laugh at her sister's efforts if that was how she planned to help her cousin get Nick's attention. Or were the girls competing? She looked at the puddle of cocoa on the floor and started for the kitchen. "I need to wipe—"

Nick caught her elbow. "Let me. You're the guest."

She wished a simple touch from him didn't do strange things to her insides. When he strode past she caught a whiff of his cologne. It made her a little dizzy. Memories once again flooded her mind. Memories she'd hoped to keep at bay tonight. She had to make it through the hayride.

In no time at all, he was cleaning up her mess with a paper towel. After disposing of the waste in the kitchen, he stood next to her again and smiled. It did more to warm her to her toes than the fire had.

"Let me guess. You came ahead of your parents, and they'll be joining us soon."

Holly sighed. "Dad came home from work sick. Mom wouldn't leave his side." When Holly saw the look on Nick's face, she knew they should have rescheduled.

"I'm sorry to hear that. Well, my parents should be down in a bit. Then we can go." He turned his attention to Cassie and Jamie who'd been looking through a book and giggling again. "You hear that, girls?"

Cassie pulled her gaze from the book and looked at him. "Is it time to go?"

As he walked past Cassie, he messed with her hair, which she hated now that she cared about how she looked. But he'd teased her the same way, pulling on strands of her hair, since she was a toddler. With one simple act, he transformed Cassie from cool teenager to little girl.

Nick looked at Holly. "I probably need to check on my parents."

"We'll be waiting."

Holly knew him well enough to recognize the strain in his face. The tightness in his jaw. She hated that his father was suffering, hated seeing Nick suffer with him. Did he remember their last hayride? She knew now, it was because of his father that he hadn't gone to South Africa. She'd always wondered if things would have been different for them if his father hadn't become ill. Though she felt guilty for thinking selfish thoughts—after all, Nick's father, his family, were suffering—it was to resolve her feelings for Nick that she'd been sent home. Had Mark, her team leader, known that she really loved Nick? Mark hadn't said it in so many words, but she suspected he did.

Holly rubbed her neck. Could she find something else to think about tonight?

She took a seat next to Jamie on the sofa to peruse the book with her and discovered the girls had tucked a teen idol magazine inside the covers of the volume they held between them. So that explained the squeals and giggles over a coffee table book on evergreens.

"What's taking so long?" Cassie got up and wandered around the room, lifting knickknacks and examining the bottoms like they still had a price on them.

"Shh. Don't be rude." Holly noticed Jamie had set her cup on the side table along with Cassie's.

She took their empty cups into the kitchen then rinsed and placed them into the dishwasher.

Drawing back the curtains at the window over the sink, she looked for stars as she considered the chain of events that sent her home from South Africa. It all seemed ridiculous now that she was here. If Nick had any feelings for her, he would have said something that night. And if not, he'd had months afterward to tell her. In all of that time, he'd sent her only one e-mail—though, in truth, her connection at the base had been sporadic, nor had she had much time to spend on the Internet.

"Excuse me." Nick reached across her and opened the cabinet, pulling out a glass.

Startled, as usual, she turned to face him. His enigmatic expression worried her. "I didn't hear you come in. I was putting away the cups. Is everything all right?"

Nick's half smile flattened as he got water from the tap. "Fine. But they're not going to join us." He drank the entire glass before setting it on the counter.

"So. . .are we still going?" Holly bit her lip, glancing at the girls in the living room. "Listen, I would suggest that we reschedule, but Cassie and Jamie have been looking forward to this."

"I probably won't have another chance, not that I'm a necessary ingredient." Leaning against the counter, Nick stared as if searching her thoughts. "We might as well go."

She noticed he wore the cream-colored sweater she'd given him two Christmases ago and fought the urge to run her hand down the soft wool.

He pushed from the counter. "You ready?"

"Okay, girls. It's just us. Let's make the most of it." Remembering Jamie's predicament, Holly frowned at her cousin and touched the sleeve of Nick's sweater. "Jamie forgot her coat. Left it at our house."

"No problem." He tossed his coat to Jamie. "This will be too big, but roll up the sleeves, wrap it around you. It'll keep you warm enough. I'll grab one of Dad's."

After finding what he needed in the coat closet near the door, he followed them out onto the porch, shutting the door behind him.

Holly donned her beanie. "Life is so hectic that even our parents couldn't join us on the so-called family hayride."

"Right, which makes this a good time. This will probably be the best opportunity we'll have to talk."

Holly's throat constricted.

Chapter 6

"Perfect night for a hayride, huh, ladies?" Tim winked at the girls as they climbed onto the bales of hay on the trailer.

Nick assisted Holly as she climbed up.

"Thank you." She smiled then searched for a place to sit.

Even in the dim light he could see her soft cheeks redden. Or was he mistaking the healthy color she'd gotten under a South African sun for a blush? It was, after all, summer in that part of the world.

He followed Tim to the tractor and squeezed his shoulder. "Thanks. I owe you, again." For safety reasons, he'd ended up calling Tim back to have him drive the tractor. He didn't want the girls by themselves on the trailer.

"Your debt is accumulating. Exponentially." He grinned and climbed into the seat. "But you know I'm glad to do it."

Tim started the engine, making it difficult for Nick to say more without shouting. He nodded and walked to the back, climbing onto the bales where Holly, Cassie, and Jamie already sat huddled together. Any colder and it wouldn't be enjoyable, but the hay and body heat would go a long way until they made it to the campfire.

Nick took the only spot left in the small circle of huddled women, sitting next to Holly. He wanted to wrap his arms around her to keep her warm. Looking at Cassie and Jamie, he wondered if he would get time to talk with Holly after all. The tractor lunged forward, knocking Jamie off her seat. Laughter and giggles erupted.

"Wait!" His mother and father hurried toward them.

Nick hopped off and got Tim's attention. When they stopped, Nick helped his parents onto the trailer.

"What are you guys doing here?" Nick thought better of pursuing the question when his father shook his head. He winked at his mother. "Glad you could join us. The more the merrier."

After everyone was situated, Tim returned his attention to driving the tractor.

Holly smiled and rubbed her gloved hands together. "Wouldn't it be funny if my parents showed up, too?"

"We could wait here to see?" Nick offered.

She shook her head. "Hey, it's not Christmas yet, but how about we sing some carols?"

Jamie stuck her hand up like she was in class. "How about 'Joy to the World'? That's one of my faves."

Holly's smile and beautiful voice made Nick wonder why he'd worked so hard to avoid tonight.

After singing several rounds of various carols and coping with the jarring of the hayride, Nick was relieved when the tractor finally came to a halt at the campfire. A small table was already arranged with thermoses of hot chocolate and coffee. His mother really had made sure things were ready ahead of time. Everyone climbed down as Tim made quick to start the fire.

After settling on logs used for seating, Nick's mother began a rendition of "O Tannenbaum," singing some in German then again in English so the others could join in.

"Tell us the tale of the Christmas tree again, Nick," Cassie said from across the fire.

"Yeah, come on. No one tells it like you," Jamie added.

"I love that story, too." Holly took a sip from her cup, gazing at him over the rim.

He could easily look into her eyes forever, but others were watching. "All right. You'd think you'd get tired of it, though."

Clearing his throat, he leaned forward and placed his elbows on his knees. "It was the eighth century when St. Boniface went to Germany to share Christianity. He decided he'd cut down an oak tree, one that the pagans dedicated to their god Thor and considered sacred and holy. Boniface dared the pagans' god to kill him. That is, if he were real."

"Ew." Cassie dragged out the necessary sound effects.

"What happened next?" Holly coaxed him on.

"As if you don't know." He winked, then fell back into his storytelling voice. "When he raised his ax, a strong wind blew the oak over. It crashed to the ground, splitting in half. It's said that an evergreen grew inside of the stump. And because Thor didn't kill Boniface, but instead their sacred tree fell over, people converted to Christianity. From there Boniface used the shape of the evergreen to talk about the Holy Trinity, making the tree, specifically a fir tree, a German symbol of Christianity."

He blew out his relief at finishing the short tale.

"I wish my mom would put one up. But she probably needs to hear that story first." Jamie laughed.

Holly quirked a brow. "But do you remember what Boniface said to them?"

"Is that a challenge?" He pushed off his elbows to sit up straight.

A smiled played across her lips.

He liked that and stood this time, jamming his hands into his jeans. Again, he cleared his throat. " 'This humble tree's wood is used to build your homes: let Christ be at the centre of your households. Its leaves remain evergreen in the darkest days: let Christ be your constant light. Its boughs reach out to embrace and its top points to heaven: let Christ be your Comfort and Guide.'"

No one said anything for a few seconds. Only the fire crackled, filling the silence.

Then, his father slowly clapped. "Well done."

Suddenly glad his father had come with them, Nick nodded and smiled.

"I know I'm impressed," Holly teased.

"What? You don't think a tree farmer can know stuff?" When they laughed, Nick joined in, but even as he did, he thought about the words he'd spoken. Somehow he needed to let Christ be his comfort, be his guide, and lead him to do the right thing where he and Holly were concerned.

"Hey, you should make that into some sort of play or something," Cassie said.

Nick's mother stood and began collecting empty cups. "There's an idea. Let's find out if there's a script to that effect, then we could see what the drama team at church thinks."

"And it makes you consider Christ when you see the Christmas tree, instead of the commercialization of the holiday." Holly stood and brushed her pants off.

When the flames tapered down, Tim tossed on more logs, sending sparks into the air.

They'd need to head back soon. It was getting late. Believing no one would notice, Nick escaped the circle and hiked up the small hill, which overlooked the farm.

In the moonlight, he could see rows of Christmas trees, seeming to go on for miles. With a quick glance back, he saw his mother handing Holly another cup of steaming liquid. Would he have to endure this every Christmas? Holly and her family on the hayride? Her subsequent return to South Africa? How much time must pass before he'd stop caring?

Soft footfalls approached from behind, bringing the scent of citrus mingled with smoke.

Holly stood next to him, sharing the view. "Aren't you cold over here?"

He hesitated. "Not anymore."

She laughed. "I'm glad to see you doing so well. I mean—considering your father's illness."

Is that what she really meant? Or was she talking about them and their parting? There was so much he wanted to say and now might be as good of a time as any, unless they were interrupted.

Nick rubbed the back of his neck as he worked up the

nerve to plunge forward. "I hope you know that he's the reason I didn't go with you. Mom needed—"

She stopped him with a hand to his arm. "Your family needed you. The farm, too. Nick, I don't blame you. I was sorry to hear about your father."

Now what? He couldn't exactly say that if he'd gone or she'd stayed, he would have asked her to marry him.

No. A year and thousands of miles had changed things. He needed to know where things stood between them first. If she'd found someone else.

"How do you like living in South Africa? I'd like to know more."

She looked up at his profile. "What do you want to know?"

"I want to know if you think that you are going back to Africa?"

Holly gazed up at the infinity of stars. "They look different, you know, over there." There, too, she'd gained a different perspective, one that she was only now realizing. Nick truly had let her go.

"And now you have a different view of life, I'm sure."

Surprised at his unexpected understanding, a pang of joy hit her. "Yes, that's it, exactly." He knew her better than anyone, didn't he? Maybe even better than Grams.

He cleared his throat. "I've missed you."

Holly's heart pounded so loudly in her ears she was afraid she hadn't heard correctly. She swallowed, uncertain how to respond. She wanted say the words back to him. That she'd missed him, too, thought about him every day.

"I could tell, listening to you talk about it, how much you loved caring for the people. I think that you're doing the right thing."

"Thanks." Holly sighed. So. . .that's how he felt about her. She was doing the right thing in South Africa. She hurried before her voice began to shake. "To answer your question, yes, I'm going to stay there. I'm only here on furlough and will return after Grams's wedding."

Holly drew her gaze from the valley below to look at Nick. A knot caught in her throat as tears threatened. She managed to croak out, "It's what I've always believed I was supposed to do. If only you could. . .be there with me." Horrified by her show of emotions, Holly rushed away a few steps, burying her face in her hands.

He caught her arm and pulled her to him. Too upset to resist, she allowed the tears to flow. Basking in the comfort of his arms, awareness dawned. It felt good. Right. Contentment calmed her frazzled nerves.

But—how could this be right?

She pushed away and looked him in the eyes. "I'm—sorry. I shouldn't have done that."

"No, it's okay. I wanted. . ."

Wanted what, Nick? When he didn't finish, she left him and headed back to the fire. She had to regain her composure, act like nothing had happened.

In his eyes, she thought she'd seen love—the love she wanted from him. Why couldn't he just say it? Yet rather than saying it, he was pushing her away. Letting her go—because he loved her? And she thought she'd been the one to sacrifice. His had been the greater.

Why did God call her to missions if she had to leave Nick behind?

It wasn't fair.

Chapter 7

At the shopping mall, Holly stared at the holiday-attired mannequins and yawned.

"No more late nights for you, young lady." Her mother winked.

Holly laughed. "It always amazes me that the retailers just skip over Thanksgiving and decorate for Christmas." She glanced at her watch. "And look, Grams is late. You sure you won't join us?"

They stopped in front of the mall restaurant entrance, waiting on Grams.

"I'd love to, but I know you like your time alone with her. It's not like you can see her anytime you want. Besides, I've already arranged to meet Margaret."

"I enjoyed our time together this morning."

"So did I. But you've been distracted. Mind telling me what's going on?"

"I'm just tired, that's all."

"Well, maybe Mother will have a better chance at getting the truth out of you. Before I forget, did your father tell you about the call from South Africa?"

"What call?"

"That man." Her mother huffed. "You received a call from one of your coworkers at the mission base. A Mark something."

Holly felt herself blanch. She was supposed to call him once she arrived in the States. "Oh? Did he say anything?"

"I don't know, hon. You'll have to ask your father. Is he someone special?"

Holly looked at her mother. "Why would you think that?"

"Your father got the sense that he had an interest in you, personally, that is."

"He did?" *Funny, he didn't seem to have that sense where Nick was concerned.* "He must have said something to give Dad that impression."

Her mother shrugged.

She was glad she would soon be able to bare her soul to Grams. She'd had that same feeling about Mark herself. But he was her team leader. So she'd laughed it off as ridiculous. But now. . .

Could that be part of the reason he'd sent her home? Holly found a bench and sat down, half aware that her mother had followed and was studying her. Maybe Mark had sent her away because she'd been a distraction for *him*. That, or she was driving herself crazy.

She sighed. What should she tell her mother?

A large poster emblazoned with THE SPIRIT OF CHRISTMAS CHARITIES caught her eye where it stood in the center of the walkway, next to a twelve-foot Brohns' Farms blue spruce. The sign read CATCH THE SPIRIT. "Mom, what's this?"

"You don't know? I'm sorry, hon. This is Nick's big idea."

"There you are." Grams strolled toward them and hugged Holly first, then her mother.

"I believe that's my cue. Enjoy your lunch. I'm off to meet Margaret." Her mother waved and hastened out of sight into the crowd.

Holly and Grams entered the restaurant and were quickly seated at a cozy booth. After ordering drinks they browsed the menu and chatted.

"I'm so thrilled for you, Grams. It was such a surprise to hear that you're getting married."

Grams closed her menu. "I'm sure that surprise came in more than one way."

Holly frowned. "What do you mean?"

Grams reached across the table and squeezed her hand. "I believe there was a young lady who thought she'd be getting married soon. Or at least engaged."

"Oh, that."

"And then the next thing you know, her grandmother is getting married. Before her."

What could she say? Grams had read her deepest thoughts, ones she hadn't even wanted to admit to herself.

Grams's smile softened. "Tell me about Nick."

Deciding on a salad, Holly closed the menu and laid it over Grams's. "What's to tell? I thought he loved me. I thought. . ."

"Go on, dear. It's all right."

"Well, you already know that when I finally realized I loved him, I'd hoped he would tell me the same. I even dared to dream what every girl does, that maybe we would someday marry. He could have asked me in South Africa, except he didn't go. He never told me anything about how he felt, but six months later, I received an e-mail that sounded as if he'd moved on."

"Oh, I don't believe a word of it. Could you be mistaken?"

"How so?"

"Nick seems to be a very self-sacrificing sort of fellow. I think he loves you. From my perspective, seems to me he was simply releasing you to go to South Africa. You've always talked about going. It was important to you. Nick loved you enough to let you go. But if he's what's important to you now, perhaps you should let him know."

"It's not that simple." Holly released a slow breath. Grams's wisdom had always helped her before, why not now?

A waitress appeared, dressed in a starched white shirt and a bow tie. They placed their order—Holly's salad, and Grams's bowl of the soup du jour—cream of broccoli.

"There's something else." Holly played with her napkin, finding the words difficult to express, even to Grams. "I haven't told anyone else. My team leader requested that I take time off because, well, he thinks I'm distracted. He's not sure if South Africa is the place for me." She decided not to complicate matters by sharing her suspicions of Mark's interest in her.

"I see." Grams frowned and toyed with a spoon. "I know that was hard for you to say."

"I feel like I've failed."

"Oh no. Not at all. Not very many of us even risk going after our dreams, even when we believe God has called us to do it. And some of us that do—well, those who do sometimes find things weren't what we thought." She smiled gently at Holly. "And now, you love Nick. I see it. I'm sure Nick sees it."

"My parents don't."

"I think you would be surprised at what your parents see. But they learned a long time ago that any suggestions from them could send you running."

Holly shared Grams's laugh.

"Well, it really doesn't matter how I feel or how Nick feels. He lives here and will stay here. I live in South Africa."

"Because God has called you to missions? Apparently He's sent you back here to reconsider that." Grams lifted her left brow as she tipped her drink to sip.

The waitress set their food before them and refilled the drinks.

"You know He has, Grams. It brings me great joy to do the work. I love it."

Grams salted her soup. "I want to hear more about it."

"You know the thing that bothers me most is when I tell people I'm a missionary in South Africa, they comment that it's not a third world country—the need isn't that great."

"I'm sure it's frustrating. What do you say?"

"Not much, usually. But the truth is if you drive outside of the city a few hours, people live in the poorest conditions. Even America's poor or homeless live like kings compared to them."

Grams smiled and nodded. "It's always a matter of looking below the surface, of going deeper, isn't it?"

Holly nodded, but she wasn't sure what Grams meant and took another bite of salad.

They finished their lunch, the conversation turning lighter. Grams looked at her watch. "Well, dear. I promised Alex I'd meet him at two. Shall we?"

Holly sighed, disappointed their time would soon be ending. "What can you tell me, Grams? Do you have any advice?"

"Why, I thought I'd already given it." Grams smiled again. "God has called you to help others. Anyone can see how you enjoy it. I suggest while you're here, look below the surface. Go deeper. Maybe the Lord will even give you a new dream."

Grams's words puzzled Holly. She usually wasn't so vague.

They exited the restaurant into the mall where Holly once again spotted The Spirit of Christmas Charities poster.

Nick had started a charity. How exciting!

Maybe Grams's words had done their work after all.

Nick swung the ax, sinking the blade deep into a thick log. He yanked it free, swung it over his right shoulder, then downward into the wood again. The strong scent filled his nose. Chopping wood had always helped Nick to work through problems in the past—why not today?

With each chop of the ax, he sent up a silent prayer. If he were to tell her how he felt about her, would it be for selfish reasons? "Lord, if You want me to tell her, give me a sign." Nick thought he would go crazy, waiting for an answer.

At the hayride, there'd been something in her eyes, he was sure. Love—the same love he'd seen in her eyes a year ago. But why had God put them on two separate paths? Was theirs a love that was never meant to be?

He began splitting the smaller logs he'd honed. He wasn't

technically wasting time—the family always needed more wood, but he had so many other things to do. The day after tomorrow was Thanksgiving. Many people shopped for their trees on Friday, making for a busy weekend. He also had the charity to run. They'd compiled a long list of families needing trees along with other items this Christmas. Thankfully, financial donations had already started pouring in.

But *his* need wasn't being fulfilled. He wanted a wife. He wanted Holly. His thoughts wouldn't leave him alone no matter how hard he tried to vanquish them. Nick dropped the ax to his side as he swiped his brow, cold droplets of snow mingling with his sweat. He felt like a kid again, when he had to give the star up to his dad—sad even though he knew the feeling was selfish.

"There you are." His dad appeared from around the shed behind the house, followed by Mr. Rivers.

"Hi there." Nick searched his dad's eyes. Apparently, he was having one of his good days.

"Your mother is busy in the kitchen, preparing for Thanksgiving. I felt it best to stay out of her way."

"Smart man." Nick winked but imagined himself married to Holly, helping her in the kitchen. *Stop it!*

Mr. Rivers adjusted his cap and cleared his throat. "Your father tells me you have a tree you've been saving for a special occasion. He wasn't sure if there was a particular occasion, so I thought I'd ask."

Panic swelled in Nick's chest but he hid his reaction. He'd already told his dad that the governor wanted his tree. He must have forgotten. Nick hated that.

He had to be careful. He didn't want to embarrass his dad. "What did you have in mind?"

"My mother-in-law is getting married the day after Christmas. We thought we could make this a special season for her to have that tree in her home."

Nick scratched his head. "So you've seen it?"

"Not yet."

"Carl." Nick's mother rushed around the corner, wiping her hands on her apron. "I need you."

"Go ahead," Mr. Rivers said. "I'll be along in a minute."

Nick's dad excused himself with a shrug and a smile.

Nick stacked the split wood. "First off, the tree is a good seventeen feet tall. So, unless her house can accommodate the size, it won't work. And even if it could, it's wanted at the Governor's Mansion."

He'd tried not to think it, but just talking about giving up the tree was more difficult than he'd thought.

Mr. Rivers trudged over to Nick and put an arm around his shoulder. "I've been worried about you, son. Is there anything you'd like to tell me?"

"I'm not sure what you mean."

Mr. Rivers released him. "A year is a long time. Truth is, I'd like to see my little girl hang around here for a while. A good long while."

Nick furrowed his brows. Wasn't her father considering that God had called her to South Africa, into missions?

"But she needs a reason, son."

"Yes, sir?"

"I see the way you look at her."

Chapter 8

Holly finished wishing Mr. and Mrs. Brohns a happy Thanksgiving then stepped outside their front door, after delivering the pies her mother had made. Her mother always liked to prepare things ahead of time, and this year was no different. Thanksgiving was still two days away. Holly was just happy the mincemeat pies wouldn't grace her mother's Thanksgiving table. She scrunched her nose at the thought. At the edge of the porch, she wrapped her arms around herself. Snowfall had been teasing the region, but the weatherman predicted heavy snow within the next couple of days.

Where was Nick? She'd hoped to give him the gift she'd brought from Africa. He must be at his home, in the converted barn across the yard, or still working. He'd been working harder than she'd ever seen him, most likely due to the new charity and his father's withdrawal from the business. She peered at the windows of Nick's house, trying to see light or movement. Sadness filled her. At one time, she'd imagined she and Nick would live in that house as man and wife.

It didn't appear now that Nick had the same dream. Growing up as close friends, they'd talked of becoming missionaries, of going to Africa. Plans had been made but life had interfered. All of it was out of her control. Yet, the verse Grams had given her circulated through her thoughts. *Commit your works to the Lord and your plans will be established.*

Yet, hadn't she done just that? She felt so torn between the country she'd grown to love and the man she still loved. She let out a heavy sigh. *Lord, if You want me to stay here, I'll stay, but I need to know Your will.*

As she opened her car door, she noticed the lights on in the farm office. In three days, their busy season would begin. A smile came to her lips. She'd pay him a visit, after all. Maybe he'd have time to tell her more about the new charity he'd started.

She'd taken Grams's advice and conducted research, discovering the vast number of needy families near Boulder, though she couldn't say the families were more needy than those at the missionary base where she was stationed.

She took Nick's gift from the back of the car. Now probably wasn't the best time, but she feared she wouldn't have another chance to give it to him alone and wanted to see his reaction. She tromped up the steps of the office.

Once inside the door she saw no one. "Hello? Nick?"

When no response came, she removed her coat and laid it over the back of a black swivel chair, thinking that he'd return soon. He'd left the door unlocked, so he wasn't finished for the day. Familiar with the office, she moseyed around, looking at a new picture his mother must have hung, then a beautiful fall bouquet of mums. Had that been Rose's idea? Or, had Nick's mother placed them there, too? Holly had always thought of her as the smothering type. If something were to happen between her and Nick, how would his mother react?

Flyers in the far corner displayed the charity's banner. Papers were strewn over someone's desk and against her better judgment, she lifted a page and read what appeared to be wording for more marketing. Perhaps a press release for the paper or other media venue. The thought of a community coming together to give for such causes warmed her heart, almost as much as the sight of Africans crowding around her in welcome, rhythmic music surrounding her.

She couldn't shake the excitement she felt about Nick's charity. Nor would she want to. Thoughts poured into her mind and heart. Could she work with Nick on the charity? She plopped into a chair on wheels, her mind spinning. The idea invigorated her. What if she stayed in the States rather than returning to South Africa? Oddly, she felt no regret at the idea.

Maybe God was giving her a new dream. Grams had tried to tell her that it was possible. And with a new dream, she and Nick would have a chance. She pushed the chair and it rolled backward, bumping another desk. Holly turned to stare at the familiar face in a frame on the desk.

She leaned against the edge to look closer and gasped. Angie Collins stood in a group of people, smiling back. Nick's Angie. He'd been infatuated with her for the longest time. Why hadn't he told Holly she was working at the farm?

Had Nick and Angie become. . .close—again? Frowning,

she tried to shrug off the dismal thought.

The sound of the door slamming scared her. Holly pushed away from the desk and stood, still gripping a slip of paper. It dropped from her fingers and floated to the desk.

Nick stood in the doorway, removing his coat. He looked from her to the desk. "What are you doing here?"

Nick cringed inside. Couldn't he have thought of something better to say? "I'm sorry. I didn't mean that the way it sounded." A nervous laugh escaped him. "Have a seat."

Though he'd gone to look at the tree and pray about what to do, he'd forgotten to lock up the office. Then he'd seen her car at his parents' house and gone there, but she'd left.

Holly's face deepened in color. "I wasn't snooping, if that's what you think."

"Nope. Not thinking that." He shoved his hands into his jeans. "I was thinking how glad I am that you're here."

"I came to see you and decided to wait." She smiled, sending waves of a long-forgotten emotion rolling through him. "I have something for you."

"Ah, you shouldn't have." He winked, not wanting to let on how surprised and pleased he was.

She strode to her coat and lifted a box from the chair. "I got it in Africa. It reminded me of you."

He took the box from her, happy to hear that she'd thought of him while there. He wondered if she'd thought of him only once. Or daily. He shoved his hair back as if to shove the thoughts from his mind.

Gripping the box, he looked at her. "Do you want me to

wait for Christmas or what?"

She stared at the box. "You can do that if you like, but I really wanted to see your reaction."

This was getting better all the time. Not wanting the moment to go too quickly, he held the box and studied the red and white striped paper.

"Well?"

"Oh, I'm going to open it, all right. Just thought I'd try to guess what it is."

"You won't be able to. Just go ahead."

"Impatient, are we?"

She smiled again. "I'd think you would be the impatient one. After all, it's your present. What's the matter? Have you forgotten the excitement of receiving a gift?"

He burst out in laughter.

"Come on. Open it!"

"I wouldn't trade this moment for the world." He put the box down and tugged his coat back on, then held hers up to help her.

"What—what are you doing?"

"Come on. I want to show you something."

"But my present. You're hurting my feelings." She slipped reluctantly into her coat.

"No, I'm making this moment last longer."

She turned to face him, and the look in her eyes—he wanted nothing more than to kiss her. Instead, he grabbed her hand and tugged her behind him out the door. The evening darkened and snow was falling as Nick held Holly's hand, pulling her between the rows of trees. He must be out of his mind, but his father's declining condition and his mother's desire to make every moment count had affected him.

"I want to show you my tree."

"I remember your tree. Do we really have to go there now?"

"It won't take long. I promise." He wasn't sure why, but he had a sense of urgency.

"You're walking too fast," she panted. "Can you slow down?"

He slowed, allowing her to walk beside him when possible. They approached the end of the field where the beautiful spruce stood in perfection, topped with a star.

She gasped. "A star! You put a star on."

He hung back as she went closer, reaching up to run her fingers over the silver needles.

"Ah, I'd forgotten how beautiful it is, Nick."

He swallowed. That was how he felt about Holly. "I wanted to show it to you before it was too late."

"What do you mean, too late?"

"Well, I've had a couple of inquiries. It's wanted at the Governor's Mansion." Nick sighed. "I'd been saving it for something special—someone special."

"Can't you use another tree?"

"This tree is the perfect one." *Just like you. . .*

Nick moved closer. He loved feeling her nearness, especially now that they'd lost all awkwardness. He wanted to treasure the moment.

She giggled. "When did you put the star on?"

"Just tonight. Since I knew I'd be giving the tree away soon, I wanted to see what it felt like to put it there."

She gently punched his arm. "You were always such a little boy at heart."

"I guess you're right. When I was growing up, my father always put the star on. He wouldn't let me do it. But of course, he didn't want me to knock the tree over, hurting me or my mother."

"Well, what you need, Nicholas Brohns, is a son of your own, so you can put the star on—for—him." Her last word came out choked.

He held her gaze. "You know, you're right. That is exactly what I need." But what could he say next? She'd already told him she would go back to Africa to stay.

What is Your will, God?

Chapter 9

Holly wanted to die. Why had she told Nick he needed a son? For an instant, she'd imagined Nick not only married with a child of his own, but herself as the mother. Nick's wife. And her heart had leaped.

But could she be the one to declare her love first? Wasn't it supposed to be the other way around? Why wouldn't Nick tell her, unless—he truly didn't love her?

The cold seemed to gnaw at her bones despite her warm coat. She wrapped her arms around herself. "Mind if we go back so you can see your gift?"

He nodded his agreement.

Holly wasn't sure what happened, but the excitement that had filled Nick's expression had fled. She wished she knew how to bring it back. It disappointed her that he wasn't a little excited to see her gift. They walked back in silence through the rows of trees, a light layer of snow crunching underfoot.

Once inside the office, she handed him the box again and forced a smile. "I hope you like it."

Nick lifted the box from her grasp and worked at the

opening with his large fingers but without much success.

Snickering, she took it from him. "Here, let me. You were never good with the small things."

She opened the box and handed it to him. He peeked inside before lifting out a giant ostrich egg, featuring delicate paintings of a variety of trees. "Oh, Holly. This is beautiful."

She looked closely at the egg. "Do you think?"

Nick rotated it as he stared at the intricate paintings. She wished he would say something. Tell her what he was thinking. But such was Nick. His eyes were full of emotions that he never shared.

"I know it's not useful and it's not exciting like a Zulu spear, but it made me think of you, Tree Man."

Nick looked at her, a twinkle in his eyes, and winked. He looked back to the egg and pointed. "What's this marking?"

Holly tried to see what he was pointing at, then noticed how close she was to him. His warm breath touched her cheek as she inclined her head toward him. Maybe he would kiss her. She lingered there, waiting.

But he pulled away. "I can't tell you how much this means to me."

After looking forward to seeing Nick's reaction, Holly wasn't sure what she'd expected. She sure hadn't imagined an almost kiss and then—nothing.

"I'm. . .glad you like it." Maybe—maybe Angie really did stand between them. Tugging back on her coat, she continued, sounding too hurried. "I really must get going."

"Did I say something wrong?"

"Of course not." Stifling her disappointment, Holly leaned

up and gave Nick a quick kiss on the cheek. Even the small possibility that Nick had an interest in someone else made her realize what she would lose if she couldn't have Nick. Why had it taken her so long to realize that Nick. . .

. . .was her dream.

"Listen, I—" She wanted to tell him everything now. But she needed time to wrap her mind and heart around her discovery. Instead, she said, "I hope you get to keep your tree. I mean, I think you should do everything you can to keep something that's so special to you, don't you?" Then she fled the office.

After she climbed into the car and started the engine, she pressed her forehead against the steering wheel while the car warmed up. She needed to heed her own words to Nick. With everything in her. If only her thoughts weren't burdened with the fear that she was too late.

Nick placed the ostrich egg on its stand on his fireplace mantel. Fortunately, the mantel was wide enough. He leaned his elbow against the wall and rubbed his chin while looking at the gift. He'd not known what to do with it, but it was the thought that mattered. And she'd said it had made her think of him.

Truthfully, it was beautiful.

She'd referred to him by the nickname she'd given him years ago. Tree Man. Did she mean it as a compliment, or that he was just unbending? If that was how she saw him then she was right.

He should have told her how he felt. But, he reminded himself yet again, she'd been called to the mission field and answered that call. He could not, would not stand in her way.

Unless. . .he got his Father's permission.

He'd already gotten her father's permission, but he wasn't certain that Holly's father wasn't simply being selfish, wanting to keep her stateside.

"I think you should do everything you can to keep something that's so special to you." Her words wouldn't leave him. Were they God's answer?

He made to dispose of the box when a small piece of paper fell to the floor. Picking it up, he recognized the handwriting as Holly's. She'd not made mention of the note at the office. It read,

Dear Nick,

As soon as I saw this it reminded me of you. Only problem was, I'd run out of money so I had to go home to get more. When I got back, the egg was gone. I panicked at first but then learned it had simply been moved from the display. But in order to buy it, the man required that I purchase several other items. Such is bartering. It brought to mind the scripture from Matthew 13:44: 'The kingdom of heaven is like unto treasure hid in a field; the which when a man hath found, he hideth, and for joy thereof goeth and selleth all that he hath, and buyeth that field.' I know that's an extreme comparison, but it was important to me. You are important to me.

Love always,
Holly

His heart pounded. This had to be his answer. How could it not? She was his treasure. He'd let her go but she'd come back. But he wouldn't know if it was to him, unless he told her.

Tomorrow. . .

The next day, Holly woke up feeling tired but hopeful. She'd promised her mother she'd help make a few casseroles. It would keep her occupied as her mind swirled with a whirlwind of ideas—staying here and working with those in need and—loving Nick. In truth, she'd fulfilled her dream already—one of them—working as a missionary in Africa. As Grams said, dreams change, and hers had.

She could hardly contain herself. She needed to contact Mark to let him know her decision. Maybe she should even thank him for his insight in sending her back home to rest. But first, she needed to make sure she wasn't jumping to the wrong conclusions. She needed to know that Nick and Angie weren't an item. Last night, at his tree, Nick had spoken of someone special, but was that her or Angie?

After dressing, she went into the kitchen. Her mother had left a note stating she'd gone to buy a few more items she'd forgotten and could Holly make two more pies and then work on the casseroles? Holly got out the ingredients to make the crusts and started to work.

"Oh, there you are." Cassie strolled into the kitchen and leaned on her elbows against the counter. "Say, who's Nick's girlfriend?"

Holly's mouth went dry. She looked up from the crust she'd just rolled out. "I—I don't know. Why do you ask?"

"You two used to be so close." Cassie started to lift the plastic wrap from a pumpkin pie resting on the counter to stick her finger into it.

Holly swatted her away. "Don't you dare. Mom would kill you."

"Well, apparently he's pretty serious about her. I forgot to give this to you before you took those pies to Nick's mom yesterday." She set a box on the counter. "Jamie found this in Nick's coat. She was bummed to learn that he had an engagement ring in his pocket."

Cassie looked up at her.

"Angie Collins. . ." The name escaped in a whisper. She cleared her throat. "I can't believe you didn't immediately give this to me or Mom or Dad."

"I said I forgot. But Angie. That makes sense. You told me once he'd had a crush on her." Grabbing a brownie before Holly could stop her, Cassie took a bite and rushed out of the kitchen.

"Hey!" Holly started to follow but changed her mind. Cassie hadn't even considered the possibility that Holly was Nick's intended. Not even a remote possibility.

It never had been, obviously.

Chapter 10

Standing outside of the Brohns Farm offices, Holly gripped the small velvet box. Her newfound dream from the night before had crashed to the ground, shattering into a thousand pieces with Cassie's untimely revelation.

Holly didn't want to hold on to the ring a second longer. She rushed through her chores, hoping she'd finish in time to beat the snowstorm the weatherman cautioned was coming the next couple of days. As she worked, she thought of calling Nick to make sure he knew she had the ring, but some small part of her held on to the possibility that the beautiful solitaire diamond was meant for her.

This was awkward. How would she approach him?

If only Jamie had contacted him directly, once she'd discovered the ring in the pocket. After Holly finished up for her mother, she explained that she needed to run to the farm to return Nick's coat.

She saw no life in the office, but it was the day before Thanksgiving. Maybe Rose and...Angie had taken the day off. But surely Nick, with their busy season starting Friday, would be working today. The office door was unlocked, which told her Nick was around somewhere.

Holly couldn't help herself. She strolled to Angie's desk to look, once again, at her picture. Angie had her arms wrapped around a little boy. Holly hadn't noticed that before.

The phone rang and Holly reached for it then paused. It wasn't her business. The answering machine came on, then a voice followed, "Nick, this is Angie. I tried your cell. A change in plans. I'll be able to make it tomorrow, after all."

Holly eased into the office chair. So, Angie was sharing Thanksgiving with the Brohns. How could she have been so presumptuous, so blind? She would never know if Nick ever had feelings for her before she left, because he'd moved on—just as she'd thought, from the e-mail he'd sent months ago. In the middle of encouraging her about her life in South Africa, he'd also encouraged her to move on, leaving their unspoken imaginary romance behind.

Holly set the velvet box on Angie's desk. Blinded by tears, she rushed out the door. She ran through the tree fields, needles brushing against her sleeves. She was breathless by the time she found Nick's tree—or rather, the place where his tree should have stood.

No. . .

He'd given it up. She sank to the cold ground as snow began to caress her face like cold feathers. He'd given up on them, too. But Holly had no right. She had no right to hold him to an unspoken promise. Without a second look back, she'd left him behind when he wasn't able to go to South Africa. Why hadn't she realized then what her heart had known all along, that her true dream was right here at home, not in some faraway place?

God could use her here just the same. And Nick could have loved her. . .here.

~❦~

After Nick cleaned up from an unpleasant task, he planned to go to Holly's house and speak to her. He went to the dresser where he kept the ring and opened the drawer. It was gone. His pulse hammered in his ears. He pulled the drawer completely out and dumped everything onto the table. No velvet box.

His coat. He'd given it to Jamie. He blew out a heavy breath. Hopefully, the ring hadn't fallen out. How could he have been so careless? He reminded himself that he'd had too much to think about lately. Nick phoned Holly's mother first because he had no idea how to get in touch with Jamie, but suspected that they'd kept his coat, planning to give it to him soon. As he waited for someone to answer, he stared out the window. The snowfall was thickening, already covering his driveway.

He hoped the weatherman was right in his prediction that the storm would blow over tonight, leaving tomorrow a beautiful day. The business counted on families being able to come to the tree farm, and he didn't want to lose money to something more convenient like a plastic tree.

After speaking with her mother, he hung up the phone, confused. Holly had left at least an hour ago to come see him. He jogged over to his office, spotting her car parked out front. At the thought of facing her, his palms grew sweaty.

If only he would have realized sooner how he felt and not allowed anyone to stand in his way. Still, perhaps this had been

God's timing all along. Holly was supposed to go to South Africa. Deep inside, he knew that she had to get South Africa out of her system before they could ever be happy. He thanked the Lord for His perfect timing, remembering St. Boniface's words, to let Christ be his comfort and guide.

Nick stepped in, closing the door behind him. Seeing no one he called after her, "Holly?"

The message light on the answering machine beeped. He paused to listen, hoping Holly would step from the restroom. Something small yet familiar sat on Angie's desk. His breath caught in his throat. Lifting the velvet box, he popped it open to see the ring.

How had it gone from his coat pocket to Angie's desk?

"Oh, no. . ."

"What's the matter?" Tim stood at the door.

"What are you doing here? I gave you the afternoon off."

"I forgot my cell phone." Tim strolled to the desk where he'd set his things. "So, what's got you all knotted up this time?"

Nick heaved a sigh, unsure how much he wanted to say. "I think there's been a big miscommunication."

Tim came to stand next to him. "It's snowing like crazy out there."

"Yeah, and I need to find Holly." Instead of taking the time to walk to his parents' house, he phoned. She wasn't there. He called her cell but got no answer. He scratched his chin, wondering where she could have gone and how long she'd been there.

Guilt descended on him for trying to control their lives, for not allowing Holly to decide between him and South Africa herself.

Lord, I need You to be my comfort and guide, to be my light in this storm. Help me find her. Help me to make her understand how I feel, and why it took me so long.

"So she's not at your parents' house and she's not here. Where in the world could she go?" Tim found his phone and flipped it open.

"I think I have an idea." Nick shoved the ring into his coat pocket, hoping this time it would find a permanent home with the woman he loved, then rushed out the door and down the steps into the increasing cold. He tugged the collar of his coat up to protect his ears and jammed his hands into his pockets, walking as fast as he could through the Christmas trees.

Though he hoped to find her at his blue spruce, he hated to see the look on her face at what she'd see there. He broke into a run and rushed around the last tree on the row, plowing right into Holly and knocking her backward. Before she fell, he grabbed her, pulling her into his arms. There wasn't much point in wasting any more time.

She tried to yank free. "What—what are you doing?" She wiped at reddened eyes, clearly upset.

"I'm holding you, and I'm never letting you go. Again, that is."

"What about Angie?"

"Holly, there is no Angie. There never was. It's always been you."

"But the tree—it was special—and you let it go." Her teeth were chattering as she spoke.

Not good. He drew her closer to him and wrapped her in his warmth. "The tree is gone because my father allowed the governor to take it for a special ceremony on Friday. I'd decided not to let it go, especially after what you said to me last night. But I had to cut it down this morning. It's the first time, since his Alzheimer's diagnosis, that Dad's done anything with the business. I couldn't hurt him that way."

"That sounds just like you. Always thinking of the other person. And the someone special? Are you letting her go, too?"

He heaved a sigh. "I'm sorry that I didn't tell you how I felt last year before you left, but I never wanted to stand in the way of your dream—and that's always been South Africa. You said you were going back, but I mean to convince you to stay."

Snowflakes fell lightly on her hair and stuck to her eyelashes. "Oh, Nick. You are my dream. You always were. I guess I couldn't see it until I was on the other side of the world without you." She looked away. "I'm sorry."

"There's nothing to be sorry for. You had to go. I know that." He swiped at a tear on her cheek.

She bit her lip and studied him. "And I know, now, that it was for a season. God has brought me to a new season, Nick. A season with you."

A lifetime.

Now that he had his heavenly Father's permission, Nick was in no mood to hold back. He lifted her chin and kissed her. Thoroughly. Completely. When he pulled away, she blinked then smiled slowly, sending a tingle all the way to his toes. He grinned, wanting to put that look on her face as much as possible. While he felt the absence of the blue spruce he'd saved for this moment keenly, the cost of waiting for the perfect time and place was too high. He knew that now.

Though nervous, he smiled as he tugged the ring from his pocket. He dropped to one knee as he popped the box open for her to see it. "Holly Rivers, I love you. Will you be my wife?"

A small cry escaped her. "Yes! I'll marry you."

He removed the ring from its velvet home and gently pushed it onto Holly's finger, then stood to watch her, snow falling around them. In the heat of his proposal, he'd almost forgotten the chill.

Her eyes shimmered as she admired it. "Please forgive me for having to go so far away to find out what you mean to me."

He smiled, savoring their closeness. "In that case, it was a journey well worth it. You've always been like the star on top of the tree for me when I was a kid. Always just out of my reach."

"Not"—Holly tilted her head up expectantly—"anymore."

Nick sealed her lips with another kiss, rejoicing in the new season of their lives.

 **ELIZABETH GODDARD** is a seventh-generation Texan transplanted in southern Oregon near the Rogue River. When she's not writing, she's busy homeschooling her four children and serving with her husband as he pastors a local church. Beth and her husband, Dan, have been married for twenty years. She enjoys hiking in the Redwoods and camping on the Oregon coast with her family. Beth's passion is to fulfill her lifelong dream, answering God's call to write.

THE FIRST NOELLE

by Paige Winship Dooly

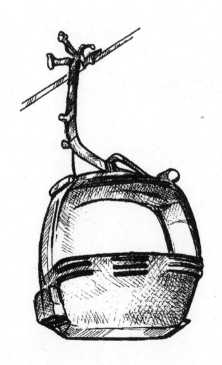

To my precious granddaughters:
Elizabeth, Nevaeh, Journey, Ella, Tempest, and Ashton.
I love each and every one of you!

The fear of the LORD is the beginning of wisdom;
all who follow his precepts have good understanding.
To him belongs eternal praise.
PSALM 111:10 NIV

Chapter 1

"A wedding. At Gram's age? What could she possibly be thinking?" Noelle slapped her hand against the steering wheel but didn't slow her rant. No one was in the car to hear, but she'd feel better if she finished her tirade. She hoped. At least she'd have it out of her system before she reached Gram's house.

She could be thinking she's lonely. That she misses having a husband by her side. A best friend who's always there.

"Like I'd know anything about that." Noelle snorted and pushed the irritating thought to the back of her mind, but it bounced right back to the front. "So my sixty-six-year-old grandmother is getting married, again, while I sit here a thirty-year-old spinster, left at the altar by my fiancé, *my* supposed best friend. Why should that bother me? I'm a wedding planner. I *plan weddings*. It's what I do. Gram needs me, and I have to be there for her."

Gram had always been her rock. Her stability. Noelle's flaky mom and absentee father were both deceased, and Gram was the only person Noelle could count on when life threw her curves. Which seemed to be pretty often.

For once, Noelle would toss aside the wayward Evans traits and be there for Gram.

She drew in a deep breath and exited the highway. The area hadn't changed much over the years, at least from what she could see from this vantage point. Dark clouds loomed low over the mountains, reflecting Noelle's mood. Yet as she drove closer, a flicker of warmth sparked in her heart, threatening to thaw the ice that the winter cold of her hometown had placed there.

Tears pushed against the back of her eyes. She didn't want to come home. Hadn't even returned for her mother's funeral. Though that wasn't really Noelle's fault. She blamed Rocky. The man she'd once loved. And now hated. Or at least disliked strongly. Gram strongly disliked for people to hate. But the thought of having to face him kept Noelle away from home.

Her mother had been in the hospital often—accidentally overdosing on painkillers, drinking too much and trying to drive, depressed and admitting herself over some bogus ailment. How was Noelle to know that the last time would be different? That her mother's appendix had ruptured but the painkillers she took masked the severity until it was so bad they couldn't reverse the infection?

Noelle had lost more than one job while running to her mother's side. Which was why she'd finally given up on the corporate world and now worked for herself, planning weddings—or other special events—for those who managed to hold on to a groom long enough to actually see the event through to the end. Noelle had planned each and every step of her own special day. So when Rocky cut her dream wedding off in its budding, she felt the need to help bring others' dreams to full bloom. She loved planning events, loved the freedom to set her own hours, and found she actually had a knack for making the dream in each bride's mind come true.

She turned onto the main strip, a few changes now apparent as she neared the town center. Several businesses had changed hands. Several existing businesses had undergone renovations. Each mile brought back more memories and brought the past to present.

On that horrible day, her mother had been in their hometown of Boulder, not in Kansas City. Noelle refused to rush to her mother's side—and risk running into Rocky—just to find her mother had cried wolf yet again. Only she hadn't cried wolf. She'd died.

"Ugh!" Now she wanted to slam her forehead against the steering wheel, but she figured since the car was still moving, that wasn't such a hot idea. "I have to stop thinking about the negative. I need to think of Gram and Alex." And her cousins, Chris and Holly, whom she hadn't seen in years. She couldn't wait to see them again. But not Rocky. She'd face anyone but Rocky. If all went according to plan, she'd avoid seeing him. Though nothing usually went according to plan. Except her weddings and events. With those, she had full control and could troubleshoot anything that came her way.

"That's it!" She smiled, made her second-to-last turn before Gram's house, and began to put her plan into motion. If she ran into Rocky, she'd let him know that she'd grown past the hurt and humiliation and silliness of their plans together, and had moved on, a much stronger woman for making it through the pain. He'd never know how weak she'd been or how much she'd hurt when he left her. And if she dug down deep, how much she still hurt now. But if she took control, things would be all right.

Her spirits lifted as if a huge burden had been cast aside. Gram's street came into sight. Noelle laughed out loud. Her grandma was getting married. She, Noelle, was going to make the event everything Gram could possibly want. And if Noelle ran into Rocky, she'd set him straight on how perfect her life was and how little she missed him.

She would be proactive, not the helpless little flower he'd left at the altar. Well, in all honesty, according to Rocky, she'd never really been the helpless flower sort—more like a haphazard lawnmower that ran down the unfortunate flowers that graced the outer edges of the garden—but still, she hadn't had much time to sort out her emotions, let alone to verbalize to Rocky all she felt back then.

As long as she stayed on guard and met him under her conditions, she'd maintain the upper hand. And as far as she was concerned, her conditions didn't include a face-to-face with Rocky anytime soon, or even in this century. She'd avoid him like the plague. He was nothing more than an irritating gnat. A bothersome pesky little detail that was barely a bump in her road. She was over him. The maturity of her thought processes over the past ten minutes showed that. She mentally dusted her hands together as she turned up the radio and sang along with her favorite song while increasing the pressure on the gas pedal. Now she began to see other changes to the area. Why didn't anything ever stay the same? Then again— if everything stayed the same, she would dread coming home even more.

This trip would be a turnaround point. Nothing could dampen her enthusiasm as she approached Gram's house and prepared to meet the gang. In a perfect world, they'd all be out front to greet her. Maybe she should call and suggest just that. She'd pull onto Gram's street in moments. For the first time in a long time, she was happy to be home.

~✦~

A few moments later, the sound of a siren directly behind her made Noelle cringe. As she braked, she sent a desperate glance toward Gram's front window. Contrary to her earlier thoughts, she now prayed the entire family would *not* be witness to her embarrassing driving infraction.

She rolled down the window. "I'm sorry, officer. I didn't realize this was now a seventeen miles per hour speed limit."

At least she'd heard the siren before she could push the TALK button on her phone. Of course, if she hadn't been busy tapping in the numbers, she might have seen him in time to slow down.

"The speed limit hasn't changed since you moved away, Noelle, and you know it. Don't act like this is the first ticket you've received on this stretch of the road."

"Really? Oh. Well, I get excited when my grandmother's house comes into view." Noelle returned her gaze to the man before her. She tipped her head sideways and peered up at him. "Guffy? Is that really you? You're the *law* now?"

267

Laughing, she stared at her old schoolmate, then threw open her door with such abandon that he had to hop backward to avoid impact.

"Officer Guffy to you. And if that door had hit me, I'd have had to write you up for assault on an officer. And yes, I'm the law. Is that really so hard to believe?"

"Only because all memories I have that include you and the law were with you by my side while we were on the receiving end of situations such as I find myself in right now."

"Don't say another thing about it. And don't try to talk me down with your old-time memories. You've committed a very serious crime here. A small child could have been bowled down."

"You clocked me going twenty-four miles per hour. I hardly think that's as serious as you say."

"Seven miles per hour over the speed limit is plenty serious. And need I remind you of the dangers of using a cell phone while driving?"

"*Need you remind me?* Guffy, what kind of talk is that? Did that lingo come in some police training guidebook?"

Guffy's face turned red and a vein throbbed at the side of his throat. Though he'd obviously changed in a lot of ways over the dozen or so years since they'd graduated—and apparently his losing upward of a hundred pounds wasn't the least of them—his telltale sign of anger certainly hadn't changed at all.

"You're really serious. You're mad at me." Noelle raised her eyebrows in surprise. "Guffy! What kind of homecoming is this? You were my best friend, my partner in crime.

We grew up together."

He hitched up his pants and pulled a ticket pad from his pocket. "Well, not anymore. You'll have to tear through the town on your own. I've changed. Some of us grow up at some point." He dashed a few words onto the pad, then tore off the top sheet and handed it to her.

"I've grown up," Noelle muttered as she wrinkled the ticket and shoved it in her purse. Guffy's raised eyebrow said he didn't agree.

"Now that we have the business stuff out of the way, get over here and give me a hug." He opened his arms for a bear hug.

"You give me a ticket and then think you get a hug?" Petulant, she crossed her arms in front of her. "Not gonna happen. Go find a model citizen to give you a hug. If someone sees us, they might think I'm offering you a bribe."

"Aw, c'mon, Noelle. Be a sport. You were speeding, and you got a ticket. That wasn't my fault."

"You could have given me a warning."

"Did you even look at the paper I handed you?"

"Noooo—not really. It's the holiday. It's my homecoming. I'd rather not see the large numbers I'm going to owe the town of Boulder before enjoying my reunion. Why?"

He stared her down.

She capitulated and yanked the paper from her purse, smoothing it with the palm of her hand. A cartoon character smiled up at her with the words "Welcome home" scribbled across the front.

A slow smile shaped her mouth.

"That's the best dog you could draw? After all these years, you still can't properly do justice to one of the greatest super-hero animals out there?"

"Go figure. One of the main reasons I went into law instead of deciding to be a cartoonist. I had to lose that dream years ago." He opened his arms again. "Welcome home."

This time she threw herself into Guffy's embrace. "It's good to be home. Thanks."

Her first encounter with an old friend had gone well. She could do this. The trip home wouldn't be the dreaded inquisition she'd expected. Everyone had grown up and moved on. Likely, no one even remembered her engagement, let alone who she dated.

"So, have you talked to Rocky lately?"

Or maybe they did. She huffed out the name in a frustrated syllable. "Rocky."

"Yes, remember him? Your fiancé? 'Here comes the bride' and all that?"

"Ex-fiancé. *Yes*, I remember him. From my distant past. That was a long time ago. Memories of all that should be in your distant past, too."

"Not really. I have coffee with him every morning."

Noelle noticed the cold mountain air for the first time. "Coffee?" she squeaked. "With Rocky?"

"Yes. Speaking of which, a nice hot cup sounds really good right about now."

He didn't seem to notice her distress.

"Could you do me a favor and not mention our little meeting with him? Or the fact that I'm back in town?"

Guffy used his superhero powers from their childhood and stared her down once again.

"Oh, I *hate* it when you do that!" She fought off the urge to stomp her foot.

"C'mon, Noelle. If he's in the distant past—why do you care if he knows you're back or not?"

"I just—do. That's all. Promise me." She held out her pinkie.

Guffy covertly glanced around. "I'm an officer of the law, and you want me to stand out here on the street, in plain view of every house on the block, and pinkie promise you?"

"Yes."

He wrapped his pinkie around hers and used that connection to yank her into another bear hug. As she stood there with her face squished out of shape against his chest, trying to breathe as he slapped his hand against her back, he quietly laughed. "Though I'm not sure what good it's gonna do, since everyone around has been buzzing about your visit and looking forward to seeing you ever since we heard that you were coming. I think they have a parade scheduled in your honor for later in the day."

She wouldn't be surprised. Though the town had changed, the people living in it obviously hadn't. "The neighborhood always has a parade on Thanksgiving Day, Guff."

He held her away. "Well, don't be surprised when you see the banner with your name on it. 'Boulder's most notorious runaway has returned.'"

She rolled her eyes.

"Will I see you at church on Sunday?"

"Church?"

"Yeah, the quaint little building your grandma goes to every week—several times a week, actually—and where she's attended for about as long as she's lived here?"

"I know what the church is; I just didn't realize you attended."

"I sure do. And we'd love to see you there."

Things had changed even more than Noelle had imagined. Guff attending church. Who would have expected that?

"I have to leave early Sunday. It's a long drive home. I'm only home this early today because I did the majority of the trip yesterday evening. I want to go straight through on Sunday."

"Another time then." He adjusted his hat and turned toward his car.

She felt slightly bereft. She hadn't realized how much she'd missed him until she saw him. "Love ya, Guff."

"Love you, too, Noelle. Good to have you home."

"So she really followed through, huh? She finally came home." Rocky sat in a booth across from Guffy the day after Thanksgiving and stared through the plate glass window of Lucy's Café. The aroma of frying bacon and sausage floated around them. "I didn't think she'd do it."

"Yeah, but you didn't hear it from me."

"Right. I didn't. I heard it from MaryAnne over at the hardware store."

"Wow, if it's made it that far, this whole end of town must know."

"Wait a minute—you knew she was back and didn't tell me?"

"She made me pinkie promise."

"Noelle asked you specifically *not* to tell me she was back?"

"Oh man. You *really* didn't hear that from me." Guff shifted in his seat. "She'll kill me."

"Nah, she'll only maim you. And you can arrest her if she does."

"You'll stitch me back up, right, doc?"

"I'll do my best." Rocky motioned for the waitress. "I think we're ready to order."

"The usual?" Before they could answer, Phoebe wrote their orders on her green pad, slapped the paper on the hook, and spun the rack toward the chef. She then leaned against the counter in front of them and smiled at Rocky. "So?"

Perplexed, Rocky stared back. "So. . .what?"

"Have you seen her? I want details. You two haven't spoken since you left her at the altar, have you? That's what I heard, anyway."

Rocky suddenly wished he could go back in time and right all the wrongs he'd done. Poor Noelle. She'd be hightailing it out of town in no time at this rate, and he very much wanted to talk to her before she left here again.

He changed the subject without answering and they chatted for a few minutes.

"Order up!"

A blast of cold air blew by as several other customers entered the café. Phoebe set their plates in front of them.

The thought of eating had lost all appeal. He pushed his plate away. Guff took one look at him and reached for it, scraping Rocky's food on top of his own. "Talk to me."

"I want to make things right. I want Noelle to know I've changed. I made such a stupid choice."

"Medical school was a stupid choice?"

"Med school was a great choice. Choosing it over Noelle was a stupid choice."

"So. . .fix things. Make 'em right."

"I'd love to. But I don't know if she'll give me a chance. For all I know, she could be seeing someone." Guff's earlier comment suddenly sunk in. He narrowed his eyes at his friend. "Wait a minute."

Guff glanced up mid-chew. "Uh-oh. . .what?"

"You not only saw her but you *talked* to her? You *touched* her?"

"I hugged her a couple of times."

"And you didn't see this as something I should know?"

Guff raised his arms in surrender. "Of course I did."

"But you pinkie promised."

"We pinkie promised."

"Hey, Guff." Rocky stood to his feet and threw some bills on the table. He slipped his arms into his coat. "Next time you come out on the bad side of an arrest gone wrong and come to the clinic all banged up?"

"Yeah?"

"Don't come running to the clinic expecting me to put you back together." Rocky spun on his heels and moved toward the door.

"But we pinkie promised, Rocky! I thought you said you'd changed. A changed man wouldn't hang his favorite lawman out to dry. What could I do?"

Rocky could only imagine what the other patrons would

make of Guff's comments. He kept his smile turned away from his friend as he pushed through the door and walked out into the brisk morning air.

Chapter 2

S ay you'll go, Noelle. What else do you have going on?"

Guff's voice carried loudly through the phone receiver, and Gram motioned for Noelle to cover the mouthpiece. Noelle held up an index finger, indicating she'd be free in a moment.

"I have wedding plans to finalize with my grandmother."

"I didn't realize." Guff's tonality chilled and became more impersonal. "Who's the lucky groom?"

"Alex Knight."

"Wow. Complicated. I, uh, I thought he was running around with your grandma."

"What?"

"He seems a bit—mature for you, too."

"Guff! *I'm* not marrying Alex, Gram is! I'm just helping with the details."

Gram looked over at her. Noelle rolled her eyes and grinned.

"Oh, right." His embarrassed laugh made her smile. "That works a lot better."

"I agree."

Though his words made light of the situation, she figured they were both thinking of Noelle's last wedding experience in town.

Guff had enough sense to change the subject. "Back to the reason I called—please say you'll come skiing? Surely you can take off for a few hours. That'll leave all evening tonight and all day tomorrow for you to work on the wedding."

Again Gram motioned for her to cover the phone. Noelle did as she asked.

"You should go. It will be nice."

"But, Gram, the wedding. . ."

"Isn't for a month. We had a great time catching up on things yesterday with your cousins during Thanksgiving dinner. We covered most of the important details. The stores will be crazy today and should be better tomorrow. Take today to have fun with Guff." Gram's eyes took on a pleading note, one Noelle couldn't ever resist. "For me?"

Noelle never could deny Gram anything. The fact that she was even back in town was a perfect example of that.

"Fine, I'll go."

"I'll pick you up in an hour. Do you have all your gear?"

"I'm sure it's around here somewhere."

An hour and a half later they arrived at the slopes.

"The mountain looks higher than it used to. And steeper. And. . .dangerous."

"Would you stop?" Guff laughed. "It's like riding a bike. You're going to do fine. C'mon. I see the others."

"The others?"

"Yeah, didn't I mention our singles group planned this event?"

"No, you didn't mention that." Noelle felt duped. Guff was up to something. She didn't know what, but why else would he omit the fact that they were meeting a group? Maybe he thought she'd say no if she knew it was a church group. She hadn't been real receptive to his invitation to church. "I hope you bluff your arrestees better than you do me."

"Arrestees? Seriously, Noelle. We call them suspects, or criminals, or prisoners." He seemed momentarily distracted.

Noelle followed his line of vision, her eyes honing in on a tall figure at the far end of the group. Her heart skipped a beat, and she stared at the man in horror.

"Guff!" she hissed. She grabbed his sleeve and ducked behind him. "Tell me that isn't Rocky."

"Okay. . .but I really don't like to lie."

"You knew he was coming, didn't you?"

"I did."

She tightened her hold. "I'm so furious with you right now."

"I can kinda tell that by your grip on my arm."

She released him. "I didn't want to see Rocky. And I especially didn't want to see him in a group setting, while skiing after an eight-year break! I didn't want a scene."

"I hate to say this, but you hiding behind my back, yelling at me, isn't helping the not-making-a-scene angle."

He had a point.

Guff glanced around. "I tell you what. How about we slip over to the group classes on the bunny slope and get you a refresher course. That will increase your confidence and let you avoid Rocky all at the same time."

"I hardly think a class with twenty preschoolers will do much for my confidence." She watched the brightly dressed kids snowplow down the hill and tried not to picture what her hulking form—in comparison to the munchkins—would look like trailing along after them. She clasped Guff's arm and turned him toward the slopes. "I have a better idea. We catch the next lift out of here and get ourselves lost on the mountain."

"But. . .the group. . ."

"Will do just fine without us. Let's go."

They shuffled over to the line, and the wait seemed to go at a turtle's pace. Noelle saw the rest of the group head their way.

Guff shifted beside her, edging out of line. "I have to go to the bathroom."

"Guff, you aren't five. Hold it."

"I'm serious. I'll be right back."

"Guff, we're almost at the. . ." He'd shuffled out of range.

"Ma'am, move into place. You're up next."

"Sorry." Noelle scooted forward.

"I have a single." The man bellowed to the line. "Any other singles need a partner?"

Only a whole slew of them from Gram's church at the back of the line. Please, God, please, God, please, God, don't let it be any of them.

She hadn't prayed in a long time, but she hoped her rusty—make that desperate—prayer would be heard.

A tall figure moved into place beside her just as the chair-lift came up behind them. Not ready, she stumbled and a firm grasp steadied her. "Here we go."

She recognized that voice. No way—it couldn't be. In a panic, she stared out at the snowy view as they were whisked up the mountain. She tried to steady her breathing. She was going to hyperventilate. Or faint. And if she fainted, she'd fall from the chair to a certain death. She glanced down at the ground which rolled by a few yards below her. Or maybe just fall to a very unflattering landing. Which was preferable considering the situation she now found herself in.

"First time up? You'll do fine. It's wonderful once you get the hang of it."

She guessed her death grip on the bar and silence gave her away. She couldn't not speak. What should she do? *Rocky* would likely fall off the chair when he realized it was her. She didn't want to be responsible for his broken neck. This was all Guff's fault. His devious plan couldn't have gone better—for him.

"I've skied before, but it's been a long time." Her voice came out in a squeak and she realized with her goggles, hat, and fluffy ski gear, he might not recognize her. The thought gave her courage, and she sent him what she hoped would pass for a quick, but friendly, smile.

They'd moved away from the lower expanse of the slopes and were now passing over the trees.

"I'd forgotten how beautiful the mountains are. And the quiet..."

Speaking of quiet, Rocky hadn't uttered a word since she'd

smiled at him. She risked a quick peek in his direction only to see him staring at her in speechless wonder. With his goggles on top of his head, his emerald green eyes studied her. He wore his hair long; tufts of brown stuck out from beneath his black beanie. He was more handsome than ever.

"Noelle."

Her breath hitched and she stared back at him for a moment. His rugged face had filled out, the thin boyish features long gone. She bit her lip and turned away. Her left hand clutched tightly onto the lift, her ski poles dangling from her wrist. A multitude of emotions poured through her. Pain caused by their last meeting eight years ago. Loneliness from the long months after he left. Dashed dreams and what-could-have-been.

"I'm so sorry."

"Don't." She didn't want to cry. Not here. Where had her well-laid plans about acting mature and aloof and taking control of the situation gone? This moment was beyond her worst nightmare. She couldn't leave. They were completely alone. And she'd picked the longest chairlift. They weren't anywhere near the top.

"I've wanted to talk to you."

"There's no need. I'm really sorry about this."

"You planned it?" Amusement rang through his words, and she glanced up at him to see his achingly familiar grin.

"I hardly think so. But Guff. I think *he* planned it. Guff is a dead man. If he dares come up this mountain, I'm pushing him off the other side."

"Ah, there we go. Familiar signs of the woman I used to know."

They both grew silent as his words sank in. They didn't know each other anymore. The thought disturbed Noelle more than she would have imagined. After eight years, shouldn't she be over him? Why couldn't they have the natural camaraderie she had with Guff? She and Guff had jumped right back into their friendship as if a day hadn't passed. And here was Rocky, the man who'd held her heart, who knew her every dream and life goal, yet he remained a stranger.

"What have you been up to?"

"I moved to Kansas City and started an event planning company."

"I thought I heard you were working in interior design? All those years to get your degree, including an early start to college, and you aren't using it?"

"I did for a while, and it comes in handy now with the party and wedding décor. I just took things in a slightly different direction." How much did he know and how much should she tell him? Part of her wanted to bare her soul to him, but the other part wanted to hold him at arm's length until she could get away from him. "When I first went to the city, my job demanded a lot of hours. My mother and her drama also demanded a lot of hours. Her demands always won out, which caused me to move through a lot of jobs. I finally realized if I was ever going to get anywhere, I'd best go into business for myself. Since I had experience planning weddings. . ." she winced. What a stupid choice of topic.

Rocky ignored the comment. "How's the company doing?"

"Pretty good. I'm starting to make a name for myself. I have a lot more flexibility—not that I need it as much now."

"I'm sorry about your mother."

"Thanks." She hoped he wouldn't mention the funeral. She turned and focused on the scenery, effectively shutting him out. After Gram's wedding, she'd have no reason to return, not for a long, long time. Sunbeams glinted off the snow-covered trees, making the ice crystals sparkle. Festive skiers flew down the slopes below them. She watched as one errant novice sped straight toward a tree and breathed a sigh of relief after the person crashed safely into a snowdrift.

They'd neared the top of the lift—finally—and Noelle mentally rehearsed her dismount from the chair. Though she'd skied avidly in the past, she now felt apprehensive about falling and tripping the entire line of people coming behind them.

In the end, she only managed to trip one person, Rocky, and much to her horror, instead of stopping to apologize, she found herself barreling forward, full bore down the hill, much like the skier she'd watched from the lift.

"Noelle! Slow down! You're—"

Rocky's voice drifted off behind her, and she breathed a momentary sigh of relief—until she realized what Rocky had tried to tell her. Judging from the amount and size of the moguls scattered across the hillside in front of her, she'd inadvertently, in her panic to get away, chosen a difficult black diamond slope instead of a leisurely bunny slope for her beginning debut back onto the slopes.

Unprepared, she caught air off the first mogul and felt her limbs awkwardly flail out in all directions. Graceful it was not. She tightened her muscles and managed to land on two feet, but immediately another mogul threw her off balance again.

She bounced her way through a few more bone-jarring landings before she reached an open clearing. Only after she began to pick up speed did she realize she'd ended up in the fall line and was heading straight down the hill at a breakneck speed. She fought for control as her body began to remember the sport and the moves gradually came back to her.

"I can do this!" Exhilarated, she relaxed a notch and tried to plan her best descent. The firmly packed snow only served to increase her speed. A large mogul loomed ahead and she tried to veer around it. No deal. She hit the icy mound of snow, flew up into the air, and knew this landing wouldn't be anything like the others. She overcorrected her balance on the landing and her ski caught at the edge, tripping her, which threw her toward the trees that lined the slope. She tried to sit back on the skis, and finally tipped to the side, hoping to slow and avoid an impact with the fast approaching trees. Just as she closed her eyes and ducked, she felt her ski twist underneath her. Searing pain shot through her right knee as she flipped and rolled toward the nearest tree. Thankfully, she sank into a welcome darkness before the final impact.

Chapter 3

A myriad of figures flashed through Noelle's muddled mind; the images coming and going far faster than she could keep up with. Wedding plans with her cousins. Her grandmother's happy face as she oohed and aahed over Noelle's engagement ring. She and Rocky at the altar after long months of planning. Rocky starting to fade. Suddenly he was in a boat, standing just offshore, still wearing his tux. The boat drifted even as she reached for its edge. It moved toward the horizon.

"Rocky, no! Come back. Don't leave me." A sob tore at her throat, but he drifted farther and farther away, finally sinking into the water and disappearing from sight. "Rocky." Her voice was an agonized whisper.

"I think she's coming around."

Gram?

Noelle fought against the urge to open her eyes. Gram would be so disappointed. She'd loved Rocky.

Rocky's deep commanding voice called her name, and she felt a firm grip on her chin, forcing her head to the side.

"Noelle. Open your eyes. Now."

She tried to turn her head away but he held tight.

"Noelle, look at me."

"Rock?" She squinted into a bright light. "Can't. Hurts too much." Her voice sounded raspy.

"Dim the light," her grandmother's quiet voice washed over her, soothing with its familiarity.

"Gram?"

"Right here, darling."

"Rocky's gone." Noelle tried to open her eyes again. "He sank into the ocean."

Soft laughter filled the room.

"You might wish that to be true," Rocky said with amusement, "but I'm here with you, warm and dry."

She smiled and patted Rocky's hand. "I'm warm, too."

The warmth fled as cold, hard panic rolled over her. Dry? Warm? Suddenly bits and pieces of her recent skiing debut flashed through her mind. The moguls. Catching air. Flying sideways toward the trees. Wrenching her knee. The cold.

Rocky was alive and well.

Grimacing, she peered into the dim room and saw her grandmother, Alex, her cousins, and Rocky gathered around a hospital bed. *Her* hospital bed. She gulped, the sound audible in the now quiet room.

"How'd I get here?"

Rocky ignored her question and continued to check her vitals. The others sat quietly, waiting. Beneath his firm touch, her wrist tingled and her heart rate increased. He reached for his stethoscope.

Whatever had happened on the mountain had certainly messed her chemistry up, and she wasn't about to let Rocky know how he affected her. Yet if she didn't admit he was the cause of her soaring pulse, he might think she had some medical condition and would keep her in hospital longer—or maybe even force medications upon her to slow her racing heart. She began to panic.

Frowning down at her, Rocky took her pulse again. She jerked her hand away. He reached for a button on the wall, discreetly pushed it, and summoned a nurse.

Before Noelle could say a word, her grandmother stood and motioned the others to leave. "We'll just be going now and leave you to your work, doc." She moved to Noelle's side.

"Gram, no. . .don't leave."

"You're in good hands, dear. We'll be back early in the morning. You just let Rocky take care of you, and get a lot of rest."

"But. . ."

Gram kissed her cheek, and both of her cousins stepped forward to do the same.

"Take care, Elle. I'm so glad you're all right." Chris leaned in and gave her a tight hug.

"Enjoy your uh, recuperation." Holly raised her eyebrows and nodded toward Rocky with an exaggerated motion. "Bye, Cuz. Love ya."

They hustled out the door before Noelle could utter another word.

The nurse sidestepped around them and entered the room. She sent Noelle a reassuring smile. "You're looking a bit better than when I last saw you. How do you feel?"

Noelle glanced at Rocky through lowered lids and leaned toward the nurse. "Is there another doctor on call?"

"You're in wonderful hands with Dr. Carmichael." The nurse sent Rocky an appreciative glance before returning her attention to Noelle. "And he's the only one on call this evening. We run a sparse crew on holiday weekends."

"Can't I go home with Gram?" Noelle pushed up onto her arms, but the pain shooting through her leg caused her to lie back down.

"You've torn several ligaments in your knee. You won't be going anywhere for a few days. Not until the surgeon has a chance to fix you up."

"Surgeon!" This time Noelle ignored the pain and pushed to her elbows. "I can't have surgery. I don't have time. I have to get back home on Sunday."

Rocky sat at the edge of the bed, much too close for her comfort. Her pulse sped up again. "You aren't going home. You might as well settle in and plan to stay through your grandmother's wedding."

"That's four weeks away! I have a career. Responsibilities. A life. I can't just laze around while my assistant does everything."

"She's not capable?"

"Well, yes, I guess she is," Noelle sputtered. "But—"

"But nothing. You could go home, but someone would have to drive you. You won't be able to walk on your leg and will have to keep it extended for a few weeks. Your surgeon will be here, so you'll have to come back for the follow-ups."

"And you're keeping me overnight because of my knee?

I thought these types of things are done as outpatient treatments these days." She tried to ignore the fact that he absently caressed her wrist with his thumb as they spoke.

"Most of them are. But I want to keep you under observation for at least twenty-four hours. You took quite a tumble and about gave me a heart attack up there on the mountain. And your vitals are causing me a bit of concern."

"My vitals are fine. You're just. . ." Noelle yanked her wrist away from his gentle ministrations. His green eyes were melting her resolve to stay immune to him. "You're just stressing me with all this talk of surgery."

The corner of his mouth quirked up. "Am I?"

She felt a telltale blush creep up her face. "You are."

"Sorry." His knowing smirk said he wasn't sorry at all. "Just the same, I'll feel better if you stick around and let the staff watch over you."

"Well. . ." She sighed. She knew Rocky well enough to know that she wouldn't win this battle. And she found herself curious about this new side of Rocky. The old-fashioned bedside manner he portrayed worked for him. She could only imagine the nurses tripping over themselves, wanting to assist Dr. Carmichael. The thought gave her pause, and a tinge of jealousy made her frown. "Okay. You win."

The nurse stepped out of the room, and Rocky leaned close. "The only thing I want to win, Noelle, is your trust. I know I don't deserve it, but I'd like a chance to make amends."

Surprised by his candor, Noelle leaned back against the pillow and studied her former fiancé. Like the town, Rocky had changed in more ways than she'd first realized. His reckless side seemed to have tamed, and though she'd loved his spontaneity—right up to the moment he spontaneously left her at the altar—she liked this new persona he portrayed.

"You've changed."

"I hope so." He stood and paced a few steps away. "I don't much like the person I was back when we were engaged."

His words cut deep and she inhaled sharply. She forced herself to release her breath and rallied, hoping she'd be able to speak with a steady voice. "I noticed."

A look of remorse passed across his features. "I don't mean I didn't like us. I cared for you more than you'll ever know. I still do."

He hesitated, and Noelle's heart skipped a beat. Was he saying what she thought he was saying? Did he still have feelings? And if he did, would she ever be able to trust him enough to give him another chance? She shook the cascading thoughts away. The man, who also happened to be her doctor at the moment, likely sensed her agitation over his presence and had determined to keep her as calm as he could. He'd surely be mortified if he could read her thoughts; that she'd taken his comment from "I care" to "Will you marry me?"

"You're smiling." Rocky returned her grin. He leaned against the wall and crossed his arms. His dimples had deepened, but his eyes still crinkled at the corners. "You find my statement amusing?"

"I know this might surprise you, but sometimes I can be a tad impetuous and my thoughts get away from me."

He looked wary.

She laughed.

He continued to stare, his perusal making her nervous. "You're more beautiful than ever."

"Right." Noelle's hand instantly smoothed her hair at his statement. "I can only imagine. First, I wore a hat for a couple of hours that always gives me a bad case of bed head. I rode in Guff's overheated car, sweating to the oldies that he still blares through his cassette player speakers. I stepped out into the cold, where ice crystals formed on my hair, before he feigned a trip to the little boy's room so he could. . ." She nibbled her lip in embarrassment.

Now Rocky laughed, the sound of his husky voice warming her heart. It had been far too long since she'd heard him laugh. He surprised her with a wink. "I was there for this part of the story. So he could pawn me off on you."

"Something like that, yeah." She grinned up at him. "That threw me slightly off-kilter—"

"Slightly? You tripped me coming off the ski lift so you'd have a head start, and then you threw yourself over the side of the mountain." This time Rocky's laughter erupted from deep inside of him. Three nurses passing along the hallway stopped to stare incredulously into the room.

Noelle stared from them to her physician. "I take it from their reaction that they don't hear you laugh very often." She motioned toward the hall where the nurses double-stepped out of sight.

"I guess not." Rocky shrugged. "In my line of work, I don't often have much to laugh about while on duty."

"Good point." She picked at an imaginary piece of string on her mint green hospital gown. "And just for the record,

I didn't 'throw myself over the side of the mountain.' I momentarily panicked and picked the wrong trail. You might not have noticed, but I haven't skied in a while."

"No." Rocky emphasized the word way too heavily, his eyes huge with overdramatic sarcasm.

Noelle surprised herself by giggling. She *never* giggled. She knew at that moment she was in over her head and that meant trouble. But she couldn't stop herself from asking, "What gave me away?"

He pretended to think. "Hmm. It would have to be a toss-up between your ungraceful mount onto the ski chair or the dismount where you caused a ten-person pileup."

She gasped, mortified. "I didn't!"

He laughed again. "No, you didn't. But not for a lack of trying."

"I told you I was a bit rusty. No one else got hurt?"

"Nah. I happened to remember how dangerous you could be when dismounting and counterbalanced. I just couldn't regroup in time to catch up with you before you barreled down the mountain."

"Thanks for painting me in such a graceful picture."

"Let's just say that if I'd had a video camera, I'd have won quite a bit of money on a certain TV show."

Noelle snatched up her ski cap from the bedside table and hurled it his way. He caught it easily and twirled it on his finger.

Her nurse popped her head around the open doorway. "Doc, our patient really needs her rest."

"Of course." Rocky smoothed her cap and gently laid it

back on the table. "I'll be close by if you need me." He raised the rails of her bed and tucked the call button into the sheets at her side. He lowered the head of the bed and smoothed the blanket up to her chin. "Use the call button if you need a nurse. If you have any pain, or—well, whatever, call. Try to sleep, and I'll be back to check on you in a bit."

Noelle pulled her arms free and nodded. She had a feeling she wouldn't sleep much at all with Rocky so close. But he hadn't even cleared the doorway before the day caught up with her and her eyes began to close.

Rocky practically skipped down the hall. He'd made a lot of mistakes in his life, but leaving Noelle at the altar was his biggest and most regretted by far. When he'd turned his life over to the Lord several years ago, she'd become his biggest prayer request.

Now it seemed that after all those years, God had answered his prayer and was giving him the chance he'd desired for so long. He just had to make sure he made the right choices and made the opportunity everything he hoped it would be.

A nurse stopped in a patient's doorway, and her mouth dropped open in surprise as he walked past her. He winked and she hurried on, shaking her head as she moved out of his sight.

So they'd never heard him whistle before. Rocky hadn't felt like whistling for a long, long time. And now, suddenly, he did. He moved into the empty call room and sank down onto the nearest bottom bunk. He leaned back, slung his legs straight out across the worn mattress, and tucked his arms behind his head. He knew he'd never sleep, not with Noelle just down the hall. But he would use the time to petition God with his desire to work his way back into Noelle's good graces, and just possibly, permanently back into her life.

She'd changed, but not as much as he'd worried. Through her grandmother, he'd kept up on bits and pieces of her life. But her grandmother hadn't been completely free with her information. She had this odd notion that if he really wanted to know about her goings-on, he could call or write to Noelle himself and find out anything and everything he wanted to know.

Noelle still had the same beautiful auburn hair. On the slopes she'd worn it in a braid, but after her tumble down the hill and subsequent trip to the hospital, her grandmother had brushed it out and it now lay in unruly curls over the pillow. Her brown eyes still twinkled with amusement, even through her wariness. He'd missed her spunk. He'd missed her every-thing. The realization could only mean one thing. He was a complete and total idiot. He should never have let her go, and now he had a chance and needed to win her back. He vowed not to mess things up again.

God, I know I had a chance with Noelle once before, and I blew it in a major way. I thought I had to choose between my commit-ment to her and the practice of medicine. You've brought her back into my life, and I promise if You give me another chance, I'll never blow it with her again.

He wanted to check on her. He actually wanted to stay with her and never leave her side again. But he didn't want to scare her with his presence. He'd go slow and let God lead.

He had no idea where she was spiritually. He needed to make the right decisions this time. She'd attended church with her grandmother through the years, but he supposed any seeds that were planted had scattered by the wayside judging by her actions. Then again, he and Guff hadn't done much better at harvesting those seeds, in her or themselves. They'd been a pretty wild bunch in their formative years. Each of them had their own baggage to lug around. He and Guff had become followers of Christ and Rocky hoped that at the very least, if Noelle wasn't a believer, he could at least plant some new seeds leading her in that direction.

His glance returned to the clock. Ten minutes had passed. Not exactly enough time for him to make an excuse in seeing to her well-being. The nurses would never let him live it down. His reputation as the steel-hearted loner would be ruined if he ran back to her room now.

Fifteen minutes. Finally. He hopped up from the bunk. He needed to go check her out. Well, check on her. He needed to make sure her blood pressure hadn't spiked, and that her pulse remained normal.

Several nurses surrounded the work station outside Noelle's door. He heard their titters of laughter as he stalked into Noelle's room. The machines in the room hummed. She lay against her pillow, sound asleep, her face that of an angel. He lowered himself onto a chair and watched her. Her breathing had become steady, and when he checked her pulse, he felt relieved that it moved calmly under his fingertips.

He smiled. His presence had most definitely affected her pulse earlier. Perhaps that was a sign from God that he still had a chance, that Noelle still felt something for him. He hoped she still felt something for him. The speeding pulse could have been a sign of her anger, but the blush at his touch told him otherwise. He slid his hand over to her palm and wound his fingers between hers. "I've missed you, Noelle. So much. I'm glad you're home. I'm going to try my hardest to win back your heart." No way was her being here an accident.

She didn't move or respond, but still Rocky smiled. Here he sat, at the bedside of his beloved, because God had given him another chance.

Chapter 4

Gram poked her head around the edge of the kitchen door to where Noelle lounged upon the couch. "You're looking awfully melancholy for someone who's about to be sprung from two weeks of post-surgery recuperation." She frowned and wiped her hands on a tea towel. After a few moments' perusal, she tossed the towel on the table and joined Noelle in the living room.

Noelle sat with her leg propped up on the coffee table in front of her, straight out in its brace as it had been since surgery. She'd looked forward to this day. "I'm excited about going shopping."

"Then why so glum?" Gram sat on the couch and tucked an errant strand of hair from Noelle's ponytail back into place.

"I wouldn't say I'm glum, just contemplative."

"Okay, contemplative." Gram settled back against the cushions. "What are you contemplating?"

"The day before Thanksgiving, as I was driving into town, I gave myself a major pep talk about Rocky and how I'd behave if I ran into him. I felt ready. But when I did go face-to-face with him on the slopes, I panicked. Then later at the hospital, I was all too ready to forgive and forget. My heart ran away from me, and I remembered just how much I've missed him."

Gram laughed. "And that's a bad thing?"

"It is after what he did to me." Noelle shook her head. "I don't want to be like my mother. She made such awful choices in men. They could treat her horribly, yet she'd take them right back if they sent her the right smile or gift."

"Honey...you're so different from your mother you couldn't be more opposite. I can't believe you'd even think you were like her, rest her soul. You know I loved her with everything in me, but she had a different attitude about her from birth. She was the most difficult baby I've ever seen, the most headstrong toddler, and it went downhill from there."

"But her track record with men—"

"Is nothing like yours. You gave your heart to one man, and when he hurt you, you never let another one in. You've held us all at arm's length ever since. Your mother would hop from man to man, take their abuse and for whatever reason, would bounce right back for more."

"I feel so angry with Rocky in my head, yet my heart misses him so badly I can hardly stand it. He never even showed remorse."

"Oh yes he did." Gram stood and walked across the room, adjusting some pictures on the fireplace mantel.

Noelle's head snapped up at her grandmother's change of tone. "When? What are you talking about? I never even spoke to him again until we met at the ski slopes."

"He showed up at your mother's funeral. He risked getting

kicked out of school to be there. He said his first year of training was so busy it was pretty easy to push back the guilt of what he'd done." She walked back over to settle next to Noelle and took her hand in her own. "But when he heard about your mother, he knew he had to make things right. He was so disappointed when you weren't there."

"I never knew."

"No, you didn't."

"Why didn't you tell me? Why didn't *he* tell me? Maybe things would have been easier. . . ."

"He wanted to, but we told him to wait. The time wasn't right."

"Gram, who knows what would have happened if he'd contacted me?"

"Right or wrong, we made our decision. I well remember that day. We were all on edge from the funeral, and I think we all thought it best to let you alone to heal. We told him we couldn't be the go-betweens, and that he had to talk to you himself. He was ready to fly to your side, but we advised him to get back to school before he turned one bad choice into two. You were too angry back then—with your mother, with Rocky, and with us. Do you honestly believe you would have wanted to see him?"

Noelle thought a moment before answering softly. "No."

A knock at the door had Gram hurrying off to answer.

"Gram! You never did tell me." Noelle struggled to get off the couch, hurrying to get her crutches balanced under her arms and catch up. "Which of your delightful friends got stuck with escorting us around?" She hated that she couldn't just pop in her car with Gram and head out for their shopping trip. "Is it Gail or Terri? I want to see them both!"

Her crutch caught on the carpet and she pitched forward. With a squeal of panic she twisted and hopped sideways on her good leg, praying she wouldn't fall and injure something else. The odds of avoiding that weren't very good. The floor rushed toward her way too fast, and she braced herself for more searing pain. Instead, strong arms caught her and pulled her firmly against a solid chest.

It definitely wasn't Gail or Terri. Alex? Embarrassed but grateful, she tilted her head and peered up at her rescuer. Green eyes twinkled back at her, but a trace of concern lingered in their depths.

"Oh. You." She tried to push away, but he didn't release his hold. "My knight in shining armor. Here to rescue me." She always resorted to sarcasm when cornered.

"I'm glad you consider me such. You obviously need one."

A knight or a rescuer? But technically they were one and the same. She tried to think, a hard task with him so close.

"I'm sure Gram appreciates your stopping by, but we were just about to head out. . ."

She gasped as Rocky swung her up into his arms and headed for the couch. She thought she heard Gram giggle from behind them. She tried to peer over Rocky's shoulder at the traitorous woman, but Gram quickly busied herself with reaching down to retrieve Noelle's crutches.

"I can walk," she hissed.

"No. You can't." Rocky settled her back on the couch.

"I can hobble."

"Not very well."

Noelle folded her arms across her chest. "I'm back where I started from. Thank you. Whether you like it or not, I'm getting ready to go out with Gram and finalize the wedding plans. We have just over two weeks until the event, and we haven't done a thing."

"I know about your plans. But you aren't going anywhere until we cover a few ground rules."

"Ground rules!" Who did the man think he was? She was going shopping with two older but spunky women. Maybe three if both of Gram's friends came along. She hardly needed Rocky to give her rules to follow. "You aren't even my doctor at the moment! The surgeon has seniority, right?"

Gram had quietly fled the room. Smart woman. Noelle felt jealous of the ability to do such a thing. As it was, she could only sit—Rocky's captive audience. Captive being the operative word.

"Oh, fine." She added a glare to her defensive pose. "Have your say. It's not like you'll be sneaking along behind us, watching to see if I break any of your precious rules." She narrowed her eyes. "Or will you?"

Rocky actually laughed. "I won't be sneaking."

"Good."

"I'm escorting. I'll be right by your side."

"But—but—I thought. . ." She narrowed her eyes at him. "Gram!"

Rocky flinched as she raised her voice. Gram didn't materialize. Noelle heard the washing machine begin to fill with water. A moment later, the old dryer added to the noise.

"Next she'll start the vacuum," Noelle muttered.

"She might have to if she hopes to tune out any more bellows like that." He rubbed his fingertips back and forth over his ear. His grin was contagious and she found herself smiling back.

"Traitor."

"She cares about you. She wants you safe. And your attempt to welcome me a moment ago—before you fell into my arms—shows just how much you need me."

Could he now read her thoughts? Noelle felt her face color. She was sure he didn't mean the double entendre, but it was there just the same. And with the way she reacted, he had to know her true thoughts on the matter.

"I mean—how much you need me along on this trip." Now his face colored. "It's icy out there, and the last thing you need is to take a spill on a hard walkway."

He had a point. If she slipped and the ladies tried to catch her, she'd likely bring them all down with her and they could end up with broken hips or something.

She sighed. "Okay. You win. What are the"—she made air quotes— "*rules?*"

He sank down beside her, his expression unreadable. "Actually, I only have one. And it isn't a rule, it's a request. Let me be there for you, Noelle, in every way." He took hold of her hand, his touch gentle, and wove his fingers in between hers.

The room felt small. Overly warm. She couldn't breathe. Was he referring to their shopping expedition? Or was this his way of making amends and offering her much, much more?

Before she could vocalize any of the questions, Gram re-entered the room.

"I guess I'm set. What do you two say about hitting the road?"

Now you decide to come back. Noelle wanted to hit something, but it wasn't the road.

Rocky winked at her and tugged her to an upright position. He didn't release her hand. "Do you want to try to walk out to my truck, or would you rather I carry you?"

"I can walk."

He let go of her hand and retrieved her crutches. Her hands were shaking. She pressed them against her stomach to still them. His nearness still unnerved her. She watched him as he walked back across the room. His blue, black, and emerald green sweater did double duty, accentuating his strength while highlighting his vivid green eyes. Not that he'd ever given a thought to either, she was sure. Black jeans hugged his muscular legs. No longer was he the thin, gangly man she'd dated in college. Time had been good to him. She could only hope he found her changes as appealing.

When he handed her the crutches, she took things slower. She secured them under her arms, the padded top digging in and making her already bruised upper arms ache. She admitted only to herself that she'd much rather be carried in Rocky's arms.

Gram picked up both their purses and headed for the door. True to his word, Rocky stayed by her side. He held her elbow as she hobbled down the two steps on the front stoop. He wrapped an arm around her waist and removed the nearest crutch as they moved along the slippery cement to his vehicle.

After he opened the door, he stowed her crutches in the back. Effortlessly, he lifted her onto the front seat. "Scoot back toward my side. You'll be able to lean against me, which will allow you to keep your leg straight."

Noelle laughed. "And where's Gram going to sit—on my lap? My leg will take up the entire seat."

"Your gram's already settled into the other vehicle with Gail and Terri." He nodded toward the far side of his truck. The three women waved. Rocky waggled the fingers of one hand back. The other hand held her purse, which he now handed her. He closed her door and walked around to open his. He slid inside and suddenly the interior of the cab felt very intimate.

"They set me up."

"Are you sorry?"

"Sorry for you."

"Why would you be sorry for me? I volunteered for this adventure. It isn't often I get to go pick out a trousseau with four beautiful women."

"An adventure you'll never want to repeat, I can promise you."

Rocky threw his head back and laughed. "It won't be that bad."

"Have you ever shopped with those three? I have. And as an event planner, I can tell you wedding shopping changes a personality ten times over for the worse. The most charming and sweet woman becomes a barracuda if you get between what she envisions her special day to be with words of reality."

"Well, then. I'll double as your bodyguard."

She glanced up at him, an action which put her much

too close to his face. Their lips were mere inches apart. If she leaned in just barely, she'd feel their gentle warmth once again. His eyes darkened to a deeper green and time slowed. She felt a precious moment of hope before fear pushed it away. She missed him. She wanted him back. And the thought of how much she wanted him back scared her. She closed her eyes in panic and turned away, resting her head against his upper arm. She felt safe there. Close enough, but not too close. Today was only one day. They'd take things slow. If Rocky had indeed changed, he'd understand.

After a few moments of quiet, Rocky started the engine. She could see his profile in the reflection of the passenger window. Though he stared toward the rearview mirror as he backed out of the drive, the sweetest smile rested upon the lips she longed to kiss.

Chapter 5

"Okay, give me the basic rundown. What are we looking for on this shopping expedition?" Rocky edged into traffic and headed toward downtown. "Where do we start?"

"Aha! Spoken like a true man. Make a to-do list and knock off each item as quickly as possible." Noelle teased.

"Nope. Just wanting to know the best place to park so we'll be central to our destination." Rocky's mouth curved up in a smirk.

"Oh. Well, we're meeting Chris and Holly first, so we can pick out dresses. Gram needs to find a dress, and then we'll choose our dresses according to the theme we end up with."

Rocky raised a skeptical eyebrow at her. "Dresses come in themes?"

Noelle giggled. "Weddings come in themes. There's traditional, Victorian, medieval, contemporary, old-fashioned, romantic. . ."

"I'd think all weddings would cover the romantic theme. That's kind of what the whole idea is, right?"

"Well, yes. But I'm talking about the style of dresses and—well, you'll just have to see as the day goes by."

"You don't know these themes ahead of time?"

"Some brides do, which can be very time-consuming."

"Not knowing a theme makes the job less time-consuming?" His confusion made her laugh.

"Right."

"How can that be?" He made a left turn and followed Gail's large car as it moved down a narrower road.

"If they come in with a theme, we have to look for that style right from the start. A good bridal shop will be able to direct us to that type of dress, but brides tend to be very particular about which dress will suit them best." Noelle couldn't believe they were having this conversation. The Rocky she remembered would have never taken the time to listen to her explain such a thing. He hadn't even wanted to give input on their own wedding. He told her to take care of it, and he'd show up for the event. But he hadn't even followed through on that one important detail.

"Why are you scowling?"

Noelle pulled out of her depressing reverie and ignored his question. "If we go shopping as we are today, we just look at all dresses available until Gram finds the perfect one that jumps out at her. Then we start all over and find dresses for the rest of us that will look good with hers."

"That makes sense." He pulled into a parking spot a few spaces down from the others and helped Noelle ease from her seat. Once she had her crutches solidly underneath her, he escorted her to the sidewalk where Chris, Holly, Gram, Gail, and Terri waited.

"Hey, Noelle! I didn't know we were supposed to bring

dates," Holly blurted. "I would have loved to bring Nick, but I doubt he'd have been very excited."

Chris elbowed her. "I don't think he's her date," she hissed.

Noelle kept her eyes forward and didn't look to see how Rocky reacted to the topic.

"It's not a date. I'm just here to serve Noelle, to be at her beck and call." Rocky's words, laced with humor, caused Noelle's heart to skip a beat. His firm grip on her arm tightened briefly and he sent her a teasing wink.

"Isn't that the best kind of date?" Gail inserted.

The others laughed. Noelle wanted to crawl into a hole. "Ahem, well, yeah. Um. . .we'd better get down to business."

They entered the nearest boutique, but it wasn't until five shops later that Gram found what she'd been looking for. The winter white, knee-length formal suit fit her perfectly. Modest lace trimmed the collar. The rest of the suit was simple, yet elegant.

"Gram, it's beautiful. Perfect." Noelle motioned for Gram to spin, which Gram did to the oohs and aahs of her granddaughters and friends.

Rocky gave his approval, which made Gram beam.

"That only took. . ." Rocky looked down at his watch. "One hour and forty-seven minutes. And now we have, what"—he looked at the group surrounding him—"five more dresses to go? We should knock that out in another eight or nine hours. At this rate, we'll be home in time for a late dinner."

"Very funny, Rock." Noelle rolled her eyes. "We only have three dresses to go. And all we have to do is agree on one that we all like."

He raised a skeptical eyebrow.

Amazingly, the cousins found dresses they all liked one store later, just in time for lunch.

"What do you say we all grab a bite to eat at Lucy's, and then we'll finish up with the florist and caterer?"

Holly frowned. "I'd love to, but I have plans this afternoon."

"Same here. I thought we just needed to do the dresses this morning." Chris glanced longingly toward her car. "If you really need me for this part, I suppose I can rearrange my schedule. . . ."

Gram waved them on their way. "We can handle things from here. We just wanted to make sure you knew you were invited to help with the plans."

"You're sure?" Chris gave her a quick hug, ready to make her getaway.

"Positive. Noelle has the details for the rest of our day lined up. She just wants to get a peek at what we've ordered firsthand."

"Great. Then you all have fun, and we'll be on our way." Holly hugged everyone and the two scampered toward their vehicles.

Noelle looked over at Rocky with a challenging grin. "Longing to follow suit?"

"No way. I'm ready to eat."

Gram looked over at her friends. "I tell you what. There's a darling little café over by where we parked. Gail picked that area because it's near both the florist shop and the bakery. Why don't you two head on over while we three go back to one of the first stores? I want to look at a necklace and earring set I saw.

Now that I think about it, it'll look perfect with my suit."

"We can wait and go with you." Noelle turned to retrace their steps. "I'd love to see it."

Gram exchanged a look with her friends. "You can see it later, after I've made my purchase."

"But. . ." Noelle frowned. "We might as well all go over together."

Rocky put his arm around Noelle's waist and urged her in the other direction. "It takes us longer to get around. I'm sure by the time we arrive at the café and arrange for a table, they'll be right behind us."

"Oh. Of course." She sent Gram an apologetic look. "I didn't think about how I slow everyone down."

"It's not that, honey." Gram gave her a quick hug. "You've already been on your feet more today than in the past two weeks put together. I don't want you to overdo it."

"And you still have two more stops, dear," Gail added. "You go rest, and we'll catch up to you later."

"If you're sure. . . ." Noelle looked up at Rocky and he shrugged.

"We're sure." Terri waved and the trio hurried away.

"That was abrupt." Noelle stood staring after the women. "I almost feel like they were trying to get rid of me." She returned her gaze to Rocky. "I wasn't overbearing, was I? I guess I can be sometimes when it comes down to finalizing details."

"Overbearing? You? Never," Rocky teased. "I'm sure they're thinking of your best interests. And as your acting physician, I have to agree. It's long past time for you to get off your feet and to rest that knee."

"You aren't my acting physician," Noelle grumbled. But she did as requested and hobbled her way over to the café.

The Greek eatery looked new. They stepped into the warm entry. Spicy, exotic scents mixed with the inviting aroma of fresh-baked bread. Soft music played from hidden speakers overhead.

"Wow, what a quaint little atmosphere. It's very. . .cozy." Noelle peered into the softly lit room where most of the light came from the candles centered on each white linen-clad table. "It seems a bit fancy for a quick lunch."

"It is cozy. As to the fanciness, I guess your grandmother wants to keep with her wedding theme today. It's a very romantic setting."

The man had most definitely changed. The Rocky she'd known before wouldn't have been able to define romance if someone pointed the word out in a dictionary. She didn't know how to react to being alone with Rocky in such an intimate setting. She hoped Gram would hurry.

The host approached them. "There'll be just the two of you today? I have the perfect corner for a little romantic luncheon." He pulled two menus from the holder as Noelle quickly calculated how many of them there would be total.

"Yes, only two. . . ." Rocky's voice drifted off.

Noelle looked up in confusion as he agreed to the inaccurate number and followed his gaze to the clear glass door. Across the street, Gram and Terri were practically shoving each other into Gail's car. Gail backed out with caution and then actually screeched her tires as she sped off down the street.

Chapter 6

"Well, this is awkward." Noelle lowered her voice. "We could always just leave."

"And miss having lunch in this wonderful place? No way."

He motioned for her to move forward where the host stood waiting. He led them to an isolated, quiet corner.

"A perfect table for two lovers to be alone with their words, no?" The host wiggled his eyebrows.

Noelle's eyes widened in horror. "Oh we're not—"

Rocky interrupted, "This will be perfect. Thank you."

"Have a wonderful meal." He started to move away, then eyed Noelle's knee brace. "Unless there's anything else you need?"

"No, we'll be fine, thank you." Rocky put a reassuring hand on Noelle's arm.

"Then I'll leave you to your lunch. Your waiter will be along shortly."

The man disappeared around a corner.

Noelle stared at the table, not sure how to situate herself.

Maybe they should have left. Rocky pulled out the chair opposite her and motioned for her to settle into her seat. She did as he said, resting her leg on the other chair. The relief to her overworked leg was immediate.

"I had no idea how good this would feel." Noelle closed her eyes and sighed. The softly padded seat hugged her aching leg. She could get through this meal. They were simply two friends, rebuilding their relationship, while sharing a lunch.

"Neither did I, but now that we're here, I wouldn't have missed it for the world."

Noelle's eyes popped open. Rocky had settled into the seat beside her. It made them appear even more—*couplish*.

"Missed it?" Confused, Noelle thought back over their words. Oh my, he thought she'd been all dreamy over their aloneness.

"I m—meant. . ." She stuttered over the words.

Rocky laughed. "Relax, Noelle. I know what you meant. I've seen many a stubborn patient push their recovery, only to realize later how nice it is to rest. The look of bliss on your face right now can only be caused by getting off your sore knee, not from my company."

"Mostly because of my knee," Noelle mumbled. The admission embarrassed her, but she couldn't let Rocky think she didn't have feelings for him. "I'm glad you're here with me. I've. . ." To her horror, tears flooded her eyes.

Rocky quickly hugged her close. "Noelle. I've missed you, too. More than you'll probably ever believe."

He handed her a linen napkin and she dabbed at her eyes, trying hard to get under control. But the intimate setting—with the two of them alone—threw her into a spiral of memories and past pains. They'd never dined in a place like this while dating, but they'd shared a lot of meals in similar fashion. She focused on the flickering candle.

Rocky silently waited for her to regain her composure, but he kept his arm around her shoulders and caressed her hair in such a way she couldn't gather a thought. "Do you want to leave? I know your grandmother and her friends sort of threw us together here."

Noelle half sobbed, half laughed. "Sort of? They might as well have stood outside, holding up signs 'Enjoy your alone time.'"

"So will we?" Rocky tugged a strand of her hair, forcing her to look at him. "We have a choice, you know. We can sit here as they planned and see what happens, or we can leave and go home."

Even in the dim light she could see his beautiful eyes. A shoehorn couldn't have pried her from this seat. "I want to stay."

His relief was evident, his eyes alight with hope. "I hoped you'd say that."

The waiter arrived at that moment, so Rocky asked for a few more minutes while they perused the menu. After placing their order, Noelle fiddled with her silverware.

"Elle."

Again she fought off tears. No one outside her family ever called her that. Otherwise, the name was exclusively Rocky's to use.

"Yes?"

He stilled his hand. "Is there a chance. . ." He stopped, his expression reflective.

"A chance?" *For me to stay? For us to try again?*

"A chance that we can enjoy this moment?" He smiled.

She wanted to state that she knew he'd meant more, but it wouldn't do to push. For now, she rested in the contentment that she sat close to the man who had loved her in the past and who she secretly prayed might one day love her again in the future.

The concept surprised her. She didn't really pray. But lately she'd had an urge to do just that, a longing to pray. A piece of the ice surrounding her heart thawed and fell away.

She returned his smile. "I think there's a good chance of that happening. I'm enjoying the moment already."

"So am I."

The waiter arrived with their food, the succulent aromas distracting them for a few moments from their conversation.

After they'd savored their first few bites, Rocky glanced over at her. "Where does this put our other plans? I know you still need to visit the florist and caterer. Do we need to put that aside for another day now that your grandmother deserted?"

"No, I'm still planning to run by both. We don't have much time, and I need to solidify some things. Gram pretty much handed all the details like that off to me, but I thought she'd at least like to have some input." She shrugged. "Apparently not."

"I think the only details on her mind at this point are of the matchmaking variety."

Noelle choked on her salad. "I noticed. I'm sorry."

"Don't be. I'm not."

Her heart soaring, Noelle smiled his way. "Cool."

"We can't let her down."

Noelle played along. "Of course not."

"She's getting married in a couple of weeks. We can't have her worrying about us."

"That would be awful." Noelle pushed a potato around with her fork. "She needs to think her plan is coming to fruition."

"Can I pick you up for church Sunday?"

"I'd love that."

Rocky looked shocked.

"You wanted me to say no?" she teased.

"I wouldn't have asked if I didn't want you to go. I just didn't expect you to say yes."

"I've not been that bad, have I?"

"Let's just say more than a few fellow church members have mentioned inviting you back to the flock, only to have you turn them down."

"Maybe I just wasn't ready." She sent him a special smile. "Or maybe the right person just hadn't asked."

"Wow." He took her hand in his, caressing the back of it while staring into her eyes. "I like that."

Noelle swallowed and tried to remember to breathe.

The waiter interrupted them by placing their bill on the table. He discreetly moved away.

Rocky pulled out his wallet and slid some bills into the leather folder. "For a place that pushes romantic dinners, they sure do have an awful sense of timing."

"Agreed." Noelle pushed her plate back and allowed Rocky to help her to her feet. "We'd better get back to it."

The day had taken on a whole new light, and Noelle had to constantly push back thoughts that she and Rocky were actually planning the wedding of their dreams. Since she'd not had his input the first time around, his comments intrigued her as he thoughtfully helped her sort through the decisions that had to be made.

The mix of flowers they ended up with—deep red and winter white roses—would be perfect with the emerald-hued greenery mixed in. They moved on and ordered a simple three-tiered cake for the reception, and Rocky insisted on ordering an additional chocolate groom's cake for Alex.

"You look amused." Rocky flipped up the collar of his jacket and slipped his hands into his gloves.

"I am. I planned an entire wedding without an ounce of input from you, and almost every detail I settled on would have been wrong according to the statements you just made at those two shops." Noelle balanced on one foot so she could wrap her knit scarf around her neck. The chill air worked through the fabric and caused her to shiver. The Flatirons in the distance blocked the warmth of the sun.

Rocky's face clouded. "I'm sorry. I wish I could go back and do a lot of things different." He stood in front of her and pulled her close. She leaned against him, savoring the moment.

"It's not that. My point is, what I've come to realize, is that we knew each other so well, yet we didn't know each other at all."

"That makes no sense whatsoever."

"It makes total sense. We ran together from such an early age, we took each other for granted. We knew the basics so well, we didn't bother to dig deeper."

Rocky rested his chin on her head. "You know. . .you're right. I hadn't thought of that."

"I hadn't either, until now. I'm sure a lot of things have changed as we've grown, but even back then, I don't think we looked for the changes anymore. We thought we had it all figured out. But we didn't know how to communicate and grow together."

He pulled away and led her to a nearby wooden bench. The metal trim was cold, but Rocky settled close beside her and placed his arm across the seat back. "So what are you saying? That if we'd married back then, we'd still be stuck in a rut, plodding along next to each other?"

"Or worse. I'm not sure we'd have made it far enough to plod. We were both too self-absorbed and immature. I'm sure that's why you ran. In some way, you did sense it before now. You might not have put it into words, but somehow you must have known that what we had was wrong."

"We were never wrong. We were right for each other, but maybe the circumstances were wrong or the timing was off."

They sat silent, lost in their own thoughts. The sun sank behind the mountains. As they watched, the shops came to life. Bright light spilled from windows and doors onto the sidewalk, reflecting off the festive holiday decorations that adorned the light poles. Tiny white lights had been wrapped around the trees and now they sparkled and danced in the shadows. Christmas music played from speakers hidden somewhere above their heads.

"This is nice." A wave of homesickness washed over Noelle,

and suddenly she didn't want to return to Kansas City.

Rocky turned to her. "You know what? The past is over and gone. We can't reclaim it, though I sure wish we could. I hate that I've lost so many years with you. But what we do have is the here and now. We can grab this moment and make it whatever we want it to be."

His vivid eyes captured hers in the lamplight.

She searched them but found no answers. "And what do we want the moment to be, Rocky?"

Chapter 7

Rocky hadn't answered her question, due to an emergency call on his cell phone. He'd taken her home and hurried away. Now, a couple of days later, she mulled over what she wanted his answer to be as she waited for him to pick her up for church.

She'd taken extra time with her preparations, determined to make a good impression on her fellow churchgoers. She wore black slacks to hide her leg brace and a colorful holiday sweater. The crutches she couldn't do anything about. Her grandmother had teasingly suggested they attach bells to ring in the holiday spirit, but Noelle had laughingly shut down that idea.

When she'd first come home from the hospital, her grandmother had told her about the pastor's messages on tape. She'd listened to a few to make Gram happy, but something changed as she listened and next thing she knew, she'd made a daily practice of listening to his online sermons. Seeds had been planted in her heart, which had lain barren for far too long, and she couldn't wait to reacquaint herself with the man in person.

Though she'd sat through his sermons many times in the past, his words had passed right over her head. As a rebellious teen, she had been less than polite to everyone in her path. And those very people had stepped up to care for them during her recuperation by making dinners and putting her on their prayer chain. She felt today would signal a new beginning of sorts. She couldn't wait to get started.

The doorbell rang, announcing Rocky's arrival.

"All set?" He sent her an appreciative smile. "You look beautiful."

Noelle felt her face flush. "Thank you. You look pretty nice yourself."

And he did. He'd dressed more casual than her, with a gray T-shirt tucked into faded blue jeans. A blue shirt hung open over the T-shirt. The effect made him look very down-to-earth and a far cry from the professional doctor she usually dealt with.

He assisted her into her coat, escorted her down the stairs, and out to his truck. Now that she'd had practice, she felt much more confident maneuvering the crutches. The pain in her leg had subsided, and she could even bend her leg a bit.

He slid on a leather jacket before slipping into the truck beside her. "Did you see your surgeon on Friday?"

"I did." Noelle was flattered that he'd remembered and cared enough to ask about the visit. "He said I was healing well and should be able to walk down the aisle for Gram's wedding without the crutches. I'll have to take it slow, but we'd already planned on that for the procession anyway."

He grinned. "That's great news!"

"I thought so. I'm ready to be rid of these things."

They entered the church and worked their way through the crowded foyer. Everyone seemed to want to say hi. Once more Noelle had the impression of coming home.

Gram waved her over to where she sat with Alex. Alex waved and leaned back, allowing her a view of her two cousins and their fiancés sitting on the far side of him. They all four waved as the music started. She and Rocky slid into the pew, with her sitting nearest Gram.

Noelle again toyed with the idea of moving back home. Her cousins were back. The family relationships were being repaired, and suddenly, the idea of returning to her lonely life in Kansas City didn't sound so hot.

The music minister opened the service by leading them in several lively songs, not anything like the older songs she remembered from her youth. Before she could decide if she missed the tradition, they sang a couple of hymns. She liked the balance.

The pastor stepped forward and began to speak about the prodigal son. Noelle fought off tears as she listened. The story so perfectly mirrored her life and how the people who loved her had welcomed her back with open arms. She glanced over at her cousins and saw the same emotions reflected on their faces.

"Are you okay?" Rocky's concern almost made her lose the precarious hold on her emotions.

She could only nod.

As soon as the service ended, he guided her to a quiet spot outside the sanctuary.

"Talk to me."

"I want to come home."

"Home?" He searched her eyes. "But you're already here."

"I don't mean for a visit. I want to come back like the son in the pastor's message. I want to return to Boulder and rebuild my life and my relationships."

His face lit up. "That's the best news I've heard in a long, long time." He pulled her close against him in a tight hug. "It's an answer to my prayers."

"Mine, too." She laughed, pulling away to wipe at her tears. "I have a lot to think about."

They watched as the parking lot emptied. Rocky lounged against the large trunk of a tree, looking very handsome in his dark brown leather jacket.

"I'll help in any way I can. I can drive to Kansas City and help you haul back your things."

"You do have a job, you know."

"I do, but I have a lot of vacation time built up. I don't take many days off."

She smirked at him. "Somehow that doesn't surprise me."

He ruffled her hair and pulled her against his side. "Let's find somewhere warm to talk."

"Gram expects everyone to converge at her place on Sunday afternoons. We won't have quiet, but it's warm, and I can announce to everyone at once that I plan to move back to Boulder. You're welcome to come, of course."

"Does she still make her mouthwatering pot roast on Sundays?" He started the engine and cold air blasted from the vents. He hurried to turn the heater off. "It won't warm the truck before we reach your grandmother's. Sorry."

"I'm fine."

He reached over and pulled her close to his side. She buckled the center seat belt around her waist. "Now I'm fine, too."

She leaned against his shoulder and looked at the Flatirons as they turned onto the main road. She suddenly wanted to hike. "How is it you never realize how much you miss something until you see it again?"

"I've wondered the same thing myself." He stared at her as they waited for a red light. Noelle had a feeling they were talking about two different things.

A horn honked from behind them, alerting them to the fact the light had changed. Rocky waved behind him and pulled out. They drove in silence for the first few blocks, then Rocky glanced over at her again. "What about your job?"

"My assistant can handle things. Maybe I can live with Gram until I get—" She laughed. "She'll be married. I guess they could do without a boarder."

"I doubt she'll be in a huge hurry to sell the house. Maybe you could stay there until you build your business up here?"

She nodded. "That might work. I'll talk to her today."

He pulled up in front of Gram's house. "I have a question."

"What?" Her breath hitched. Maybe he'd already realized he wanted them to move forward. That would be an answer to her prayers.

He leaned forward to peck her on the cheek. "Will you go to Bible study with me Thursday night?"

Bible study. Not quite what she'd been hoping for, but it was another date with Rocky. She tried to hold back her laugh.

"You find it funny that I asked you to a Bible study?" Rocky's lips twitched.

"I find myself happy that you asked."

"Ah, I can live with that. You have a beautiful laugh." She allowed him to tug her from the truck. When she slipped on the icy walkway, he was there to keep her on her feet. She longed for him to do the same for life, but this time around she'd try her best not to rush things.

They entered the door and everyone hushed with their arrival. The pungent aroma of roast and veggies floated through the air. Noelle just stood for a moment, her hand clasped in Rocky's, and absorbed the moment. Everyone she loved was gathered in that room.

"I have an announcement to make." She smiled up at Rocky and he returned her grin.

Before she could speak, a squeal carried across the room. "I knew it! We're three for three on rekindling our old romances!" Holly barreled across the room and gathered Noelle into a bear hug.

"Well, my romance isn't exactly rekindled, more like brand-new. All the same, it's wonderful, and I'm so happy for you both." Chris dragged Marcus along and wrapped her arms tightly around both Holly and Noelle.

Noelle stood speechless, not wanting to embarrass her cousins, but mortified for herself.

Chapter 8

Before she could form words to clarify, Rocky pushed her farther into the room. Gram stood waiting, her own eyes full of tears. "I'm so happy for you, dear." She turned to Rocky. "For you both."

How they could miss the deer-in-the-headlight expression on her face, Noelle didn't know.

"I'm glad to know you all approve of our dating again, but that isn't all the news Noelle has to share." Rocky the diplomat smoothed the way for her real announcement in a way that didn't cause her cousins or grandmother any embarrassment.

"There's more? Tell us." Holly grasped her hand.

"I've decided to move back home."

"Oh, that's even better!" Gram pulled her into a hug. "I've prayed for this for a long, long time."

"I know you have, Gram, along with many other prayers, I'm sure."

The men dragged Rocky off to watch the football game while Noelle joined the women in the kitchen to finish up dinner preparations.

"So, tell us about Rocky."

"Like what?" Noelle nibbled on the piece of roast she grabbed before Gram could slap her hand away. She grinned at the older woman. "I'm not sure there's much to tell."

"C'mon! We know you two are an item again. We need details." Chris pointed her long-handled spoon toward a nearby chair, and Noelle hobbled over to it. "You talk while we work. It wouldn't do for the wedding planner to miss the wedding."

"Seriously, there isn't much to tell. We've talked a lot. We had a nice lunch the day we all went shopping." She sent a pointed glare toward her grandmother. "The day Gram and her friends set us up."

Her cousins' guilty laughter clued her in to the fact that they'd been in on the plan. She buried her face in her arms on the table with a groan.

"Well, you have to admit it worked." Holly set a stack of plates on the counter and reached for the silverware.

"I'm not sure it did work. Our next big date is a Bible study."

~❧~

Rocky picked up Noelle just after six the next Thursday and took her to a local pizza place. A large arcade attached to the eatery with an opening in between.

"I love your choice of restaurant. I wouldn't have imagined we'd end up here if I'd spent an entire week thinking on it."

"Did you?"

"Did I what?"

"Spend the week thinking on it."

He stepped close to her, and the raucous noise dimmed in

the background. His lips were only inches away.

"Um." What was the question again? Oh, had she spent the past few days thinking about their date. "No. Technically, it's only been four days since I last saw you. I've been busy and didn't have much time to worry about our date."

"Our date?" Rocky grinned.

It was a date, wasn't it? Or had she put her foot in her mouth yet again?

"Darlin', if I wanted to take you on a date it wouldn't be to an arcade."

"Sorry. But at my grandmother's last Sunday. . ." She waved a hand in the air. "Oh, never mind. I know my cousins put us on the spot."

He tucked a strand of hair behind her ear. "Don't be sorry. I like the thought that we're dating. This Bible study doesn't count. I consider it a bonus. I want to experience everything with you. And I want to take you on dates. Real dates. When I do, you'll know we're dating."

"Oh."

He scooped down and handed her a skeeball. "You're up."

She sent the first ball up the wood ramp and it slid into the fifty-point hole. She helped him spend the rest of his quarters before he led her through the opening and into the pizzeria.

"You know. . .I'd have been fine with this being a date. I had fun."

"Really? So the nice place where I made dinner reservations for Friday is unnecessary?"

"I don't think you need to rush off and do anything drastic like canceling already made plans."

"You don't, huh?"

She loved his teasing grin.

"No." She settled in the booth he led her to and frowned as the owner walked to the door and locked it. "I hate to tell you this, but I think the pizzeria side is closing."

Rocky glanced over his shoulder as he scooted in next to her. "Nah. That's Rick. He owns the place. On Thursday nights he closes the place early so we can have our meeting here." He flipped open the menu. "What kind of pizza would you like?"

"Pepperoni, onions, green peppers, and black olives."

"We'll do a half and half."

She laughed. "You don't like my choices?"

"Let's just say I have no problem if a couple doesn't feel the need to have everything in common."

"Point taken."

A small band warmed up in a dim corner. Noelle loved the cozy place. "I can see why so many people attend this study."

Guff arrived at the door and tapped on the window. Rick hurried over and let him in. Guff slid in the seat across from Rocky, and a friendly man stepped up to the microphone on the small stage. "Welcome, and I'm glad you all could make it. It's getting colder out there, and I wasn't sure how many of you would brave the freezing temperatures."

"It's Colorado, dude," someone called out from a far corner.

Everyone laughed.

Rocky leaned close. "He's from Florida. He's having a bit of trouble acclimating."

"I see."

Just like they had on Sunday, they sang a few songs to open the meeting and then the teacher began to speak. Also like on Sunday, his words watered the seeds planted in Noelle's heart long ago, and more seeds began to take root. She felt comfortable, loved, and a warmth spread through her that she'd not felt before. They stayed with the topic of homecomings, same as the preacher earlier in the week.

She knew without a doubt that nothing felt more right than sitting here in Boulder with Rocky by her side. She was glad they'd picked one of the dimmer back corners where she could rest her leg upon a chair.

Rocky leaned over. "Are you doing all right? Does your knee hurt?"

"No, I'm fine. I'm better than I've been in a long time."

She felt Rocky reach for her hand. He continued to hold it throughout the rest of the lesson.

After the study, Guffy pulled her aside and asked if everything was okay. She assured him they were both fine. Noelle could tell something had changed in her and Rocky's friendship.

"Well, I'm glad things are going well for you." He slapped Rocky on the back. "By the way, I volunteered you both for nursery duty Sunday."

"You did what?" Noelle frowned and looked down at her knee.

"We'll do fine." Rocky assured Guff. He turned to Noelle. "You can hold babies, I can cart them around."

Guff hurried away.

"I was looking forward to the sermon." She tried to quell

the disappointment at the thought of missing out.

"Depending on how the morning goes, we can always catch the second service."

"In that case. . .I bet we'll have a blast. They're only babies after all, right?"

Chapter 9

"I hope you're ready to chase babies all over." Noelle lowered herself into one of the nursery's stuffed rocking chairs. "They look a little more active than I expected. I'm really sorry I can't help more."

"I didn't realize they'd put us in with the toddlers. I guess Guff forget to tell us that part." Rocky didn't look any too distressed. He actually looked excited. "And for the record, you don't look very sorry. You look comfortable. I'm not sure you won't rock yourself to sleep in that padded chair."

She put her foot on an ottoman. "Hmm." She leaned her head back and closed her eyes. She could get used to this type of chair. And she kind of liked the busy sounds of the toddlers crawling around at her feet. She could imagine a future with a baby or two toddling around, and Rocky at her side—she reined in the thoughts and her head whipped up in shock.

Rocky looked over at her and laughed. "What, did you start to doze off already?"

"Not exactly," she muttered.

Much to the kids' amusement—and hers—Rocky plopped

down onto the carpeted floor. Five toddlers immediately piled on top of him. One grabbed hold of his hair and flipped over onto the floor.

Noelle loved this side of her former fiancé. He looked cute with his hair tousled, his shirt coming loose from his waistband, and happy babies crawling all over him, vying for his attention. Their ecstatic giggles had her smiling.

One lone girl stood near the door, and Noelle watched her lip curve down into a frown before she howled in distress. Noelle started to rise, but Rocky stayed her with a hand.

"I'll get her."

He hurried over to the small child and scooped her up into his arms. Noelle got a glimpse of the name tag on her back. Emilie. The other toddlers wandered off in various directions as he cuddled the frightened girl close and walked over to the wide windows overlooking the play area. He whispered into her ear and she gradually calmed.

Yeah, baby girl, I can relate. He has the same effect on me. He looked over just as she completed the thought.

"You look happy. A penny for your thoughts."

"Oh." She grasped for an explanation. "I didn't realize you had such a way with kids. You certainly charmed Emilie just now."

He smiled down at the little girl. She had her thumb in her mouth and her eyes half closed. "I work with a lot of kids at the clinic and in the ER.

"Hey, Em, I'm going to let this nice lady rock you, okay?" Emilie nodded, but didn't lift her head from Rocky's shoulder. Smart kid.

The children immediately swarmed him again, and he dropped down to their level. He made funny faces and noises until they all chortled with laughter.

"You're a natural. Ever think of opening a day care center?"

"Not hardly." He pushed his hair back. "But I do have a heart to work with children."

"Then why are you in the ER and running a family practice if that's how you feel?"

He snuggled a blond boy on his lap as he analyzed her question. A look of realization crossed his face. "To be honest, I buried that dream a long time ago. I'm not sure why." Again he looked thoughtful. "That's not entirely true."

"You lie, Mr. Wocky?" The towheaded toddler squinted up at him.

"No, I didn't lie. I just had another thought."

"What's the thought, Mr. Wocky?" Noelle teased.

He glanced down at the little boy on his lap. "The ER keeps me busy, as does my practice. When I'm busy, I don't have a lot of extra time to think about. . .things."

"What kind of things?"

This time he stared deep into her eyes. "Well, the one main thing that comes to mind is how stupid I was to leave a beautiful woman at the altar. A woman I love."

Noelle didn't know what to say.

She watched as the blond boy tugged at Rocky's shirt. "Mr. Wocky."

Rocky didn't seem to hear him. "Working with kids would make me happy. I think deep down, I've been punishing myself in a way. I guess since I left you for medicine, I didn't feel I deserved to do what really makes me happy."

"Mr. *Wocky*!"

"That's crazy." Noelle wanted him to be happy. "I've never wished you harm or unhappiness." She hesitated and grinned. "Well, not recently anyway."

He laughed. "Well, without you in my life, and after I left you like I did, I didn't feel I deserved to do what I wanted."

"Rrrrr." The small boy folded his arms dramatically across his chest.

"What is it, Jeffy?"

"You said a bad wowd."

Rocky looked stumped. He looked up at Noelle. She shrugged.

"What bad word?"

" 'Tupid."

Noelle tried so hard not to laugh that she snorted.

"I'm sorry, Jeffy. I'll not say it again." Jeffy jumped up and ran across the room and picked up a truck. Rocky sent Noelle a fake glare.

She could tell he fought off his own urge to laugh.

"Out of the mouths of babes."

"Yep." Noelle lowered her voice. She was dumbfounded by his comment. "You aren't 'tupid, you know."

"I left the best woman in the world at the altar. That wasn't one of my finer moments. I want to make it up to you."

"You don't have to make anything up to me, Rocky. The past is the past."

"I know, but until I know you're truly happy, I don't want to chase any more of my dreams."

"Because of me?"

"Because of you."

The babies were all content at the moment, and Rocky scooted closer to her and took her hand in his. "Noelle, when I left you, I didn't think things through. But I think in some way, I expected you'd just put your life on hold and be there for me when I returned home. I might have been smart enough to get into medical school, but I wasn't smart enough to hold on to the most important thing in the world. You."

One of the babies squealed. He turned and lifted her up into his arms before he turned back to Noelle. "I want another chance. I want us to make a fresh start. I'll follow you anywhere, if you'll only give me a chance to make up to you what I took away."

She considered his comment. "You have nothing to make up for. As I said the other day, we were both young and train wrecks waiting to happen. You just put into motion what we both probably knew somewhere deep inside. Marriage at that point wouldn't have fixed all that was wrong with our lives, relationships, and immaturity. I'm not sure we would have made it."

Rocky frowned as he analyzed her words and leaned back on his heels. "Do you think things are different now? If so, in what way?"

She nodded. "We've both matured—in all the ways that matter. Not counting the arcade. . ."

They laughed, remembering their competitiveness before the Bible study.

"We've both realized how important relationships are.

And"—she hesitated—"I've found my way back to Jesus. He was there all along; I'm the one who diverted from His path."

"I'm so happy to hear that!" Rocky's face lit up and he whooped quietly, while bouncing the baby in his arms.

A parent showed up at the door and Rocky stood to take over the process. "We can finish this talk later."

Noelle's heart pounded in anticipation.

Chapter 10

After the last child left, they walked toward Rocky's truck. He held her close to his side, not wanting her to slip on the icy walkway. Snow began to fall, and the crisp air made Noelle homesick again. "I definitely don't want to leave, Rocky."

"I know you said that the other day, and I've been praying you meant it. Are you sure?"

She nodded.

Rocky stopped and stared at her. "I don't want you to leave, either. Ever."

Noelle shivered, and he took her in his arms. They walked to the truck and he started the engine to warm it. "Marry me."

"What?" The question popped out before Noelle could bite it back. She wanted more than anything to say yes. But what if he got cold feet like before?

He seemed to sense her distrust. "If you want, we can elope first and then you won't have to worry about me not showing up. We can still have a big wedding. I just want you to trust me."

"You're serious."

"Completely. And more sure than I've ever been about anything in my life. I don't want to lose you again."

Noelle realized she did trust him. "No, we'll wait and do it right. On one condition. . ."

He raised his eyebrow. "You're attaching conditions?"

"I want you to do what you love. Even without me in your life, you deserved to do what you loved. I want you to let go of the past and forgive yourself. Everything happens for a purpose, and everything happens in God's perfect timing." She swiveled sideways on the seat to face him. "If we'd married when we first planned to, I don't think we would have made it." She shrugged. "Maybe we would have, but who knows? Now we come with a clean slate. I have no doubt our love is strong enough to carry through."

"You learn fast." Rocky's grin was all the confirmation she needed. "And with God at the helm this time, we can't help but do much better." He paused. "You sure we need to wait? I mean, we can slip away and be married and not miss another day together."

Noelle laughed. "We can wait. Our special day will be worth the wait, I promise you."

"I can only imagine." He lifted the back of her hand to his lips and gave it a gentle kiss.

"Besides, I need time to plan our wedding—again. And I need to finish out my commitments at home."

He scowled. "How long will that take?"

"Not long at all. But I do have the details we talked about last Sunday to take care of. Most of my work commitments are only through the end of the year. As I said, my assistant has done well, and I'll hand the rest of the business over to her. I can work from here on most events, but I'll need to go back for a few things. I need to pack my apartment and find a permanent place to live."

"I'd ask you to move into my place after we marry, but I only have a small efficiency." He looked thoughtful for a few moments. "Your grandmother is moving out to Alex's new place after they marry, correct? And you're going to stay at her place for now? Did you ever talk to her about that?"

"I did. She said I could stay as long as I wanted."

"How about we make an offer on her place?"

Noelle only had to think about it for a moment. "The location is perfect for you with work, and I can't imagine a better place to start our new life. Come on, let's go discuss it with Gram and tell everyone our news. Since they thought they guessed it last week, we'll throw them off this time."

He held her back with a gentle tug. "No."

She sat back in the seat. "No?"

"We haven't set a date. I haven't even properly asked you the big question and you sure haven't officially accepted. We're going to do every step of this right."

"So what are you waiting for?"

He took her hand and looked her in the eyes. "Noelle, will you do me the greatest honor of becoming my wife?"

Choked up, she could only nod. He reached into his pocket and pulled out a familiar red velvet box.

"My ring? You kept it all these years?"

He nodded and slipped the ring over her finger. The fit was perfect. "If you want, we can go pick up a new set to commemorate our new start."

"No way. I want this one. It feels so right to have it back where it belongs."

"And it feels so right to have you back where you belong."

"It does." She snuggled against his shoulder and enjoyed the warmth of his truck, his scent, the cold—everything about the moment.

"Valentine's Day."

"What?" She pulled slightly back so she could see his face.

"We can marry on Valentine's Day. Gram already has the Christmas wedding and you said you need time. Will two months be enough?"

She snuggled back against him. "More than." She laughed. "I've had almost a decade to perfect this thing, you know. I just need to tweak a few of our earlier plans. For instance, the honeymoon—"

"I definitely want that in the plans."

"I know *that*. But about the honeymoon. . ."

He looked wary. "What about the honeymoon?"

"You aren't going to get by with two days at Guff's parents' cabin in the mountains this time. I want more time. And a warmer location."

"Two weeks minimum and anywhere you want to go."

"It's a deal." She held out her hand to shake his, and he circumvented it and pulled her into his arms. This time the kiss they shared was long and full of promise. Only the sound of a siren behind them made them pull away.

Rocky looked over his shoulder. "Guff."

"What did we do this time? What violation can he possibly

get us for? We aren't even moving."

Guff walked up, and Rocky opened his window. "What can I do for you, officer?"

"Did you folks know we had a law against loitering here? I saw the strange vehicle and thought I'd best check things out."

Rocky looked at Noelle and rolled his eyes. "I've had this same vehicle for years, and we're parked in front of the church. I think you could put two and two together."

Guff laughed and leaned against the window. "You're right. But the windows were steaming up, and I wanted to be sure it was you. Can't be too careful these days, you know."

"Your timing is impeccable." Sarcasm dripped from Rocky's voice.

"Thank you!" Guff acted clueless as always, but Noelle had the feeling he was more perceptive than he let on. "So, what are you two up to?"

As if he didn't know. The windows hadn't fogged that fast. Noelle leaned around Rocky and flashed her ring finger in Guff's face. "If you must know. . . *This* is what we've been up to."

For once Guff was speechless. "So soon? I mean. . . You just got home. I thought you all were. . ."

Noelle and Rocky laughed.

"Soon?" Rocky pulled her close. "Hardly. We've waited far too long to get back to this point. I'm not letting this lady get away again."

They swore Guff to secrecy, hoping he could keep their engagement quiet for a week.

⚜

On Christmas Eve, Rocky and Noelle waited until all the gifts were opened and then stood before the family. "I know you jumped the gun a bit a couple of weeks ago when I wanted to announce my plan to stay in town." She paused and they all laughed. "But tonight we have another announcement to make."

This time her cousins sat in place, and her grandmother listened expectantly.

"I'd like to announce"—she waggled her finger in front of them—"our engagement."

Noelle's family circled around, each woman bearing her own beautiful ring. Noelle looked up at her grandmother, who had tears of joy in her eyes. They hugged.

Alex stood nearby, beaming.

"Grandpa Alex?" Noelle placed her hand on his arm.

He froze in surprise before sending her a huge smile. "I like the sound of that."

"Good, because I know I'm a couple days premature on the endearment—but will you walk me down the aisle?"

Alex cleared his throat a few times before he could speak. "I'd love to, and I'd consider it an honor."

Epilogue

Carol had to fight the tears of joy as she stood in the bridal dressing room at the back of the church. Sandy gave her a hug then took off toward Clark, who ushered her to her seat in the front pew. Garland stood at the door and offered a forced smile before he turned and headed out to usher one of the late-arriving guests.

Noelle bustled about, making sure everything was as it was supposed to be. Carol couldn't help but smile as she saw herself in her granddaughter.

She turned to Gail. "I can't believe all this is happening."

Gail hugged her, careful not to smudge their makeup. "Believe it." She pulled away and gave Carol's shoulders a squeeze. "You've worked so hard to make everyone else happy, and now it's your turn."

Carol blinked and felt her chin quiver before nodding. "It's like a fairy tale."

"Alex does make a handsome prince." Gail winked. "And we need to get this show on the road before your chariot turns into a pumpkin."

Chris and Holly stopped by for hugs before joining their fiancés at the front of the church. Carol was delighted that her engagement had sparked the romance that sizzled among her granddaughters.

She closed her eyes and said a prayer of thanks for everything coming together so well. After a few tense incidents, her family had come through for her. Every last one of them rearranged their lives to witness one of the most joyful days of her life.

"Mom?"

She opened her eyes and turned to see Michael grinning from the doorway. "Okay, I'm ready." She took one last glance in the full-length mirror and smoothed the front of her winter white suit.

Michael kissed her cheek then crooked his arm. "Let's go."

A giggle escaped Carol's lips as she linked her arm with her son's then began the walk that she never thought she'd take again. Once they approached the altar, Michael squeezed her hand then turned her over to Alex before taking his position as best man.

Carol listened intently to the pastor's words about the love between a Christian husband and wife. When she glanced at Alex, she saw that he took everything to heart. She had no doubt their love was blessed, and it would only get better over time.

After they said their vows, the pastor completed the ceremony then turned to Alex and winked. "You may now kiss your bride."

A collective sigh resounded through the church as Carol

and Alex shared their first kiss as husband and wife. When she turned around and looked at her family, she noticed that there wasn't a dry eye among them. Garland offered a smile and gave her a thumbs-up, making her laugh.

The photographer didn't waste any time before snapping pictures so Noelle could get back to her wedding planner duties. Chris took off to help her cousin, while Holly hung around and chatted with Carol and Alex while they waited to make their entrance at the reception.

Carol gasped at the elaborate decorations in the fellowship hall. White linen cloths topped with poinsettias covered each table, and white skirts were draped beneath each, hanging to the floor. The centerpiece of the room, the three-tiered wedding cake, sat upon a table skirted by white linen and lace. The lace overlay revealed a hint of the red linen cloth that graced the top of the table. Delicate red icing roses with tiny green leaves graced the confection, and the cake topper matched the poinsettias. Gold confetti sprinkled across the tables sparkled in the room's soft lights. "Noelle! It's beautiful! You really went all out!"

"It was fun," Noelle said. "I'm just glad I could do it. Now come on and let's get this show on the road."

After Noelle announced the happy couple's arrival, she finished orchestrating all the events, including the cake cutting. Then she pulled Carol over to the side to toss the bouquet.

"Just a minute," Carol said. She scanned the crowd until she made eye contact with Sandy, who nodded.

"What's going on?" Noelle asked. "Why did Aunt Sandy bring two extra bouquets?"

Carol chuckled. "I needed three—one for each of my granddaughters." She gave Noelle a gentle nudge toward Chris and Holly. "Don't let me down, girls," Carol said loud enough for the cluster of young women, all waiting to catch the bouquet. "Get into position."

She turned her back to the group and tossed each bouquet, one by one, then turned around to see that she'd made her targets. Chris, Holly, and Noelle all stood there, holding the flowers, looking stunned. The girls behind them dispersed into the crowd.

"You set this up, didn't you?" Noelle asked. "No one else even tried."

Carol shrugged. "Well, I am the bride today, so I get to call the shots, right?"

Alex joined her and slipped his arm around her waist. "Yes, you do get to call the shots. Just let me know when you're ready to leave."

She turned her face up to his and smiled. "I'm ready now."

 **Paige Winship Dooly** is the author of over a dozen books and novellas, with four more books due out in the next year. She enjoys living in the coastal Deep South with her family, after having grown up in the some-times extremely cold Midwest. She is happily married to her high school sweetheart and loves their life of adventure in a full house with six homeschooled children, a cat, a dog, and a hamster.

A Letter to Our Readers

Dear Readers:

In order that we might better contribute to your reading enjoyment, we would appreciate your taking a few minutes to respond to the following questions. When completed, please return to the following: Fiction Editor, Barbour Publishing, Inc., P.O. Box 719, Uhrichsville, OH 44683.

1. Did you enjoy reading *Christmas Homecoming*?
   ❑ Very much—I would like to see more books like this.
   ❑ Moderately—I would have enjoyed it more if _____
   _____
   _____

2. What influenced your decision to purchase this book?
   (Check those that apply.)
   ❑ Cover   ❑ Back cover copy   ❑ Title   ❑ Price
   ❑ Friends   ❑ Publicity   ❑ Other

3. Which story was your favorite?
   ❑ *Silver Bells*   ❑ *O Christmas Tree*
   ❑ *I'll Be Home for Christmas*   ❑ *The First Noelle*

4. Please check your age range:
   ❑ Under 18   ❑ 18–24   ❑ 25–34
   ❑ 35–45   ❑ 46–55   ❑ Over 55

5. How many hours per week do you read? _____

Name _____

Occupation _____

Address _____

City _____ State _____ Zip _____

E-mail _____

$$\heartsuit$$

HEARTSONG

PRESENTS

If you love Christian romance...

$10.^{99}$

You'll love Heartsong Presents' inspiring and faith-filled romances by today's very best Christian authors. . .Wanda E. Brunstetter, Mary Connealy, Susan Page Davis, Cathy Marie Hake, and Joyce Livingston, to mention a few!

When you join Heartsong Presents, you'll enjoy four brand-new, mass-market, 176-page books—two contemporary and two historical—that will build you up in your faith when you discover God's role in every relationship you read about!

Imagine. . .four new romances every four weeks—with men and women like you who long to meet the one God has chosen as the love of their lives—all for the low price of $10.99 postpaid.

Mass Market, 176 Pages

To join, simply visit www.heartsongpresents.com or complete the coupon below and mail it to the address provided.

✂ -

YES! Sign me up for Hearts♥ng!

NEW MEMBERSHIPS WILL BE SHIPPED IMMEDIATELY!

Send no money now. We'll bill you only $10.99 postpaid with your first shipment of four books. Or for faster action, call 1-740-922-7280.

NAME _____

ADDRESS_____

CITY_____ STATE _____ ZIP _____

MAIL TO: HEARTSONG PRESENTS, P.O. Box 721, Uhrichsville, Ohio 44683 or sign up at WWW.HEARTSONGPRESENTS.COM